Carla Kelly started writing Regency romances because of her interest in the Napoleonic Wars. She enjoys writing about warfare at sea and the ordinary people of the British Isles rather than lords and ladies. In her spare time she reads British crime fiction and history—particularly books about the US Indian Wars. Carla lives in Utah and is a former park ranger and double RITA® Award and Spur Award winner. She has five children and four grandchildren.

Also by Carla Kelly

'A Christmas Houseguest'
in *Snowbound Regency Christmas*
'A Father for Christmas'
in *A Victorian Family Christmas*

Lord Ratliffe's Daughters miniseries

Marrying the Captain
The Surgeon's Lady
Marrying the Royal Marine

The Channel Fleet miniseries

The Admiral's Penniless Bride
Marriage of Mercy
The Wedding Ring Quest
'Captain Grey's Christmas Proposal'
in *Regency Christmas Wishes*
'The Captain's Christmas Journey'
in *Convenient Christmas Brides*
A Naval Surgeon to Fight For

Discover more at millsandboon.co.uk.

NAVY CAPTAIN'S CONVENIENT WIFE

Carla Kelly

MILLS & BOON

All rights reserved including the right of reproduction in whole or in part in any form. This edition is published by arrangement with Harlequin Enterprises ULC.

This is a work of fiction. Names, characters, places, locations and incidents are purely fictional and bear no relationship to any real life individuals, living or dead, or to any actual places, business establishments, locations, events or incidents. Any resemblance is entirely coincidental.

Without limiting the exclusive rights of any author, contributor or the publisher of this publication, any unauthorised use of this publication to train generative artificial intelligence (AI) technologies is expressly prohibited. HarperCollins also exercise their rights under Article 4(3) of the Digital Single Market Directive 2019/790 and expressly reserve this publication from the text and data mining exception.

® and TM are trademarks owned and used by the trademark owner and/or its licensee. Trademarks marked with ® are registered with the United Kingdom Patent Office and/or the Office for Harmonisation in the Internal Market and in other countries.

First published in Great Britain 2026
by Mills & Boon, an imprint of HarperCollins*Publishers* Ltd,
1 London Bridge Street, London, SE1 9GF

www.harpercollins.co.uk

HarperCollins*Publishers*, Macken House, 39/40 Mayor Street Upper,
Dublin 1, D01 C9W8, Ireland

Navy Captain's Convenient Wife © 2026 Carla Kelly

ISBN: 978-0-263-41876-7

04/26

Printed and Bound in the UK using 100% Renewable Electricity
at CPI Group (UK) Ltd, Croydon, CR0 4YY

To the men and women of navies worldwide,
"that go down to the sea in ships,
that do business in great waters."
—*Psalm* 107:23

Chapter One

It had been far too long since Captain John Beattie, Royal Navy, Mediterranean Fleet, had last laid himself down in his rack. Every single muscle in his body protested when he did so, perhaps considering it their right and privilege to keep him upright and moving.

21st October 1805, standing on the quarterdeck of his ship, *HMS Swallow*, he had absorbed Admiral Nelson's flag message: 'England expects that every man will do his duty'.

Every member of his crew then engaged on deck had looked to him, needing to know his feelings. Such was leadership; he accepted it.

'That's it, my lads,' he had said. 'To your posts. Master and lieutenants, a word here.'

They'd known what to do before he commanded anything because John trained his men well. Without a murmur, they dodged cannon fire from both sides, and falling masts, and French and Spanish snipers firing from their own riggings.

He stared into the dark as he swung in his wooden-sided bed, the prerogative of a man of rank, instead of a mere hammock. He knew full well that were he to die at sea, his swinging bed would become his coffin, weighted with cannon balls, nailed shut and slid into the water.

Trafalgar had been no mere fleet action. Nay, by God, not this one, this hammer blow administered to the combined fleets of Spain and France outside of Cadiz near a headland named Trafalgar. This was far more, and memorable.

After the battle, he watched little *Pickle* bravely raise more sail, even under stormy conditions, and start for England, delivering the message of a momentous battle won, even at the terrible cost of Admiral Nelson himself, killed by a French sniper.

The rest of the wounded fleet had struggled to stay afloat through four days of the storm, as if the gods of war were French and determined to keep the battle raging. From his quarterdeck, John had missed his promising First Lieutenant Fontaine, sent below deck with a small but nagging wound. John and his second lieutenant had kept a round-the-clock watch on overworked crew, and any drift towards other ships, battened down as they were.

At comparative rest now, this was John's time to second-guess his decision to send his surgeon to Admiral Collingwood's *Royal Sovereign* to help with the many wounded. *Swallow*'s only wounded man was Lieutenant Fontaine, and it had seemed a trifling matter. A bit of wooden splinter from a Spanish ship had sliced through Will's neck, giving him a wound that appeared minor.

Will himself had insisted that Surgeon Woodlawn go to the *Royal Sovereign*.

Now Will was dead, the little wound turning into a big one that had festered and bubbled in a tiny space and killed him.

John turned carefully onto his side, well-trained to avoid hasty movement in his swinging coffin. He wanted to weep, but he was too thirsty and had no tears. He closed his eyes, hoping he wouldn't see Will's trusting expression in his mind, as he gazed at his captain, the man who could do no wrong in his eyes, then sighed, as if in apology, and died.

Lieutenant Fontaine had been shrewd, even when he'd known his fate. He made it clear to John that he would sign over to his captain his funds and prize money at Carter and Brustein Counting House in Plymouth. 'See that my sister gets this, sir,' he said.

John countersigned under his first lieutenant's feeble scrawl. 'Will, your sister will be dealt with fairly. I promise.'

When death came, John couldn't bring himself to throw Will's body overboard, especially when they were so close to Gibraltar, that entrance to the Mediterranean Sea. *Swallow* anchored close to *HMS Victory*, waiting her turn for enough repairs to struggle back to home port in Plymouth.

During the long wait, his carpenter had prepared a coffin for Will. John and his crew walked their first lieutenant to the burial ground, interring him next to others from the same battle. Ashes to ashes, dust to dust, God be praised. They then prepared to sail homeward with the *Victory*, which bore the body of their admiral. Not for *this* hero the raw cemetery at Gibraltar.

It would be a rough journey of twelve days, time for Captain Beattie to plan his next step, giving Anna Fontaine, spinster, the grim news about Will's death and hopefully smoothing her path to receive her brother's funds. He had met her once, but couldn't remember much beyond a serene expression.

He would promise to accompany her to the counting house and then go to his own house to see Allan, his son, now in the capable hands of a nursemaid, a cook and a scullery maid. His dear Cathy dead these three years from consumption, he had chosen his Plymouth staff as carefully as he'd picked his crew. Maybe there would be enough time to reacquaint himself with his boy—six, almost seven now—who so resembled Cathy. Drydock in Plymouth might buy him two weeks to become a father again, before duty called him back to sea.

He could do no more; exhaustion claimed him. Captain Beattie damned Napoleon, closed his eyes and slept.

The early January seas were unsettled off Plymouth and Captain Beattie was a prudent seaman, biding his time offshore and sending a dinghy ahead to inform the harbourmaster of their imminent arrival. He knew Will's sister would be at the dock.

He knew that, because the letter he'd sent with the *Pickle* was one of many letters from other *Swallow* crew members. 'Anna loves a dockside welcome,' Will had assured him, before his wound had started to fester. 'She'll be glad to see me.'

And here they were. He nodded to Second Lieutenant Marsing to take the *Swallow* to her dockside anchorage. As captain, John maintained a calm air on the quarterdeck, even as his insides writhed with the task ahead. He had given bad news before, but not after a family member had received such a cheerful letter from a now dead man.

He scoured the dock for a barely remembered face, reminding himself it had been three years since he had done that, when he'd last sought out Cathy's lovely, pale face. He looked now for Anna Fontaine.

There she was. He was right, remembering that serene expression, part of an eager sea of faces looking for their man, or son or brother. He dreaded that expression changing, once he delivered his message.

He started down the steps to the main deck, only to be stopped by the harbourmaster's mate, a nervous fellow who seemed to always deliver bad news himself.

'Captain Beattie! Grand to see you!'

'And you, sir,' he replied, his eyes looking beyond the man. 'I have a message for…'

'Just a moment, sir. Our drydocks are full up with you heroes. You're to sail tomorrow for Portsmouth Drydock.'

Damn, he thought. *Maybe I can take Allan with me.* He held out his hand for the orders thrust his way, then handed them to his second. 'Your voice is louder than mine, Lieutenant Marsing. We're sailing on tomorrow's tide to Portsmouth.'

'Great Neptune's balls,' Marsing muttered. 'Aye, sir.'

He bellowed out the change of plan. 'Be back here at eight bells tomorrow!'

Here I go, John thought, taking a deep breath.

He staggered off the gangplank, forgetting like a pea-green landlubber that his sea legs were propelling him. He stood still, trying to stop his spell of dizziness as the wooden wharf seemed to move and buck.

'Never gets easier, does it, Captain?' Marsing said cheerfully as he staggered into an embrace with his wife, then moved away with her hand steadying him.

'No, it never does,' he said quietly to their backs.

The crowd thinned out as his crew and their loved ones hurried away to make the most of their mere one day in port before raising sail to Portsmouth drydock. A lady remained, looking at the empty deck, her expression troubled now.

John took a tentative step and another. 'Excuse my balance. I haven't been ashore long. You are Miss Fontaine? I believe we were introduced once.'

'We were,' she said calmly. She eyed him and raised her chin. Her gallantry broke his heart. 'I fear you have bad news. Tell me, sir.'

He gently explained what had happened.

'A splinter? Surely not,' she said.

'It festered and I am afraid we could do nothing.'

Miss Fontaine went pale, clasping her hands tightly together. He knew if she hadn't been wearing gloves, he would be staring at white knuckles. Thank God she was no screamer or fainter. He had seen those after other fleet actions when he'd often become the bearer of bad news to waiting families.

'I am so very sorry, Miss Fontaine,' he said. Hopefully, she could somehow tell he meant every word. 'This is a terrible loss to you, to the fleet and to me, personally. Please accept my sincerest condolences. I will see you home. I am headed to my son on Terrace Lane, which I believe is near your Covent Street, where Will told me he resided.'

She nodded, looking up when the harbourmaster's mate plucked at his sleeve again. 'Please, sir. Another moment of your time.'

'I will be fine, Captain Beattie,' she said, still so calm. 'Your time is not your own. Go to your son, once this man finishes with you.'

He nodded. 'I will, and thank you, Miss Fontaine.' He remembered his other duty. 'With your permission, I'll call on you this evening. I must discuss your brother's financial dealings at Carter and Brustein.'

'I will be home. Number two hundred and eight, Covent Street.'

She dipped a small curtsy and left him. Although it hadn't shown on her face, he sensed her utter bereavement. There were days he hated his job. This was one of them.

Chapter Two

Anna Fontaine spent the afternoon weeping for her brother. Her housekeeper and friend Mrs Moore cried, too, both of them grieving. The other woman finally left to brew tea, that English remedy for all ills, and it helped.

Finally drained and dry of eye, Anna sat close to Mrs Moore. 'I wonder what will happen to us,' she said. 'Will's captain said he would visit this evening to discuss finances.'

'Finances?' her friend asked as she poured more tea.

'Will lodges—lodged—his salary and prize money with Carter and Brustein,' Anna explained. 'He always left me with sufficient funds to manage.' She looked away, remembering that conversation. 'I wish he could have added my name to his account. Are such things possible?' She managed a smile. 'We ladies are kept in the dark about money.'

'That is why Captain Beattie is coming here?'

'So he said. Will told me that the captain is a widower, his wife having died of consumption several years ago. I imagine he treasures every moment with his child. Time is short for such a man.'

She thought about that later, as the terrible loss of her brother grew in proportion to her awareness of her situation. Unfortunately, war and national emergency had kept her brother from shore, where he could have found a wife. And she was a spinster at twenty-nine and would never see offspring of her own.

What now? She knew the rent was due soon, but after that? 'Mrs Moore, what is going to become of us?' she asked.

'There are your mother's relatives near Bristol, my dear.'

'I know, but none of them were pleased when Papa let Will go to sea.' She remembered the arguments, with Will storming off until Papa gave grudging permission for his only son to serve as a Young Gentleman in Mama's many times removed cousin's frigate. That had led to years as a midshipman, followed by second lieutenancy, and then his recent rank of first lieutenant aboard the *Swallow*. 'And who will want a spinster hanging around?'

She left the rest unsaid, the bleak prospect of being the Unwanted Cousin left to fetch and carry. She chose not to think of Will dying in battle and leaving her not only extremely sad but poor and a burden.

True to form, in moments when she had too many thoughts, Anna spent the rest of the day rearranging the linen closet and contemplating the enormity of her dear brother's death. 'Where are you even buried?' she asked the bath sheets she folded and refolded.

Supper was bread and soup, eaten in the kitchen. Anna thought of the times her housekeeper had insisted on maintaining the propriety of a house, with its mistress in the dining room and the help in the kitchen. This was different. William Fontaine was dead, changing the order of things.

'Captain Beattie *will* be here tonight,' Anna said, desperate to know more.

'We need to know something,' Mrs Moore added.

We need to know a lot, Anna told herself. They sat in silence and waited.

Was it fear or relief when he finally knocked? Anna hurried to the front door.

So much for the morning's stalwart captain who had so impressed her earlier. She opened her door on an exhausted man with desperation writ large on a face that might have been handsome in easier times.

'C…come in, sir,' she managed.

Two children stood so close to him that they looked attached with glue. It touched her heart when he gave them a gentle push forward. She held the door open wider.

Captain Beattie flashed her a look of gratitude. 'I'll explain, Miss Fontaine.'

'I know you will, sir,' she replied. 'There's the sitting room, with a nice fire. It's warm,' she added, noting the older girl's thin cloak. Who *was* she? The small boy's clothing was better, but his eyes were filled with terror. *What in the world?* she thought, forgetting for a moment her own anxiety. Some instinct told her that theirs was worse.

A widow with two grown children of her own, Mrs Moore knew hunger when she saw it. She didn't wait for an introduction. 'I have soup and bread in the kitchen. Come along, children.'

The little ones seemed to recognise a command when they heard it. So did Captain Beattie, apparently. 'Aye, go with the nice lady.'

Mrs Moore shepherded them out, but not before whispering to Anna, 'Something's afoot.'

Anna gestured the captain into the sitting room. He went to the fireplace to warm his hands, staying there so long Anna knew he was at a loss for words. She began the conversation, not sure where to start.

'Sir? You said something about Will's finances, but tell me first, was there no surgeon on board the *Swallow*?'

Anna wished she hadn't been so blunt. His look of real distress showed her a captain not used to failing his men.

'Miss Fontaine, I will regret that until I die,' he said simply. 'Your brother assured me that his injury was a trifling matter, and agreed that our surgeon should go to the *Royal Sovereign*, where there were many more wounded.'

She understood. In her heart, a greater question remained. 'Did my brother suffer?'

'I fear he did, but it was over quickly,' he replied simply.

Anna folded her hands in her lap and continued, knowing without knowing how, that this man's suffering equalled hers. 'I take comfort that he does not suffer *now*, and has done his duty.'

'Miss Fontaine, I held his hand to the end.' He took his

own deep breath, and in the deepest recesses of her heart Anna felt the cost of *his* war.

Captain Beattie took out a sheet of paper from inside his uniform jacket and handed it to her, apologising for the much folded and crumpled final will of her brother. She noted Will's shaky signature and swallowed down her tears.

He gave her a moment, leaning back. 'Miss Fontaine, let us go to Carter and Brustein tomorrow morning and settle this matter. With this signature, Shlomo Brustein will settle Will's finances on your behalf.'

'I greatly appreciate this. Thank you, sir.' She gave the will into his keeping once more.

He returned his gaze to her face, and she realised that he had a bigger issue at hand than mere money. It must be the children. But what about them? She waited for him to speak.

'Miss Fontaine, you don't know me.' Silence, then, 'Can you trust me? I need *your* help and I have nowhere to turn.'

Captain Beattie was right: she didn't know him, beyond Will's words that he was from Scotland's Kirkcudbrightshire, and that he was a widower with a child. She had known a few Scots in her admittedly sheltered life.

'I know you are from Scotland. Will named a place.'

'Kirkcudbrightshire. Spring Hill, to be specific.' He managed a smile and seemed to relax a little. 'Will probably told you we Scots are a bossy, swearing type.'

'He did mention that,' she said, keeping her voice light. There was so much here she didn't understand.

'My crew tell me they have never heard such creative swearing when we are under attack. I plead guilty to that.' His shoulders rose again as the tension returned. 'Miss Fontaine, I need your help most desperately.'

She sat in silence long enough to hear the mantelpiece clock ticking. 'You had better tell me. Then I will know if I can trust *you*.'

He had a way about him, looking directly into her eyes. Anna realised that he was treating her as his equal. How she knew, she could not say.

'Let me lay this before you,' he began, settling into the chair, not taking his eyes from her face. 'My wife died of consumption that plagued her all of our brief married life. I knew that when I married her.'

He puffed out his cheeks in an entirely human gesture that told Anna much about this man. She almost leaned forward to touch his hand.

'I have no relatives in England. Three years ago, I arranged for a housekeeper who cooks, a scullery maid and a nanny for my son. I paid them well, and I reposed much confidence in them.'

Anna held her breath as a dark look came into his eyes. 'Oh, my,' she whispered. 'Something happened.'

'Aye. For the last three years, I've sailed into Plymouth, visited a few days and reacquainted myself with Allan.' He looked down at his hands. 'It was different this time.'

He looked up in surprise as the door opened and Mrs Moore came in, her face cheerful as usual. 'Anna, you should see these little ones eat! I made more sandwiches.

Would you...' her housekeeper glanced from her to the captain, and her expression changed '...like some?'

'Later, my dear,' Anna said gently. 'Give us a moment.'

Mrs Moore closed the door.

'Go on, Captain Beattie,' Anna said as she braced herself. 'What did you find this time?'

His eyes filled with tears. He sat in silence until he could speak. 'I let myself into the house tonight. It was dark. The scullery maid, Pru, stood there with a poker, ready to strike me.'

'Good God!'

'I reminded her who I was, and Pru collapsed in tears at my feet.'

'Where...where was Allan?' Anna asked apprehensively.

'She'd told him to stay in the kitchen with the door closed.' He wiped his eyes. 'She was ready to defend him with her life.'

'But...'

'The housekeeper and the nanny?' he said, biting off the words this time. 'Gone these last two months, after warning her not to let anyone in the house or leave it, on pain of death. Evil, wicked women! They fooled me. I thought they were dependable and kind. How could I have been so foolish? God, I am an idiot!'

He was on his feet now, pacing back and forth, his face a mask of pain, as if he watched the whole thing unroll again in his mind's eye.

Anna waited, reminding herself to breathe. And think. *What would I want someone to do if this had happened to me?* she asked herself when the roaring in her head diminished.

Anna stood up and took his arm, which demanded all her courage. She knew better than anyone how quietly she lived, troubling no one and causing no disturbance to the universe. She felt his pain; it was almost palpable.

He stopped walking. She patted his arm, astounded at her own temerity. 'It's done now. It's over. They're safe in my kitchen, eating. They're…'

'Aye, they are! God help me, what would have happened to them if I had not returned alive from Trafalgar?' he asked in anguish.

Without thinking, she reached up and covered his eyes with her hands. It was a momentary, impulsive act, and she took her hands away quickly, but not before Captain Beattie had regained his composure. He sank into his chair again. He gestured for her to sit, masterful in his command of his emotions, probably earned the hard way at sea in battle. She sat, but this time her hand rested on his arm.

Her touch seemed to soothe him. He sounded almost normal when he spoke. 'For two months they survived on scraps from the pantry, and Pru kept my son safe. She's only ten years old, or as near as she can figure. Imagine *her* terror.'

Anna imagined. She waited for what she knew was coming, and had her answer before he spoke, even though the responsibility made her quail.

'Miss Fontaine, I must sail tomorrow afternoon for

Portsmouth and the drydocks there. I have nowhere to leave my son and Pru, except with you.'

Even as she wondered in her heart where this would lead, she leaned closer and meant every word. 'They can stay with me until you make other arrangements. You can trust me, Captain Beattie.' Should she? Yes. 'For my brother's sake, and for the children's, I will not let you down.'

Chapter Three

His look of relief could have been seen for miles out at sea, or so Anna imagined.

'Bless your heart, Miss Fontaine,' he said. The words were quietly spoken, but she felt his sincerity in her soul. 'I do not know how long this will last. I must leave tomorrow. I will have a better idea when I return.'

'No matter,' she said. 'You and your son may have my brother's room, though I will warn you that the bed is not a large one.'

'I am used to small spaces.' She thought he smiled then, but it was hard to say, because he was looking down and not at her. 'If you can assure me that the bed will not pitch or yaw, we will manage tolerably.'

It *was* a smile, albeit a small one. She took heart and smiled back, wiping away any grief she felt at the prospect of opening the door to Will's room for someone else. Will had told her in letters that the Old Man—that nickname given to all captains—was firm but kind. In Will's memory, she knew she must repay that kindness.

'I'll show you to his room.'

'Thank you,' he said simply, then seemed to reconsider. 'First, may I see my child in your kitchen?'

'Certainly.' She sniffed the air. 'I think Mrs Moore has been augmenting our leftover loaves and fishes.'

She rose and he followed. As she walked into the kitchen, Anna reckoned it was her first good moment in a sad day.

'That smells good,' the captain said as Mrs Moore looked at him from the Rumford, where she was turning over sausages.

'Sit down, sir,' Anna's housekeeper said. 'These two are full. This is for you.'

The captain sat, his lap immediately occupied by his son. Captain Beattie bowed his head over Allan and held him close.

Anna turned towards Pru. Efficient, capable and probably a spinster in the making since birth, Anna sat and opened her arms. Without any hesitation, Pru landed in her lap.

'I tried, ma'am,' she whispered. 'T'old witch told me she'd be watching the house and if I left for anything, the constable would nab me and haul me away.' She shivered, and not from cold. 'I've been hauled away before.'

'No one will haul you away,' she declared, even as she knew she was stepping into a great unknown. 'Allan is alive and so are you. How did you manage, Pru, when those odious women left?'

It was Pru's turn for silence. Anna knew the captain waited for an answer, too, some explanation of what had gone so horribly wrong. Anna wondered if anyone had ever listened to the scullery maid before. What to say? She knew. 'Pru, you kept both you and Allan safe for... for...two months? I think you are amazingly brave and creative.'

'I know how to get by on nearly nothing,' Pru replied, her hesitation replaced by something close to pride. She turned towards Allan on his father's lap. 'We managed, didn't we?'

Allan nodded.

'I wish I knew why they abandoned you two,' Captain Beattie said. 'I trusted them.'

'I think I know,' Pru said in a small voice. 'Sir, maybe I was nosy.'

'Hardly matters,' the captain replied. He surprised Anna by winking at the child. *You do have an instinct for children*, she thought. 'I've been known to snoop around when I thought something was amiss. Did you think that, too?'

Pru nodded. 'When you're raised in a workhouse, you get...cautious.'

'I hear that from some of my crew,' he said gently. 'What was amiss?'

His question, asked with nothing except interest, nothing overt, seemed to open the floodgates. 'They whispered together a lot, and I heard about someone named Faro. Do you know him?'

Anna gave the captain oceans of credit. He didn't laugh.

'I have, indeed. It's a card game, Pru, and I've lost a few coins at the table, too. They gambled, then?'

'Only Miss Driscoll, I think. She said she had some money from you.'

'That money was to keep you fed and comfortable until I returned.' His voice hardened as he gave Anna a side glance. 'Two hundred pounds. Some of that was supposed to be your wages, Pru. Did you even see a penny?'

She shook her head. 'No, sir. Miss Driscoll went out at night and when she came back…well, I heard her crying a few times.' She shrugged. 'Maybe she wasn't too good with Faro.'

'I wasn't either, so I stopped. I gather she didn't.'

'Miss Driscoll got angry at Pru over everything, Papa.' Allan leaned back and looked up at his father. 'Pru didn't steal anything. Why was Miss Driscoll so angry that she hit Pru?'

The captain sighed.

You look so tired, Anna thought.

'I'm sorry, Pru,' he said.

'It didn't show,' the scullery maid said, as if that was somehow allowed, which chilled Anna to her marrow. 'I also heard them talking about jewellery. Did…? Was that…?'

'My wife's jewellery,' he said, his voice dull, like an ache. He kissed the top of Allan's head. 'Allan's mother's. Oh, God.'

'You didn't lose that, Papa,' Allan said. 'I knew where you kept Mama's pretties, and Pru hid them behind the commode in my dressing room.'

'Pru, you're so resourceful. You can sign on my crew any time you wish,' Captain Beattie said approvingly.

'Sir, I could never,' she said softly, as though a compliment was too much. 'You're teasing me. I knew they wouldn't look behind the commode because night soil is my job.'

'Mama's pretties weren't anything valuable, I suppose,' Captain Beattie said, gathering his son close, reminiscing in a way that seemed almost too intimate to Anna. 'Before the war, and even before we married, I liked to bring Miss Cathy Fergusson baubles from my ports of call. Some necklaces, a bracelet from Ceylon, a cameo brooch from France before the situation got so nasty. Thank you, Pru. I'll collect it tonight after you're all in bed here.'

'We're not going back there, Papa?' Allan asked.

'Never.' The captain looked at Anna. 'Miss Fontaine is letting us stay here tonight. She has agreed that you and Pru can remain here while I am in drydock in Portsmouth. Tell us what happened next, Pru, when they couldn't find Cathy's baubles.'

'They left. They told us not to leave the house or say anything.' She looked down again. 'As if anyone would have believed us.'

'I doubt anyone would have,' Anna said. 'You both could have ended up in the workhouse, with Captain Beattie none the wiser. Pru, you are my hero.'

'And mine,' the captain said.

Captain Beattie deposited his son back in his chair. While the children ate—Mrs Moore had brought more biscuits and their appetites seemed bottomless—he gestured towards the open door.

Anna followed.

'I'll return to my house and see what I can recover. Would you show me where Allan and I will sleep tonight? I know it is an imposition, but I don't know what else to do.'

'Never fear, sir,' Anna said. 'We have room. It's a small house,' she said at the top of the landing. 'We're renting it, with the rent paid quarterly.'

'Is it time to pay?'

'Soon,' she replied, wondering where that would come from, now that Will was gone. There was so much to consider. She glanced at the man beside her, and saw him not only as a captain with firm command and many lives in his hands, but also as a father with no idea what to do, beyond asking for help from a stranger. *May I never be that desperate*, was her first thought, followed by, *but if I am, I hope someone will help me.*

'I will leave you money to pay the lease, and also funds to cover all expenses, until I return.' He nearly smiled. 'Provided you don't pawn jewellery or frequent gaming hells.'

She laughed. 'Not in recent memory, sir.'

It gave her a pang to open the door to Will's room. She hadn't meant to hesitate, but she couldn't help leaning her head against the door and taking a deep breath.

'Death is hard, Miss Fontaine,' he said in that matter-of-fact tone she was already recognising, no matter how short their acquaintance. 'I couldn't have asked for a better first lieutenant than your brother.'

She couldn't look at him, knowing she would disgrace herself with more tears. She kept her forehead against the door, liking the solidity. 'He said the same thing about you, sir.'

'Then we were both fortunate,' he replied. 'Buck up, my mate.' He chuckled. 'That's what I would tell my crew. I am a plainspoken Scot, and time is moving on.'

That was all she needed. Captain Beattie was a busy man, trying to arrange the welfare of his son at short notice. He didn't need to deal with a tearful lady. She opened the door.

She took a deep breath. There it was, Will's favourite blanket when ashore, his books, even the sweetmeats she knew he liked, because he was coming home. She stepped back involuntarily, unable to enter the room. To her surprise and then her complete relief, Captain Beattie put his hands on her shoulders and steadied her.

They stood that way for a moment, then she squared her shoulders and stepped into the room under her own power. 'Thank you, sir,' she said, and meant it.

She calmly surveyed the room again, and became herself. 'I am sorry the bed is so small, sir, but I do have another pillow.'

The captain became the captain again, too. 'No matter. I look forward to close quarters with my son I so seldom see.' He turned to her. 'Miss Fontaine, I will be forever grateful to Pru for her courage.'

'I am, too,' Anna said. 'We'll find a good place for her here.'

Finding that place was easily accomplished. They came downstairs to see the children intent upon playing jackstraws, which Mrs Moore must have dredged up from somewhere in this childless house. Anna had no doubt that Pru would be looked after by her housekeeper tonight.

What now? This was her house, but something about Captain Beattie seemed to fill the place. She knew command when she saw it, and also saw a different person from the utterly distressed man who'd knocked on her door a short time ago.

'What now, sir?' she asked, her voice quiet in case she was wrong.

'The hour is late. Allan, Miss Fontaine will help you prepare for bed.' He glanced at her. 'Would you sit with him upstairs until I return from my house?'

'I will, sir.'

He looked next at Mrs Moore, who, it seemed to Anna, watched the whole scenario unfold, her eyes bright with interest.

'Mrs Moore, is it? Can you find somewhere for Pru?'

Anna knew Mrs Moore was used to command, too. 'Pru will fit quite nicely in my room. We will look after each other, sir.'

He actually smiled at that, which allowed Anna to lower her own shoulders a notch.

'Very well, then. Miss Fontaine, I would never ask you to keep your door unlocked until I return. Do you have another key?'

She did, and gave it to him. He kissed his son, and had the supreme fatherly instinct to press his forehead to his son's and whisper a few words only to him. 'I won't be long,' he told her, and let himself out. She locked the door behind him.

Anna didn't think she possessed any motherly instincts at all, but she had no trouble helping Allan into a nightshirt dredged up from a trunk in the attic containing Will's clothing. She made herself comfortable above the covers beside him.

'What should we do now?' she asked, as she remembered Mama's bedtime stories.

'Tell me something about my father,' he said eagerly, which broke her heart into small pieces, as she understood another horrible side of war: it made children and fathers strangers.

She wasn't about to tell this trusting child that she knew nothing about his father, beyond his name and his desperate plight. She said a small prayer, small because she doubted whether the Lord had time for her needs.

Maybe she was wrong. She knew where to begin, as surely as if some Superior Being *did* care.

'There isn't a braver man in the entire Royal Navy,' she said. 'He and his ship…'

'He said it's named after a bird,' Allan supplied, when she stopped.

'Ah, yes, the *Swallow*. Your father and the *Swallow* are keeping us safe from enemies across the Channel.'

Should she? She did, putting her arm around him and receiving instant gratification when he snuggled close with no hesitation. In spite of all that had happened to him, she knew he was still a trusting child.

'His duty keeps him from home and he wishes every night on...on a star that he could be here to keep you safe.'

She heard a contented sigh, then even breathing. She closed her eyes and slept, too, waking a little later to feel a hand on her shoulder, and words close to her ear.

'Miss Fontaine, I am back and the front door is locked. You and I will be in front of Carter and Brustein at eight o'clock.'

Anna sat up, wondering for a brief moment where she was and who *this* was.

'Oh, yes,' she whispered. 'In the morning. Goodnight, Captain Beattie.' She smiled in the darkness. 'He's a warm little furnace. You'll have no trouble sleeping.'

In her own room, Miss Anna Fontaine had no trouble either. She settled into her bed content, despite what a wrenching day it had been. *Captain Beattie, keep me safe, too*, she thought. And she closed her eyes.

Chapter Four

They were at Carter and Brustein's promptly, when Shlomo Brustein himself unlocked the front door of his counting house close to Plymouth docks.

Allan Beattie had taken great exception to his father leaving him. Troubled, Anna watched them both, wondering who suffered more, and resolving in her heart of hearts never to put herself in such a position. Not that anyone was in a hurry to marry her. Quite the contrary. She decided that this little boy with a father bound to do his duty would never be abandoned again, certainly not on *her* watch.

Bless Mrs Moore, who presented eggs and toast for two children—as Pru was no more than a child herself—and who had apparently decided that not on *her* watch would they go hungry again. It was Mrs Moore who held the little boy close when his father kissed him and forced himself outside the door, Anna beside him.

'You have a ferocious crew, Miss Fontaine,' he said as they hurried along. 'I dare anyone to stand in Mrs Moore's or your way.' He stopped. 'I have roped you into something I hope you never regret.'

'Call me a patriot,' she told him, wondering at herself.

They hurried through the Barbican, that warren of shops and houses rooted there for two centuries and more. Captain Beattie kindly slowed down so she did not have to break into a run to keep up with him.

'Miss Fontaine, according to my little boy this morning, you told him last night that I wish on a star every night that I could be with him.'

'I did,' she said frankly. 'He was a little upset when you left and wanted to talk about you.'

'I can imagine,' he murmured. 'I found Cathy's jewels in that damned house, exactly where Pru had said. And you comforted Allan with wishes on stars.'

He didn't say it unkindly, but more like a long-absent father who knew nothing about the routine children craved. Her heart went out to Captain Beattie and men like him, caught in a war and away from loved ones.

'I will look for that star from now on,' he told her.

He took her down a narrow street to an establishment she had passed before but never noticed because it must have been designed that way. There was only a small plaque by the door to announce Carter and Brustein.

'He's here early for me,' Captain Beattie said and opened the door. 'I sent a message last night.'

Anna saw a stooped older man who looked as though he had spent a lifetime bent over ledgers.

'Come, come, my dears,' he said. 'Captain Beattie, who is this charming lady?'

'My lifeline, sir. You read my note and know I need your help.'

Mr Brustein opened the door to his office. 'Sit, please.' He wasted not a moment. 'I know your urgency. All I need is Lieutenant Fontaine's will.'

The Captain handed over the sheet of paper.

Mr Brustein nodded. 'We can make this work.'

And so he did. Within minutes, Mr Brustein handed over his paperwork to an underling. 'Done and done. Will's account is in your name now, Miss Fontaine. Captain Beattie, name the amount you wish to withdraw from your holdings for Miss Fontaine.'

He did so. When Anna gasped, he gave her what she recognised by now as a captain's appraisal. 'You are helping me by caring for the children, Miss Fontaine. You can save Will's funds for when you need them later on. Don't argue.'

She didn't. The money appeared almost at once. When she opened her mouth to protest one last time, he took her reticule and put the money inside. It barely fitted.

'You are doing me an essential service, Miss Fontaine,' he said. 'I won't leave you wanting.'

'Where are you bound for, Captain Beattie?' Mr Brustein said in the silence that followed.

'Portsmouth for now,' he said, 'with permanent orders soon.'

Mr Brustein held out his hand to Anna. 'You are doing a kind thing.'

'Such a small thing,' she managed.

Captain Beattie closed his eyes and she felt his relief,

almost as if he'd embraced her and pressed her close to his body.

Such a small thing, she thought, then realised, perhaps for the first time, the greatness of small things.

Chapter Five

Outside on the street again, the captain put his finger to her lips briefly when she opened her mouth. 'I will have no argument from you, Miss Fontaine, about that money.'

'But…'

'I will sleep better at night, knowing that you, my son and Pru are safe. I say to you again, don't argue.'

'Aye, sir, aye,' she said, half-teasing, half-serious, which startled her, too. What was happening to her calm, well-ordered life?

'And now?' she asked, feeling the need for a monumental change of subject.

'The Drake, Miss Fontaine,' he told her. 'Look lively, now. The *Swallow* must sail soon.'

She had passed the Drake Hotel many times, always impressed by the nearly constant flow of Navy men to and from its stately entrance. But to go inside? She hesitated.

'Come, come, Miss Fontaine. I want you to meet Mrs Fillion, a remarkable woman who started here as a maid and now owns it. Will might have left something here.'

Mystified, she followed him to the lobby, which somehow gave off an air of power, further amplified by officers grouped around a doorway into a room with what looked like a card game in progress. At this hour of the morning?

Captain Beattie must have noticed her amazement. 'This is what we call the Perpetual Whist Game. It starts early and never ends.'

'It's been going on for years,' said a woman with a distinctly Irish lilt to her words.

Startled, Anna turned around to see a woman dressed in serviceable black, with curly red hair shot through with grey. To Anna's amazement, Captain Beattie solemnly kissed her cheek.

'Home from sea, Mrs Fillion, sound of wind and limb,' he said, then, 'Miss Fontaine, we always greet this hotelier with a kiss and that very reassurance. You're looking at durable Royal Navy tradition. Miss Fontaine, meet Mrs Fillion.'

Anna shook the extended hand. 'Pleased to make your acquaintance,' she said. The handshake signalled an equality that Anna relished. So did the kindness in the other woman's eyes.

Anna had to admire Captain Beattie, a man becoming more adept at explaining his fraught situation quickly. When he finished, Mrs Fillion touched Anna's hand. 'Accept my sympathy on the death of your brother. These are indeed trying times.'

'Thank you.'

'I am so glad you took in the Captain's son.' Mrs Fillion's eyes misted over. 'So much suffering at sea, and at home. It beggars belief. What may I help you with?'

'If you please, let us into your storeroom,' he said. 'I think there is something for Miss Fontaine on your shelves.'

What? Anna thought as she followed them down the steps off the lobby.

'Mrs Fillion lets us keep personal effects down here. Letters that go astray end up here. This is often the last resting place of dead men's possessions.' He took her hand. 'Steep stairs, Miss Fontaine. Before he died, your brother said there was something of his here.'

Mrs Fillion turned to Anna. 'If my officers only have time to drop off possessions, I contact their loved ones.'

'So much work for you,' Anna said. 'I admire you for doing this.'

'We all do,' Captain Beattie said. 'I've left items here, too.'

He stood close to her—it was a tight space—but there was room to back away. She didn't. Why, she couldn't have said. She could consider it when he was at sea and not smelling so nicely of bay rum and something else— probably just Captain Beattie.

'Do you alphabetize us, Mrs F?' he asked, which made Anna and Mrs Fillion laugh.

'I do, Captain B. Follow me to the Fs.'

Mrs Fillion counted off two shelves, reached up and handed her a small box—perhaps a ring box?

'When did...?' Anna asked as she took it.

'I date them. Look, last year. April.'

'Open it. It's yours now,' Captain Beattie urged.

She did, and stared at what must be a lady's wedding

ring, filigreed and lovely. 'I had no idea... He never said he'd met someone...' She shook her head. 'This makes me so sad.'

The Captain put his arm around her. 'In late winter and early spring, we were cruising off Jamaica, with time for shore leave. We returned with the fleet and anchored off Gibraltar.' He hesitated, then, 'Your brother was exemplary in his duties, but he was not talkative.'

'No, he was not,' she admitted, and then opened a small door into her heart. 'I wish we had both been more forthcoming with one another.'

'I have no idea what this meant to him, or who it was meant for.' He surprised Anna then and, from the look on Mrs Fillion's face, surprised her as well, by adding, 'I could be more forthcoming, too. Is it the curse of captaincy?'

'I wouldn't know, sir, although I am certain the Admiralty makes harsh demands on men. And women wait.' Anna touched the ring. 'And wait, never to know.'

'It's yours now, Miss Fontaine. Perhaps *you* can wear it someday,' Mrs Fillion said gently.

'That seems unlikely,' she said quietly. She closed the box, knowing that somewhere in the world, a woman waited for news that would never come. 'I will never know any more than this. I'll tuck it away.'

She waited in silence upstairs while the captain and Mrs Fillion discussed someone from the Drake picking up the boxes from his house and storing them here, in this cellar of forgotten memories.

'Please ask your man to take this to Bledsoe's.' He held out a key. 'He's the estate agent.'

'I will, Captain Beattie,' Mrs Fillion promised.

'I'm off then. My time is short.'

Don't say that, Anna thought in sudden alarm. *It's too final.* She chastised herself inwardly, well aware that it was merely conversation and nothing more.

'Good sailing, Captain Beattie,' Mrs Fillion said, giving him a firm handshake.

Someone called for Mrs Fillion at the front desk, a captain on crutches.

She started towards him, then turned back to Anna. 'I am always here if you need me.'

'Oh, I...'

'If you need me, Miss Fontaine,' she repeated.

They walked back to Covent Street in silence. She glanced at the man beside her a few times, wondering if he regretted what he was about to do. She wanted to tell him not to worry, that she would never fail him, even as she cringed inside at this enormous responsibility which had been thrust upon her.

Her street was quiet and calm as usual. When the Captain opened the door, she shook off her fears at the sound of running steps and a little boy with his arms open wide.

Captain Beattie crouched down and held him close. Anna turned to close the door and saw two of her neighbours, heads together, across the street, looking at her. She waved, but they did not respond, only turned away and continued their conversation, with a glance or two in her direction. Odd, that.

Mrs Moore had prepared a luncheon, eaten in the kitchen, the five of them close together, with Allan on his father's lap, because there were only so many chairs. Allan nestled close to his father, his cheek against gilt buttons.

'I have no way of knowing how long I will be in Portsmouth,' Captain Beattie said finally, as he set down his fork. 'I do know that when I return here it will be a brief stay—very brief. Rumour suggests that we might attach ourselves to Collingwood's Mediterranean fleet, but that remains to be seen.'

He touched his son's dark hair, a contrast to his own red hair with its many lighter highlights. 'Allan, your mother's hair was so brown and pretty,' he said, 'very much like Miss Fontaine's hair.'

Anna asked herself why a mundane observation to a six-year-old should make her face feel warm, but it did. *It's nothing special*, she wanted to tell them both, looking away.

When she looked back, he was the captain again.

'Son, mind your manners and help the ladies when asked. I must leave now.' He regarded Pru, who moved her chair closer to Allan in a protective gesture. 'You have allies, Pru. Mrs Moore and Miss Fontaine are here to help, not frighten you.'

'You can be certain of that, Captain Beattie,' Mrs Moore said, sounding militant.

Anna couldn't help but smile. 'Sir, I am most fortunate in Mrs Moore, and no, if peace breaks out you cannot steal her.'

Perfect. They all laughed.

'Miss Fontaine, don't I intimidate you?' Captain Beattie joked.

Did he?

'No, sir. You have a good heart,' Anna said impulsively.

'Don't tell anyone, will you?'

'Your secret is safe with me. God go with you,' she said quietly.

'And you, kind lady.' After a long moment, Captain Beattie set his son down. 'Walk me to the door, Allan. You, too, Miss Fontaine.'

'All of us will,' Mrs Moore said.

'Aye aye, Captain Moore,' the captain replied, and gave her a smart salute, so at least they were smiling as he opened the door.

As Anna watched, he gathered his son close. Allan cried, and he soothed him with soft words—Gaelic words, something heard in distant Scotland.

'Go to Pru,' he said, and Allan did, the two children clinging close, as they must have clung to each other when they had no idea what would happen to them. Anna put away that image because there was something equally difficult happening right now. How did Navy families manage farewells?

'Do not fear, Captain Beattie,' she said. 'You brought him to the right house.'

'I know I did,' he said. 'It may be the best thing I have done in years.'

'Do not fear,' she said again, but for his ears only.

Mrs Moore handed the captain his boat cloak. Pru found his hat and gave it to him.

He kissed Allan again. 'I'll see you when I can, you know I will.'

Mrs Moore headed the children towards what Anna hoped were biscuits in the kitchen. It only remained for Captain Beattie to close the door. He stepped out, looked down as if he wasn't quite sure of his footing, then back at her.

'Miss Fontaine, I sound like a perfect rogue, but I need a hug and here you are.'

With no hesitation, she stepped onto the wide front step. He enveloped her in an embrace that she suddenly realised she badly needed, too. Yesterday, she'd waited to hug her brother. That would never happen again on this earth. Here was a near-stranger holding her close as if his life depended on it. Maybe it did; she had his son.

'He's all I have,' he whispered as he held her close.

'I know. I will never let you down.'

Then he was gone. She couldn't watch, even as her neighbour across the street did so avidly. She closed the door, leaned against it and briefly wondered if this was how husbands and wives felt upon parting.

'Captain Beattie, I will not fail you,' she announced. 'Never.'

Chapter Six

In the following weeks, the residents of 208 Covent Street, augmented by two children, worked their way through grief and sleepless nights and came out on the other side. It didn't happen overnight, but it happened. In her quiet way, Anna was inclined to give all the credit to Mrs Moore and Pru, who was Allan's relentless protector. Upon reflection, she realised that it had begun when she agreed to help Captain Beattie. She was responsible.

Anna had debated whether to leave the boy alone with his faithful Pru, but had decided on a different tack, spending time every day with him, playing jackstraws or reading. She remembered Will's attentions when they were children and how often he'd jollied her out of pouts, considering it his duty to cheer her up.

Mere days ago, such a memory might have reduced her to tears. Instead, she chose to honour Will by remembrance.

'Will generally always beat me at jackstraws,' she grumbled, looking at her pitiful pile of slender wooden rods. 'I'm just not patient, and he was.'

'Did he make you cry when you lost?' Allan asked as he carefully tugged a stick from the jumble and nothing quivered.

'No. He was much nicer than that, you scamp!' She laughed, pleased at the memory, which could have broken her heart but didn't, mainly because she'd discovered she liked jackstraws and little boys. 'Will also let me walk with him, even though I knew he would rather have been with his friends.'

'If my father had time, would he play jackstraws with me?'

'Certainly,' she assured him, sensing in her heart that Captain Beattie would do exactly that. She suddenly wanted to give Napoleon a piece of her mind for ruining so many childhood dreams.

Luncheon always meant smiles, as she and Mrs Moore watched their young charges eat with enthusiasm. 'We could probably feed them a cauliflower and beet purée and they would smack their lips and ask for more,' she whispered to Mrs Moore.

At first, bedtime was harder, Allan inconsolable at sleeping by himself in Will's room. Pru had happily followed Mrs Moore downstairs, but here was Allan, alone.

Anna knelt by Allan, and he folded into her arms. 'Papa slept in here with me yesterday,' he said through his tears. 'Papa's gone now.'

She felt her own eyes welling. 'My dear, I don't think I could spend a night in my brother's room,' she managed. 'He meant everything to me, and it's hard, with him gone.'

God bless Mrs Moore. 'There is a boy-sized cot in the storeroom. We could put it in your room?'

'We could. Would you agree to that, Allan?'

'My feet will still be cold,' he told her dolefully. 'Pru has warm feet and so does my father.'

If you were my very own, I would keep your feet warm, Anna thought, surprising herself with a fleeting, impish thought: How would it feel to have Captain Beattie and her sandwiching his son between them? *Anna, really*, she scolded herself. *Think of something else.*

'Allan, have you ever slept with a pig before?'

'No, miss,' he said, eyes wide.

'The pig I have in mind is made of pottery and filled with hot water. I will wrap a towel around this pig and put him at the foot of your cot.'

'He'll warm my feet?'

'Yes. And we'll put your cot right by my bed. Will that work for you?'

He considered the matter, and frowned. 'What about the rest of me?'

'I promise you that once your feet are warm, you'll fall right to sleep.'

'Promise?'

'Promise.'

Allan nodded. 'I'll do it.'

And he did, after helping Anna make up the cot they carried upstairs and deposited close to her bed. The pig came next, wrapped in a light cloth, then placed at the foot of his cot, between the sheets and blanket.

He patted his pillow. 'Miss Fontaine, is Pru downstairs with Mrs Moore?'

'She is. You'll see her in the morning.'

He hung his head. 'When I cried at night, Pru held my hand. Does Papa cry at night?'

Her heart opened wider to this child of a man nearly always at sea, because evil men schemed to control the world. Here she was, answering questions that Captain Beattie would probably give the earth to answer, because he loved his son.

'He probably does sniff a bit, when no one is watching.'

'He won't mind if I cry sometimes?'

'Ask him, the next time you see him.'

She saw the sudden fear. 'He will be back, won't he?' he asked.

Even so close to her, Allan Beattie wasn't close enough. She pulled him onto her lap.

What to say? Yesterday's Anna Fontaine had vanished, replaced by a woman aware of the huge responsibility thrust upon her because she'd opened her door to a desperate father. She pushed Fear away and there stood Resolve, perhaps a little hesitant, but still a calming presence.

'He will be back, Allan. I know it.'

She held her breath, but he went willingly to bed. When he reached up to her, she lay down on her bed and held his hand.

'Are your feet warm?' she asked.

'They are.' He yawned. 'Papa needs one of these.'

'We have another one. He can use it, when he returns.'

Allan yawned again, closed his eyes and slept. She listened for his even breathing, then quietly went downstairs, wondering how Mrs Moore was faring. She found more tears, and Pru on her housekeeper's lap. She flashed her friend a *What-have-we-got-into?* look.

She sat beside Mrs Moore and touched Pru's leg. 'I hope you're not worried about Allan,' she said. 'He's warm with that pig in his bed, and already asleep.'

Pru hung her head. 'I did a bad thing, Miss Fontaine.'

'It couldn't have been too bad. The house is still standing,' Anna replied.

Her reward was a tiny smile, then the return of remorse writ large. 'Miss Fontaine, I broke a glass. I didn't mean to, but I broke it.'

Mrs Moore looked at her. Pru looked at her. Anna knew she was in charge, responsible, and resolute because Captain Beattie had left her in charge. She gently cupped her hands around the scullery maid's face. It startled the child at first.

I doubt anyone has ever touched Pru with kindness, Anna thought. She kept her hands on Pru's face, relieved to see her shoulders lower as she relaxed.

'There now, Pru. Let me tell you what I require of you in this house. We work together. When things break, as they sometimes do, we sweep them up and that is the end of it.' She kissed Pru's forehead.

Her own doubts were swept away when Pru put her hands over hers. 'I will always look after Allan Beattie, Miss Fontaine.'

'And I will look after you, my dear.'

Chapter Seven

A worse trial than a broken glass came in the morning, from a source Anna had never imagined: her neighbours.

To her delight, the sun shone, something not always seen in January on a Devonshire coast that leaned heavily towards winter fog. While Pru helped Mrs Moore with the breakfast dishes, Anna decided Allan needed the small task of unlocking the front door.

He did it with a flourish that made Anna wish his father were standing there to see how far his son had come in less than a week. Allan grinned at her over his shoulder then darted outside onto the front step, where he took a deep breath.

'It's been so long since I was outside.'

He was right, she realised with a shock, remembering what Pru had told them about those two horrid women threatening them if they ventured beyond their own front door.

Those days were over, and it was a nice morning. Anna pulled on her cloak, after calling to Mrs Moore that they were going across the street to pay a call on Mrs Dalton. She grabbed Allan's coat and handed it to him as he soaked in the sun.

'Let's cross the street,' she said. 'I want to introduce you to my neighbour, Mrs Dalton.'

'Does she like little boys, Missy?'

She smiled at the nickname as he took her hand as they crossed the quiet street. She thought of the many mornings she'd joined Mrs Dalton for tea, her usual contribution her brother's latest letter from the fleet. He had a knack for making sea life interesting for the ladies on shore.

Anna knocked and waited. A movement of the lace curtain near the door caught her attention. She waved to the shadowy figure. To her surprise, she saw a woman glaring at her and turning her back.

She stood there, indecisive, then remembered that her last view of Mrs Dalton had been around Captain Beattie's arm as he'd hugged her on the front step. Surely she didn't think…

'Should I knock, too?' Allan asked.

'I think not,' Anna said. 'She must be busy. Let's go home.'

Allan pointed to the other houses. 'I like to knock on doors. Should we try another one?'

She looked across the street where he pointed at other houses. To her horror, ladies she assumed were her friends stared back at her disapprovingly.

'Perhaps they are too busy as well.' She managed to keep her voice light. 'Mrs Moore promised to make my favourite sugar biscuits. Let's see if she has started them yet. You can sneak a bit of dough if I distract her.'

She reckoned that was all any child of sound mind needed, and she wasn't wrong. He practically towed her across the street and up the steps. He didn't bother removing his coat, but trotted into the kitchen, where, thank the Lord, Mrs Moore was cooling a tray of biscuits.

Soon Pru and Allan were seated at the table, with biscuits in front of them and glasses of milk.

'Mrs Moore, I believe I sniffed something off in the pantry earlier,' she said.

Mrs Moore followed Anna into the pantry and quietly closed the door. 'What's up, my dear?'

Anna grabbed her arm and told her what had happened.

Mrs Moore's eyes widened. 'The other ladies, too?'

'Yes! Everyone was staring at me behind lace curtains. All I can think of...when Captain Beattie hugged me on the front step, I saw Mrs Dalton. What have I *done*?'

Mrs Moore put her arm around her. 'Nothing. These old biddies have nothing to do except gossip. Don't worry.'

'I hope you're right.'

'I know I am. I'll take the children with me to market. I usually see Mrs Dalton's cook there, and one or two others. I'll tell them what's happened.' She patted Anna. 'Don't you worry.'

Anna saw them off to market. 'I am making a mountain out of a molehill,' she murmured.

She perked up when the doorbell jangled, hoping it was Mrs Dalton.

Oh, no, not you, she thought, dismayed, when she

opened the door on Reverend Edward Maddy, curate at St Andrew's, Vicar Montague's substitute.

'Reverend, do come in,' she said, wishing she could close the door on that face. There was something about the man that made her wary. He looked ordinary, except that his face was doughy and he wore an oversized cross, as if needing to announce to everyone that he was a man of God.

'What I have to say will not take long,' he assured her.

She watched his face for kindness and saw none. Anna chose to think the best. Perhaps he hadn't heard about Will, who, like so many Plymouth parishioners, was often gone.

'Reverend, I thought this house had been spared from any suffering about Trafalgar, but my brother Will…'

He slashed his hand down like a guillotine blade. 'Miss Fontaine, I never thought *you* would succumb to the lures of the flesh!'

She stepped back. What was he *saying*? 'Reverend, you must have…'

He shook his finger at her. 'Did you think your indiscretion would go unnoticed by your neighbours, who witnessed a shocking display on these steps? Heaven knows what went on *inside* this house!'

She stared at him. Was he calling her to account for nothing beyond gossip? *Mrs Dalton, what have you done to me?* she thought, perplexed.

'Sir, please understand what happened. Captain Beattie arrived to tell me that my brother, his first lieutenant, died after Trafalgar.'

He folded his arms. 'Oh, really? Surprise me, Miss Fontaine.'

Unnerved, she took up the challenge. 'His son Allan was with him, and a scullery maid. The little ones had been living alone for two months after the Captain's housekeeper and cook abandoned them. That is what Mrs Dalton *didn't* see.'

'Tell me more,' he said. 'I am all ears.'

He did have large ears, but Anna knew he wasn't hearing anything except the opinion of a gossiping neighbour. She plunged ahead anyway.

'Captain Beattie had nowhere to take his son, no family, no one. He had to sail in the morning to Portsmouth's drydocks. He begged me to keep Allan and the maid here until he could make other arrangements. That is all.'

Her heart sank as the Reverend's face hardened.

'That is all,' she repeated. 'What Mrs Dalton witnessed from across the street was a desperate man needing reassurance as he left his son again.' Anna could tell he didn't believe her. She drew herself up. 'There was nothing salacious or untoward. You have misjudged me.'

'Others on this street came to warn me.'

'They saw nothing,' she snapped, tired of this interrogation. 'It was early; the street was empty. Mrs Dalton is merely spreading rumours.'

He shook his finger at her. 'The ladies on this street are exemplary Christian women. I hear you have only been here a few years.'

'Six, since my mother died, followed by my father, a vicar.'

'A vicar? Your *father*? Shame on you. When that Navy man returns, you must refuse him entrance!'

'I will do no such thing!' she insisted, finding strength from somewhere.

He pointed his finger. 'Then you are as guilty as he!'

Guilty of what? Anna wondered. Reverend Maddy had come to the parish of St Andrew's already self-righteous, sowing distrust. Who could she complain to?

'You, Miss Fontaine, have no power to do anything. Let me be your guide.' He came closer. She backed up. The look in his eyes sent chills marching in ranks down her back. 'I'll take care of this unfortunate situation.'

'I doubt that supremely,' she said quietly.

'You are a menace to decency and rectitude,' he declared.

She had no defender. All she had was a promise made to a sad and desperate man serving King and country, at the expense of his own flesh and blood. She calmly and deliberately decided it was enough.

Three words. She didn't raise her voice, because she never raised her voice. All she had was the force of her own conviction and the mental reminder of the gratitude in Captain Beattie's tired eyes. Her words had to carry the day, because she had no other defence.

'Leave this house.'

He left, slamming the door for good measure.

Anna had one final thought.

I am ruined.

Chapter Eight

I am the world's most accomplishment actress, Anna told herself after an evening of jackstraws and bedtime rituals until Allan slept in the cot beside her bed.

She knew her housekeeper had returned from the market with her own solemn face. Anna looked around for Pru, Mrs Moore's little shadow, as Allan was hers.

'She is abed, too,' Mrs Moore said as she poured the tea.

'I knew something was wrong.'

'You go first. It might explain what happened to me.'

Anna told her housekeeper precisely what had happened, leaving nothing out. 'I fear Mrs Dalton has taken it upon herself to spread a wild untruth. Our nasty curate dropped by to condemn me.'

'This is so unfair,' Mrs Moore declared. 'I received the cold shoulder from several of the maids on the street. Miss Calder's maid seemed inclined to listen and at least appear sympathetic.' She managed a mirthless chuckle. 'We both wondered how a Navy town like Plymouth could ever consider that this hasn't happened before.'

'Nothing has happened,' Anna said quickly.

'Not to those who like to spread rumours.'

'What can I do? Captain Beattie *did* hug me on the front step.'

Trust Mrs Moore to dredge up a little humour from this reeking midden. 'It's all your fault for being a pretty lady,' she declared with a smile. 'We should spread our own rumours about captains long at sea. You know they must yearn for the comfort of wives in ports.'

'Mrs Moore!'

Mrs Moore patted her hand. 'It's a tempest in a teapot. That is all.'

'I hope you're right.'

'So do I,' her housekeeper said quietly. 'Time will tell.'

It proved to be a long week. Left to her own devices, Anna knew she would stay away from innuendo by remaining indoors. She wasn't one to invite attention, which made this entire situation so improbable. Didn't these Covent Street ladies *know* her by now?

She would have remained inside except for Allan, who for two days sat by the window that overlooked Covent Street, gazing out with a wistful expression. She chafed inside, knowing that he had already suffered cruelty by a nanny and housekeeper who hadn't had his best interests in mind.

Stiffen your spine, she told herself one morning. She held out her hand to him as he pined in silence. *Enough is enough.*

'Allan, let's go for a walk.'

His expression brightened immediately. In minutes, they walked down Covent Street to Sutton Pool, with its noise and confusion, and smells of tar and low tide. At the Hoe, she bought Allan a sweet and they started back. Allan tugged on her hand. 'Missy, when will my father return?'

It can't be a moment too soon, she thought, hoping Captain Beattie could solve the dilemma he had inadvertently turned loose on her.

'I wish I knew,' she tried, which Allan's expression told her was unsatisfactory. 'I know it's not the answer you want, but it's the best I have.'

The afternoon was warm for January, and they idled towards Covent Street again, a tidy lane that used to feel like a refuge.

They passed two of her friends, who ignored her by turning away. *Never mind, Anna*, she told herself, even as her heart broke. *They choose to believe rumours.*

So ended another dreary day, brightened only by Allan Beattie's growing confidence, and Pru, who had attached herself to Mrs Moore even as she continued her own vigilance over Allan.

'I never heard Pru laugh before,' Allan told her after dinner when they adjourned to the sitting room for a jackstraw competition, now conducted on a whist table. 'She likes Mrs Moore.'

'So do I,' Anna said.

'I like you,' he said in a most matter-of-fact way, chin in cupped hands, elbows on the table as he surveyed the battleground of jackstraws.

His quiet observation carried her through that week and the next and into February, which ended on a Saturday evening as someone knocked on the door, a novelty in itself, because no one had knocked on their door for weeks now. She prayed it wasn't the curate.

'I'll get it, dearie,' Mrs Moore said. Anna thought she heard more than a hint of militance, as if her housekeeper was ready to do battle for her and the children.

Allan concentrated on the jackstraws, even as he rubbed his eyes and yawned, sure signals that his day was done. Anna rose to her feet at the sound of firm footsteps.

'Thank God,' she whispered as Captain Beattie stood in the doorway to the sitting room, Mrs Moore beaming behind him.

'Allan!' was all he said, which ended any jackstraw competition. He embraced his ecstatic son.

Anna smiled at the sight, grateful beyond measure that there were no tears this time, nothing but a little boy so happy to announce that he was the Covent Street jackstraw champion, and, 'Why were you so long away, Papa?'

'Yes, why?' Anna whispered, her lips barely moving, her turmoil replaced by sudden calm. She hung up the Captain's boat cloak as father and son sat close together and Allan told him about visiting Sutton Pool with Miss Fontaine and even walking all the way to the Hoe, where Sir Francis Drake himself had watched for the arrival of the Spanish Armada.

'I have learned so much, Papa,' he concluded, as his father held him close.

The Captain looked up at Anna when she said that Mrs Moore had prepared a second supper. 'That is, if you're hungry, sir,' she added, unwilling to interfere, as much as she wanted to crowd close to Captain Beattie, too, and pour out her calamity.

It could wait, and it did, as they crowded together around the kitchen table, enjoying the sight of a hungry man making short work of Mrs Moore's leftovers.

Allan's enthusiasm faded when his father announced that his visit was brief.

'Allan, I have to leave again on tomorrow's tide. The *Swallow* is fit and ready, and it's back to the Channel for me.' He looked at Anna. 'Miss Fontaine, you and I must discuss what will happen now. I still need your assistance.'

'There is another matter,' she said quietly when Allan turned his attention to Pru. 'Once Allan is in bed, we must talk.'

He gave her an evaluating look. All she could do was gather up the dishes to return to the scullery.

'You're worrying me,' he said only moments later, following her with his plate and cutlery.

'Something unfortunate has happened,' she began, then shook her head. 'Oh, not to Allan. It's another matter.' She put her hand on his arm, unable to help herself because her disquiet was real. 'After he's in bed, sir. I'll be in the sitting room.'

Did some malevolent force decide to move the clock's hand back two hours? Time dragged. She waited as the Captain followed Allan upstairs. *Don't be small about this, Miss Fontaine*, she told herself, knowing that every moment with his son was precious to a father compelled to be away because duty called and could not be ignored.

She considered the matter, aware how quiet her life was, how little ever happened to her. She had blessed Will for suggesting they set up house together in Plymouth, which at least took her from the sympathy of her late father's well-meaning parishioners. Her life had remained calm and orderly. Too calm? Too orderly?

She looked at the clock again, exasperated that the hands never moved. *I can wait*, she thought, followed swiftly by another thought. *I am tired of waiting.*

Chapter Nine

It would have been a simple matter to drift off to sleep, holding his son. John rubbed his eyes as he sat up carefully beside his slumbering boy. The sad child he had parted from so reluctantly had much to say, telling his Papa that Miss Fontaine liked to sew on buttons and walk. 'Papa, we have been *everywhere*,' Allan assured him as he cuddled close.

'I imagine you have,' John told him, even as he smiled inside at his memories of the Caribbean, the Kingdom of Sicily, the cold Baltic Sea with its equally reserved inhabitants, and the exuberance of Africa. *Everywhere, son? Little do you know.*

'It's a nice room,' Allan said, 'but I liked Missy's room, too. That's what I call Miss Fontaine.'

'What, you slept in there?' he asked, then considered the matter. Probably the last thing Anna wanted to do was sleep here in Will's room, with memories of a brother, dead and gone.

'Mrs Moore found a cot,' Allan explained simply. 'And Missy held my hand when I cried.'

John put his hands over his eyes, collecting himself. He knew Anna was waiting downstairs, and from her air of composed distraction, he knew it wasn't good news.

Still, how much time did he have with this lovely child?

'Do you like it here?'

'Aye aye, sir,' Allan said, then laughed. 'Missy also told me she likes to cuddle.' Allan touched his face. 'Papa, she is softer than you are.'

'I imagine she is.' John *had* noticed that Miss Fontaine was not all angles and planes. His face warmed to think of the careful way he had patted the pillow in his quarters aboard the *Swallow*, shaping it just so… Nothing for Allan to know about.

His boy yawned, cuddled, relaxed all over, and slept.

John lay there, amused at himself for pretending that his life was this simple—a father putting his son to bed, then going downstairs to read the paper, or to tease a wife as she tried to darn socks, or even putting his head in her lap, and see where that led. Nice for some—not for him. Napoleon had dictated otherwise. *Up you get*, he told himself. *Face the bad news*.

He watched Anna from the door of the sitting room, admiring her as she sat so still. Maybe she was thinking of Will, who never could say enough kind things about her. Will said once that he doubted any human could remain in a state of turmoil, just being around his sister. 'Annie has mastered the art of being still.'

There it was before him. *Miss Fontaine, you would be the perfect wife in our world gone mad*, he thought. He quickly assured himself that idea was a bolt out of the blue and impossible. But because war waited for him impatiently, tapping its skeletal toes, he had to find someone to care for his son. Perhaps Anna had a suggestion.

She looked up. John knew he had never seen such beautiful eyes anywhere. *The single men in Plymouth must be remarkably stupid*, he thought, then mentally swatted those thoughts away.

'Captain, we have a problem.'

At least she didn't say, *you* have a problem. An optimistic man could take heart at that quiet comment, but he was a realist.

'Give me the news, Miss Fontaine. You can't keep Allan with you. Is that it?'

She blinked in surprise. 'What are you saying? Don't be absurd.'

He hadn't expected that. 'You mean, you want to continue with this responsibility?' Another stare, or maybe it was a glare. 'Well... I...he must be a burden... The circumstances...' *Shut up, John*, he told himself.

In a moment she was on her feet, hands on hips. She spoke most distinctly. 'Let us come to a proper understanding, Captain Beattie. I gave you my word that I would watch over Allan. I never break my word. Let me tell you what has happened.'

She sat down. He was smart enough to sit beside her and keep his mouth closed.

Her irritation left her quickly, replaced by worry. 'Captain, it's a most unfortunate thing, blown entirely out of proportion.' She raised her hands in frustration. 'It's my neighbours.'

That was the cork out of the bottle. Mincing no words, she told of someone named Mrs Dalton totally misunderstanding a simple early-morning hug on the front step, and spreading the news to the rest of her neighbours. The whole thing was so ridiculous that his first instinct was to laugh. A look at Anna, close to tears, stopped him from being a complete idiot.

'You mean…oh, you couldn't possibly mean… Mrs. Dalton thinks you and I are involved in a…a…clandestine affair?' he managed to choke out.

'Plainly put, sir, she saw you coming out of my house in the early morning, and assumed… Well, you can imagine.'

He could. 'Miss Fontaine, I am so sorry. Surely we can explain…'

'I've tried. She won't even open her door to me. And the other neighbours…' She shuddered. 'They turn away when I see them.' She stood and paced the length of the room, stopping in front of him. 'What's worse is she also tattled to the curate, and he paid me a visit, too.'

'The *curate*?'

'He inflicted himself on our parish several months ago. Our old vicar, a most sensible man, is not doing well, and Reverend Maddy is a substitute,' she told him, her irritation evident in her whole demeanour.

John leaned back. 'Now you will tell me that he didn't believe a word of your explanation, preferring to assume the worst.'

'Obviously I don't have to tell you that.' She sank down on the sofa beside him. 'I ordered him out of my house.'

It all sounded so trivial to him, so easily explained, and so far removed from his usual occupation that he still wanted to laugh, and tell her the whole thing would blow over. He took her hand instead.

'Miss Fontaine, as I already mentioned, I must leave tomorrow afternoon. I have no opportunity to make other arrangements for my son.'

The mention of Allan seemed to settle her, which he found touching beyond belief. If she had opened the door weeks ago on a hissing snake and invited it inside, she would have been better off than she was now, with her neighbours disapproving, and a self-righteous curate ready to pounce.

'I know I am taxing you to the limit. Dare I hope that my boy may remain here?'

'Certainly he may,' she said promptly. 'I like Allan.' She turned to face him, giving him an up-close view of a pretty face with freckles on her nose. He hadn't noticed them before; then again, he hadn't been so close except for that pernicious embrace.

'Captain Beattie, I've managed to live for twenty-nine years calling no attention to myself. I've done nothing wrong. Could you speak with the curate?'

'Consider it done,' he said. 'I still must leave by tomorrow's tide. I may be gone a month or more. Miss Fontaine, my life is not my own, but I will speak to the curate.'

'Early church is at eight o' clock.'

'We will go and I will talk to him afterwards.' He shouldn't have, but he gave her a little nudge, something he might do to Allan. 'It will work out.'

To say that his sleep that night was sweet and deep would be a gross exaggeration, beyond the fact that Allan was a little furnace and he was warm. He slept finally, hopeful that a man of God would understand.

Chapter Ten

When he woke, John had to admire the efficiency of Miss Fontaine's well-run household. Pru brought in hot water, after a light tap on the door. When he sat up, she curtsied. 'Miss Fontaine knows you want to shave.'

'She is right. Wake up, my boy. We're getting ready for church!'

Trust Pru. 'Get up, Allan. Time's a-wasting, and you know how Missy feels about that!'

So it's Missy for Pru as well, is it? he thought, as Pru closed the door and Allan woke up.

He looked at his timepiece. Had he really slept eight hours? In a row? He stripped, put a bath sheet around his waist, and lathered up his face. He savoured the simplicity of shaving on a deck that didn't pitch or yaw. He glanced at Allan, who sat up in bed watching him, his eyes lively.

'Papa, will I be able to do that some day?'

'Aye, you will grow whiskers, laddie,' he said, touched to the depth of his heart as he remembered doing exactly what his son was doing, this little boy he saw so seldom.

John dressed carefully, wishing his uniform wasn't

so shabby, then helped Allan into his clothes. 'We look as fine as five pence,' he told his son. 'I think I smell breakfast.'

John laughed as his boy darted out of the door and down the stairs. He followed at a more dignified pace, smiling to see Anna in the corridor.

'Good morning,' he said. 'I could wish my uniform weren't so worn, but I somehow have no time to see a tailor.'

'Captain, I will be the envy of nations, or at least the parish of St Andrew, to come to church with a Trafalgar hero,' she said. She paused then, and he couldn't help noticing her frown. She looked around. 'Where is Allan?'

'He ran ahead. Is there a problem?'

'A small one.'

John watched the colour rise in her cheeks. He had a momentary pang, thinking of his late wife and her consumptive pallor. Miss Fontaine looked so healthy, and a little embarrassed right now. He wanted to tease her, but knew he had no claim to do anything of the sort.

'A small problem? Perhaps I can help.'

She took a tentative step closer. 'Captain, since Allan has been sharing my room—he sleeps better if I hold his hand—he helps me with buttons I cannot reach.'

'Miss Fontaine, I am as talented as my son. Turn around.'

He buttoned her up the back of her dress, after the observation—in silence, certainly—that those freckles on her nose had companions. Pretty light brown freckles.

Breakfast was quick and efficient. Thank God for coffee. Other segments of British society might demand tea, but the Royal Navy was fuelled by coffee, the better to keep crews alert and awake.

'Miss Fontaine, you run a tight ship,' he told her. 'If you ever get the urge to run away to sea, we could find you a berth on the *Swallow*.'

He chuckled as she blushed.

Allan's eyes widened. 'Papa, do ladies go to sea?'

'Some do,' John said. 'But most wives remain in port, waiting with the patience of Job.'

Miss Fontaine rose and left the room.

'Was it something I said?' he asked Mrs Moore as the children left, too. 'What...just happened?'

'She misses her brother.'

'The children, too? But they never knew him. I don't understand.'

The housekeeper gave him a patient look, as if he were a child himself. 'Pru noticed it first. When my mistress gets silent and leaves the room, she goes to a quiet place and sits there. Pru and Allan sit with her, too. No one likes to be sad alone.'

Thoughtful, he walked to the sitting room, peering in, his heart touched to watch a sorrowing lady with her arms around two children, there to comfort her.

Anna, he thought, *I would comfort you, too.*

He thought about that on their way to St Andrew's. *Captains are always sad in solitary*, he thought. *It's the nature of the beast.* He writhed inside that he'd seldom been around to console Cathy as the consumption had manifested itself in earnest. He hadn't even been present for Allan's birth, nor yet again when Cathy had died. *We men must do our duty*, he reminded himself as he followed them inside the church. Usually that reality carried him through, but at this moment he found it distinctly lacking.

The issue stung further. He hoped the children didn't notice, but no one greeted them, as other congregants nodded and smiled to each other. Miss Fontaine was first in the pew, with the children following her.

'I should sit next to her,' he whispered to Mrs Moore. 'Something is wrong.'

'Stay where you are. I have a bad feeling that your sitting beside her would make matters worse.'

He opened his mouth to argue with her, but shut it when she gave him a look worthy of Nelson or Collingwood. He folded his arms and stared straight ahead. *What is worse than this?* he thought, miserable and not used to feeling lower than the most malingering sailor in the fleet.

Captain Beattie soon found out.

After the sacraments, he settled in for a boring homily, something dry as toast and usually forgotten. Not this time.

The ordained man of God leaned forward, his eyes searching out his victim like a bird of prey, until they landed on John Beattie. John locked eyes with him and stared back. The curate shifted his gaze to Miss Fontaine and found the perfect target. The curate pointed his finger and proceeded to ruin a life.

'We live in a sinful town!' He stared heavenward dramatically. 'Now it lurks on our better streets, where we allow evil to live among us.' He clutched his heart, or that place in his chest where a heart might beat. 'Now shameless women shelter unwanted boys and girls, hoping to turn them to a life of unspeakable degradation.'

Captain Beattie feared to move, not wanting to call attention to himself. His heart broke into a thousand pieces, aware that his simple request for a reassuring hug had been so wilfully misunderstood.

He heard people whispering around him, and necks craning. *Don't react, Miss Fontaine*, he thought. *This is all my fault and you are bearing my burden.*

The diatribe continued as the curate worked his way through the evil women of scripture, Jezebel prominent. Miss Fontaine sat calmy erect, as if chiselled from marble, unflinching.

Captain Beattie knew he was not a praying man. But he prayed now for God to end this, and seldom had he meant a prayer more.

To his relief, the steam seemed to go out of the doughy scoundrel wearing the robes of an ecclesiastic. He babbled, stumbled and ended with a feeble plea to avoid fornication. Then it was over, to John's great relief.

'I will see you now,' John told Reverend Maddy on their way out. He leaned towards Mrs Moore, who was giving the curate her own disapproving look. 'Take the others home, Mrs Moore. If you can fix me a sandwich, I'll take it with me. Tides wait for no man.'

The housekeeper nodded and shepherded her little flock past a row of puzzled onlookers. John waited.

Reverend Maddy was in no hurry. Time was passing.

After the last parishioner scurried away, John planted himself in front of the curate.

'Reverend Maddy, you were wrong to single out Miss Fontaine and me for censure,' he said firmly, mincing not a word. 'She has already explained the situation I found myself in. Nothing has changed, because I am ordered to the Channel again and there is still no one but Miss Fontaine to protect my son. I have no relatives younger than fifty, and they are far away, near Edinburgh. I am in the service of the Crown and at the mercy of events.'

'What's done is done,' the curate said, sounding so prim and righteous that John itched to wring the man's neck. 'I have merely warned my parish—my parish, Captain, not yours!—of evil lurking in Plymouth.'

'There is no evil in Miss Fontaine.'

'My parishioners have been warned,' the curate retorted.

He stared at the clergyman. *I have made matters worse* warred with, *He knows what damage he has done and glories in it.* Captain Beattie silently wished him to the devil, and soon.

John stalked past the smug curate, wondering if he should have said anything at all.

'I wonder, Miss Fontaine, if I have done the right thing,' Captain Beattie told Anna later, as he accepted a stout sandwich in a paper parcel. 'I am so sorry.'

'Don't apologise again,' she said, keeping her voice gentle in the face of his remorse. 'It will blow over. I know it will,' she added, even as her doubts multiplied.

That seemed to help. His eyes lost that hard expression and his shoulders relaxed. She wondered how peaceful he might look in a calm state of mind, perhaps even sleeping.

It was another quick goodbye. Allan grew solemn, but she rested her hands on his shoulders. 'We'll be fine, won't we, Allan?'

To Anna's delight, the Captain hugged Allan and Pru as well—Pru, who had even less idea what a family was than Allan. He sent the children ahead, then opened his arms to Anna.

'Kindly give me another of those hugs. We'll do it with the front door closed this time.'

Anna had no trouble being hauled close until he left nothing to the imagination. She wrapped her arms around him.

Then he was gone, opening the door on the children, who followed him down the steps. Anna stayed inside, wondering how a house could suddenly seem so empty, when only one person was leaving.

She asked that question again when the house was still that night. She found a psalm that her father had liked to read when he was missing Will at sea and took comfort from it.

Morning came with Mrs Moore shaking her awake. 'Miss Fontaine! We have a problem!'

Chapter Eleven

'Good heavens, Mrs Moore.' Anna glanced out of the window to see the sun barely up.

'He's waiting downstairs,' her housekeeper said with panic in her voice, so unlike the Mrs Moore who never faltered.

Anna threw on her clothes and hurried downstairs. Mrs Moore directed her into the sitting room. 'Oh, dear,' she whispered. 'Oh, dear.'

Anna steeled herself to see the curate waiting to pounce again. Instead, she saw a mild-looking man with a leather business case.

'You are Miss Anna Fontaine, sister of William Fontaine, late of the Royal Navy and current holder of the lease on this property?'

'I am,' she said calmly. 'My brother was deceased after the battle of Trafalgar. If it is a matter of this property's lease, I am quite able to continue payments.'

Mr Business Case shook his head. 'You have been evicted.'

Her heart plummeted to her stomach. 'There must be some mistake, sir. I am quite able to pay.'

He ruffled some more papers. 'Anna Fontaine? Ah, yes. The Bishop of Exeter has declared you a menace to the parish of St Andrew.' He glared at her. 'The issue is moral turpitude.'

She gasped. 'That is impossible!'

'Hardly. Most of Plymouth heard yesterday's sermon. Are you aware that this house, and many others, are the property of the Exeter diocese?' He held out a paper with wax seals. 'This eviction has been signed by Edward Maddy, curate of St Andrew's, and counter-signed by Vicar Montague.'

'I will find another house,' Anna declared.

'Unlikely. Word has got out about you. I work for Darius Bledsoe, who controls the rental properties in Plymouth and Devonport for the diocese.' He pulled out a gold timepiece, glaring at it as though it was as much a disappointment as she was. 'You have six hours to vacate the premises. If you persist in staying here, you and your possessions will be thrown onto the street and the constable summoned. I will see myself out.'

The front door closed with a distinct click. She stared at Mrs Moore, whose face probably reflected the pallor of her own.

'That beastly man,' she said finally. 'This is monstrous.'

The roaring in her ears subsided enough to hear her housekeeper's gusty sigh. 'I would like to twist the head right off that warty little scoundrel!'

Anna sat in silence, imagining such a sight. She wanted

to laugh, because Mrs Moore looked as if she could do just that—wipe off her hands, stamp on the curate's corpse and kick it aside.

'I believe you could, Mrs Moore,' she said. 'I would pay good money to see it, but that will never do.' She did laugh then. 'What would the neighbours say?'

'Do you think that wretched nuisance was teased by fellow classmates as a child? They probably turned his smallclothes inside out and made him wear them over his trousers.'

'I wouldn't doubt it for a minute. He probably tattled on them, too.' She laughed again, hoping it wouldn't turn into hysterics. It didn't.

In a minute, Anna heard the early-morning sounds of the fishmonger, who called, 'Oysters! Oysters! They're fresh as a sailor back from sea!' as she made her usual rounds. Life was going on as normal. She had money in hand and more available.

Still…she knew she bore a heavy burden, thanks to a desperate man. She possessed no more power than any woman, which equated to none.

'Mrs Moore, we have a challenge ahead.'

'Would you say so?' Mrs. Moore grinned. 'Six hours isn't much time. Do you have a plan?'

'I will. Give me a moment. Allan and Pru will rise soon and want breakfast. Let me think.'

When the door closed, she told herself, *I can do this; I gave him my word.* She put her hands over her eyes for one blessed moment.

She spent little time blaming herself. The ladies in

Covent Street had seemed welcoming, until an innocent hug had unleashed a storm of censure she could never have anticipated.

'Think,' she demanded. 'You have six hours. Have you a friend anywhere? You only need one. You've had your fill of Plymouth.'

Fill… Fillion. *I wonder*, she thought, then, *I barely know her*. Anna ordered herself to stop dismissing an idea, any idea. She made herself remember their brief conversation.

I am always here if you need me.

If you need me.

'I need you now, Mrs Fillion. I know it's a common thing that polite people say, but I pray that you meant it.'

There was one way to find out. Her promise to Captain Beattie gave her the strength to get her cloak and bonnet, then find Mrs Moore in the kitchen, staring with vacant eyes at a pot of oats.

'I have an idea,' Anna said. 'I'll return soon. After the children have breakfast, get those empty boxes in the cellar and pack the essentials.'

'Where are you going, love?' Mrs Moore asked, panic written all over the face of someone usually in charge.

'I'm going to the Drake.'

'That's in the Barbican!' Mrs Moore warned her. 'I'm coming, too.'

'No. You are to organise the children,' Anna said calmly. 'Get them up and start packing.' When Mrs Moore opened her mouth to protest, Anna kissed her cheek. 'I am twenty-nine years old and capable.' *I hope*, she added to herself.

She hurried away before Mrs Moore could voice more objections, setting out at a spanking pace, aware that people rarely bothered someone with a determined look.

Her expression was sufficiently quelling. A lounging sailor near a grog shop whistled at her, then slunk away when she glared. Even a constable backed away. Better and better.

It was one thing to walk bravely through the Barbican. It was quite another to stand at the entrance to the Drake and wonder at her boldness. *It doesn't matter*, she thought. *I need help.* She opened the door.

Mrs Fillion stood behind the front desk, sorting through papers, spectacles perched on her nose. She saw Anna, yanked off her spectacles and hurried around the desk, her arms open.

With a sob, Anna threw herself into her embrace.

'How did you know I needed this?' Anna managed to say.

'I knew I would never see you here without Captain Beattie if it weren't an emergency. What happened?'

Soon they were seated in the alcove between the front desk and the stairwell.

Mrs Fillion took her hands. 'You're freezing,' she scolded, but in that way of women looking out for each other. 'Why are you here and how can I help?'

Aware of time passing, Anna started with Captain Beattie's impulsive embrace on the steps of her home, and the rumours that had started. She only faltered on that terrible moment when the curate had pointed at her in church.

'Somebody should thrash that man!' Mrs Fillion declared.

'Then a horrible man with a leather case arrived this morning and said we had six hours to vacate our premises. Mrs Fillion, I am desperate. Please help us.'

Her tired heart seemed to start beating again when the hotelier grasped her hands and said, 'Yes, Anna, a thousand times.' Anna wept as Mrs Fillion held her, like mother and daughter. 'It's going to be fine,' she crooned.

Anna pulled herself together. 'I can pay for lodging. That is not the issue.'

'I knew Captain Beattie would never leave you penniless,' Mrs Fillion said. 'Take your money? No. I have a better idea.'

'I could use a good idea,' Anna said simply.

'I need someone at the front desk. You, perhaps?'

'At the front desk?' Anna asked, surprised and, if she was honest, intrigued. The front desk meant Navy men, who lately—especially one man in particular—had disrupted her orderly life. Her humour returned. 'Men? The old biddies on Covent Street will lose their minds if they hear I work at the Drake.'

Mrs Fillion laughed. 'It's a cliché, but living well *is* the best revenge. Officers are as gentlemanly as they can be. True, some haven't seen a pretty face in a long time, but everyone knows I run a tight ship at the Drake.'

'I'll be safe,' Anna agreed, 'but no one ever said I had a pretty face.'

'Look in the mirror occasionally,' Mrs Fillion said crisply. 'Front desk for you. Your housekeeper cooks? My chef will collapse in gratitude if Mrs... Mrs...'

'Moore...'

'... Mrs Moore agrees to help him. You mentioned a scullery maid. Pru? There are never enough choppers and dicers in my kitchen,' Mrs Fillion said, ticking off the chores on her fingers. 'Captain Beattie's son? Is he useful?'

'He will do whatever you like, and with good cheer,' Anna said, amazed at the racehorse speed of this conversation. She reconsidered. 'He can be a little tentative, but he has been through so much.'

'So has his father, Miss Fontaine. Please, may I call you Anna?'

'Certainly, you may, Mrs Fillion.'

'I am Grace.' She stood and tugged Anna up with her. 'My Ben—he's a handy man to know—will drive you back to Covent Street and help with the packing. We'll beat that six-hour deadline. I'll have rooms ready when you return.' She hesitated. 'I can put you on the third floor, which is where officers and their wives stay, or... or with me below-stairs.'

'Below-stairs,' Anna said promptly, then felt the greatest sense of belonging, knowing in her heart of hearts that it was not a step down into lower status, but an opportunity. 'I can learn a skill. Mrs Fillion...'

'Grace.'

'Grace, I am in your debt forever,' Anna said quietly.

Grace Fillion cupped her hands around Anna's face,

hands roughened by work but so tender. No one had touched her like that since the death of her mother.

'When you are settled and comfortable, we will both write to Captain Beattie,' Grace said. 'He must know what is going on. Do you have a black dress?'

'I do.'

'Good. You'll be perfect for the front desk. My clientele is always respectful. They're rowdy sometimes over at the Perpetual Whist Game, but I make allowances.'

'I won't mind that,' Anna said, dismissing her quiet life, which—truth to tell—was a boring business. Things were going to be different from now on. If she really thought about it—and why not?—life before Captain Beattie had knocked on her door *was* a trifle slow. 'I won't mind at all.'

Grace clapped her hands. 'Bravo! My dear, welcome to the Drake.'

Chapter Twelve

Anna soon acquired three things: a second black dress; the ability to organise officers unaccustomed to being told what to do into an orderly queue; and the abiding knowledge that a smile worked wonders on exhausted officers needing a bed. She also learned a fourth thing: how deeply she could love.

She'd feared first of all for Allan, who burst into tears when he was told they were moving again. Anna could never scold a heart mangled by desertion, and the absence of a loving, if often absent, father. Their eviction deadline loomed, but Anna had found a moment to sit with him.

'Will my father know where I am?' Allan asked.

'Indeed, he will. As soon as we are settled at the Drake, Mrs Fillion and I will each write a letter, so there will be no doubt where we are.' She added shrewdly, 'You may write Papa a letter, too, telling him what you're doing at the Drake.'

'Doing?' She heard interest this time, not fear.

'Yes. We will be working for Mrs Fillion.' She kissed his head and let him cuddle her, as if they had all the time in the world. 'She tells me that making officers comfortable is how *we* fight Napoleon right here in Plymouth.'

That was the clinching argument. He nodded, hopped off her lap and helped Ben strap down a box.

Pru had no trouble pitching in; change and chaos were all she knew. Anna felt a pang when they prepared to climb aboard the cart taking them to their new adventure. As they stood together on the pavement, Pru tugged at Anna's skirt.

'Am I to come along, too?'

Shocked, Anna pulled Pru close. 'I will never leave you behind, Pru. I should have made myself plain about this. The promise I made to Captain Beattie extends to you, too.'

'I hoped it might,' Anna heard her reply, and rejoiced in her heart. *We can do this, Captain Beattie. Just you wait and see.*

Grace must have explained everything to her staff, because all Anna saw were smiles when they arrived at the Drake. Willing hands unloaded their possessions and took them down the stairs to their quarters. In a matter of minutes, Mrs Moore was nodding happily to instructions from Grace's chef, a Frenchman with a cautious expression.

'Anna, you should share a room with Allan,' Grace said.

'I agree.' Anna watched Allan pat the pillow on one of the two narrow beds and give her his first smile of the whole, upsetting day. 'He needs familiar faces around him.'

'What is this war doing to our children?' Grace whispered back. 'And you, my dear?' Her expression hardened. 'Nosy gossips can cause the same damage as cannon and bayonets.'

'I intend to put it behind me,' Anna assured her. She could reflect later on how completely her own life had changed since Captain Beattie had come into her orbit, a frantic man forced to trust a stranger. 'Perhaps I was getting complacent.'

'I admire you, Anna. You will succeed admirably at the Drake.'

She did, they all did, but it took patience. Her first reminder came the next morning, when she dressed in black to follow Grace upstairs to work behind the front desk.

She got no further than the door of the room she shared with Allan. He and Pru were heading to the kitchen close by, ready to chop and dice. When he saw her, his Missy, dressed for work, his eyes filled with tears.

'Please don't leave me, Missy!' he cried.

She held him close, ready to explain that she was only going above-stairs to the lobby. A firm hand on her shoulder reassured her that there was far more to Grace than running a hotel.

Her employer knelt beside her, embracing her and the terrified child. 'Allan, Missy can stay below-stairs for a few days with you,' Grace said in a quiet voice. 'You know, until you understand that she will never leave you. I have work for her upstairs. That is all.'

'She can't leave me,' he said more quietly, as he clung to Anna.

'Don't worry, Allan. My business above-stairs with

Missy will keep.' She smiled at them both. 'Allan, Missy will chop and dice with you. When the day is nearly done, she will walk you upstairs, and you can see what we do there. It's not so far away. Agreed?'

Anna felt her own load lighten as the little boy relaxed in her arms. He nodded finally.

'Agreed,' came his soft reply.

'Very well,' Grace said. 'When Chef gives you both leave this afternoon, I will see you upstairs.'

So it went, requiring only one day of slicing, dicing, peeling and chopping, as Allan accustomed himself to his new surroundings. That first afternoon when Pierre declared Allan and Pru free from work, Allan looked towards the stairs.

'Are we going up there now, Missy?' he asked.

Anna listened for fear, but heard none. There was only a momentary hesitancy when he looked back at Pru, his lifeline. She gave him a thumbs-up.

Anna had her own encouragement. 'Allan, there are men above-stairs who probably know your father.'

'Do they have sons, too?'

'I imagine they do, and they surely miss them as much as your father misses you.'

'That's a lot.'

'I do not doubt you are right.'

Grace turned from the front desk to greet them both, giving Allan a hug, then sitting him on a chair. 'These are heroes like your father,' she told him, as he eyed the officers. 'We take care of them here. Watch us.'

Anna watched, too. She smiled to herself as her employer turned her cheek for what Captain Beattie had already told her was the obligatory kiss from each officer. Grace listened to their woes, assigned them rooms, watched as they signed the ledger, and handed out room keys.

When she was not busy, Grace explained her duties to Anna, after a glance at Allan, who rested now, his eyes drooping. 'A few hours below-stairs with Pru, compared to boredom here, might convince your shadow that the kitchen is more fun.'

Allan was a quick learner. The next morning, he announced to Anna that he preferred to chop and dice. She could go upstairs.

'Are you certain?' Anna asked.

He nodded and motioned her closer. 'I fall asleep up there. Besides, I know where you are.'

Anna smiled all the way upstairs. 'You were right, Grace,' she said.

Grace's gaze seemed to see through the back wall. 'I had a little boy once, who preferred chopping and dicing.'

Dare I ask? Anna thought. She put her hand on Grace's arm.

'He went to sea and died at Camperdown,' her employer told her. 'I miss him to this very day.' She gestured around her, the graceful movement taking in the lobby with officers and luggage. 'When I say this is our war, I mean it. Your captain will be pleased at his son's resilience.'

My captain? Anna thought. *Surely not.*

***

Days passed, then one week and another. Anna continued to watch Grace conversing with the naval officers, wishing she had that same ease of manner.

She decided that Navy men were a breed apart, men used to command and obedience. If there was a tender side to them, she wondered when it might show, until that first time she watched a lady waiting for a husband long at sea.

The lady had come to the Drake looking as shy and ill at ease as Anna knew she had felt that first time, that frantic time, here alone after her eviction.

'She's waiting for her husband,' Grace confided. 'They'll stay on my third floor. She said they've been married a mere month, and he's headed back to sea immediately. They won't need any room service.'

Anna didn't try to hide her smile. She looked up after many minutes, when the door opened and a lieutenant came in. He scanned the room, then his eyes riveted on his wife.

She rose as he hurried to her and kissed her soundly. They nearly ran up the stairs. Grace glanced up, then returned to her entries in the ledger, her shoulders shaking with amusement. 'I wish I had a pound note for every baby that begins on my third floor,' was her comment.

Anna felt her face grow warm, feeling what seemed dangerously close to envy. To her heart and mind came a glimpse of Captain Beattie as she had never seen him, joyful and eager to bed a wife. *There was a wife*, she reminded herself. *I know he loved her. He said as much.*

The greater lesson, the one that changed her, came a day later, when she was alone at the desk and a captain came in. He bore himself well, as they all did, but no amount of rank or experience could disguise his pain. His young lieutenants grouped around him, looking concerned.

This was an officer on his last legs; Anna sensed it. She thought of Captain Beattie. Would his final moments be like this, too? Alone, except for young officers inadequate to the moment?

She beckoned them forward as Grace had taught her, even as chills marched down her spine. The captain collapsed halfway across the lobby. Before he fell, he looked into her eyes. She saw a man in need.

She knelt beside the captain and pulled him close, his head in her lap. Without a thought to propriety, she cradled him in her arms. In that moment, she knew she would never again hang back. Every man keeping her, Allan and Pru safe from a continent in turmoil became her responsibility.

No help materialized; Anna knew it was already too late.

'I'm here,' she told the captain. 'I'm here.'

'You are England,' he whispered, then closed his eyes in death.

Anna bowed her head over him, as if shielding him from the previous confusion, and now the great silence. She shielded him until she was forced to relinquish him to others. She stood quietly in the lobby, then slowly walked downstairs, seating herself on the lowest tread, silent about what had happened not only to the captain, but also to her.

Her employer joined her later, sitting beside her. Anna looked at her.

'Grace, we must write to Captain Beattie,' she said. 'He needs to know how we are doing.' She took a deep breath. 'I am now ready to fight Napoleon in my own way, too.'

Chapter Thirteen

The Channel was its usual windy grind of restless waves funnelled between a continent and a large island. Winter might be wearing out, but spring was a reluctant maiden.

'She's a tease, this Channel,' Captain Beattie remarked to his new first luff after breakfast of coffee, ancient toast and highly suspect cheese, accompanied by curses from his steward, who took mouldy cheese personally.

As painful as Lieutenant Fontaine's death had been, John did not hesitate over Will's replacement. He had anticipated it for months, knowing that Will would soon be moving to his own command, and none better. Sadly, war had outfoxed them.

Second lieutenant Thomas Marsing had moved competently into Will's former place. A Welshman with dancing dark eyes, Tom knew when to be serious.

'Sir, I will never fail you, even as Will never failed you,' Tom promised, and his captain had no doubts. John knew how to nurture leaders.

Captain Beattie understood the aloofness of command, and the demands of a hard service. He appeared on deck during long night watches, when no captain usually roamed. It became a matter of course for Tom to follow him onto the quarterdeck.

Sometimes they spoke; sometimes they didn't. Lately, John found himself deep in thought, relieved that Allan was in a safe mooring on Covent Street. However, instinct told him that Reverend Maddy was a troublemaker. His only consolation was the knowledge that Anna Fontaine would never be cowed by such a fool as that curate.

On this voyage John frequently lingered on the quarterdeck, leaning his elbows on the rail and gazing towards Plymouth, wondering at his audacity in thrusting himself, Allan and Pru onto Anna. His chagrin mellowed into a pleasant reminiscence of a charming woman, and damned if she wasn't pretty, too, in a calming, serene way.

He thought of Cathy, destined for a brief life, something he'd been aware of when he'd married her. He knew he loved her still, but wasn't there a time limit on wholesale grief? Such were his quarterdeck musings, invariably followed by the utter folly of thinking that his life during war was his own. His only solace was the knowledge that his son was safe.

The monotony ended when a Fast Dispatch Vessel dropped off a message from Admiral Collingwood himself, master of the Mediterranean Fleet, commanding the *Swallow* to sail with all dispatch to Gibraltar. John nodded at his admiral's sketchy handwriting: 'I have a job for you, Captain Beattie,' he read. He turned over the note. 'I also have mail on the *Queen*, for you miscreants aboard the *Swallow*.' Mail. Thank God.

They made Gibraltar three days later. There was something about the Rock that drew even maritime veterans to it. Gibraltar was the door to the Mediterranean—Italy, Greece and North Africa. Since Trafalgar, the Royal Navy could rove almost anywhere.

'Back again, Mr Marsing,' he said to his first luff. He pointed to the *Queen*, Admiral Collingwood's flagship. 'There is mail aboard. Come with me, and you can take it back.' He couldn't help laughing. 'You'll be the most popular man on the *Swallow*.'

'Aye, sir!' Tom said, with the same enthusiasm. 'May I ask, what does the Admiral have in mind for us?'

'Your guess equals mine,' he said. 'Maybe we'll rove about the Mediterranean. Better that, than to the blockade.'

'Even if we have to deal with Americans here?' Tom asked.

'We'll manage the Americans,' he replied. 'At least we speak the same language. I think.' It was a Royal Navy joke. Nautical upstarts from the former colonies had made treaty recently with pirates from Tripoli, who had disrupted their new-found trade in the Mediterranean. So far as anyone knew, the treaty was holding. Who knew about the Americans?

Once aboard the *Queen* that afternoon, John was met by the bosun, who saluted and handed off a mail bag. 'This is your personal correspondence, Captain Beattie,' the bosun added, handing him a smaller pouch. 'Lieutenant Kelso will see you to the Admiral.'

'Toss the sack down to Lieutenant Marsing,' John ordered. 'Lead on, Lieutenant Kelso.'

No Collingwood below-deck. Lieutenant Kelso indicated a chair. 'He hasn't forgotten you, sir.'

'No worries, Lieutenant. I'll read my own correspondence while I wait.'

When the man left, John opened the oilskin pouch immediately, pawing through official business, looking for letters from Plymouth with the same eagerness as when Cathy was alive. A letter from Allan caught his eye first, and he wasted not a moment opening it. He leaned back, snapped the seal, and read, *Dear Papa, I am doing fin. Missy sayes finer than fife pens.*

He smiled, relieved that his instinct about Anna was true. Perhaps some help with spelling would be good. The smile left his face as he continued. *I reely like chopping carots, onyins and potatos. Mrs Filyun lets me help Pru mak beds.* 'What is this?' he said softly. *Missy says not to wory.*

John *was* worried. He folded Allan's letter and rummaged in the pouch, suddenly desperate for more. He found two letters, one neatly addressed to Captain John Beattie. The other had GF written in the left upper corner and the admonition, READ THIS FIRST! in large block letters.

He held his breath and opened the letter that must have come from Grace Fillion of the Drake. Damned if his hands weren't shaking. *Never fear, sir, we are all well,* allowed him to keep breathing. What followed horrified him. 'What have I done?' he asked himself.

He read the letter, which was as plainspoken as Mrs Fillion herself. An agent sent by that damnable curate had evicted Anna, she who was bearing enough burdens thrust on her by a desperate captain she hardly knew.

'What must you think of me, Anna Fontaine?' he asked the air.

Sickened, he turned the page, where, to his relief, Mrs Fillion told him again not to worry. *Sir, Anna is a solid sort*, he read. *She came right to me, and they are all safe here. Pierre, my chef, is grateful for kitchen help. Anna (such a shy, quiet lady)*—'Indeed she is,' John said to the letter—*has proved so helpful at the front desk.*

There was more, but he heard a door open and stood up to bow to the Admiral of the Fleet, Admiral Lord Cuthbert Collingwood, and his dog Bounce, who trotted up with some dignity and sniffed his crotch.

'Captain Beattie, how goes my favourite Scot?' John heard through the fog of his distress. Suddenly, John felt tears course down his cheeks. He held out Mrs Fillion's letter.

Without a word, the Admiral took it. 'Tell me more,' he ordered when he finished reading, and John did.

'This is serious,' the Admiral said.

'I've ruined a kind lady's life,' John said, barely able to get out the words. He looked at the unread letter in his hand. 'I fear to open this one.'

'Tell me, Captain, what kind of man was Miss Fontaine's brother? I know you lost him after Trafalgar.'

'Lieutenant Will Fontaine was utterly dependable and destined to captain his own ship soon. I trusted him with everything.'

'What you tell me, and what I have read, suggest that Miss Fontaine is cut from the same cloth.'

Don't try to make me feel better, John thought, angry for a moment, until he realised he was angry at himself and not his commander.

'She is.' He held up her letter. 'I haven't read *her* letter yet, though.'

'Ah, yes. It appears that Mrs Fillion, God bless her, wanted hers read first.' Collingwood gave John's knee a pat. 'Read it. I must speak to my secretary.'

John broke the seal and spread out Anna's letter. *Captain Beattie, things have not precisely worked in my favour*, he read, shaking his head over perhaps the greatest understatement since Eve bit into the apple.

Her story was much the same as Mrs Fillion's, and he heard no blame. It wrung his heart when she thanked him—God in heaven!—for introducing her to Grace. She concluded with,

We are in good hands here at the Drake, and all of us are useful. Allan suffered a little at the eviction, but he's my—she'd crossed out *my* and wrote *your—smiling lad again. Do your duty. I promised you I would never fail you, and I will not. Yours sincerely, Anna.*

From my to your. He stared at that and felt himself relax. *Anna.*

'At least you are not in a towering rage,' he whispered to the words.

The door opened. Admiral Collingwood resumed his seat. 'Well, sir?'

'She reminded me that she promised to never fail me, Admiral,' he said, still choked. 'I don't know what to say.' He held out the letter, so personal. 'Here, sir. I would value your opinion.'

The Admiral read Anna's letter, nodding a few times with what looked like approval. He tapped it a few times. 'Give me a moment.' He closed his eyes.

When he opened them, it was to give John the Admiral's Stare, but a benign one.

'Let me lay this before you, Captain Beattie. I need you and the *Swallow* here in the Mediterranean. It's roving duty, and one that I know suits you. But you need a land base.' He pointed to Anna's letter. 'I am more and more inclined to Port Mahon on Menorca.'

John nodded, dreading the letters he had to write to both Grace Fillion and Anna. *I will never be home*, he thought despairingly.

'Very well, Admiral,' he said, knowing there could be no other reply. 'I am yours to command.'

'Wise of you!' He thumped John's knee. 'You're going to do one more thing. It's something I long to do, but I have been sentenced to parade about the Mediterranean Sea and show the flag.'

Silence. 'Admiral, to what are you referring?'

'Simple. I am ordering you to Plymouth first, to see your son with your own eyes. Do one thing more, if you wish. I cannot order this or, by God, I damn well would.'

'Sir?'

'Marry that good lady and take her and your boy with you to Menorca.'

John sucked in his breath. He couldn't have heard the man correctly. 'Aye, her letter was kind, but she must be seething inside! I have made her an object of ridicule and shame in Plymouth. *Marry* her?'

'Find out what she thinks of the idea. You might be surprised. Let your new first luff take the *Swallow* to a Gibraltar anchorage. You will take a Fast Dispatch Vessel leaving from my flagship for Plymouth tomorrow.'

'But sir, I can't just… What about my late wife?' What was his admiral *saying*?

Collingwood's demeanour softened. 'From what you have told me, she must have been a lady after your own heart.'

'Aye, she was,' John said quietly.

'Napoleon doesn't care, however, and we must continue to fight.'

'But…marriage? I know how Miss Fontaine feels about my son, but not a clue what she thinks of me.' He gave his admiral an exasperated stare. '*Marriage*, sir?'

'Damn the war,' Collingwood told him almost cheerfully. 'Go and find out. *That's* an order.'

Chapter Fourteen

The FDV sailed for Plymouth in the morning, after John had writhed all night in his rack, wondering how he could possibly make Anna's life any worse.

When he emerged on deck that morning, bleary-eyed and feeling every second of his thirty-eight years, Tom handed him what he knew were official orders to Gibraltar or more likely Port Mahon, as conditions warranted, and a private note from Admiral Collingwood.

'I must say, Captain, you're keeping rare company,' the Welshman joked. 'I am to proceed to Gibraltar and wait there.'

John said something he should have regretted but didn't, and took the letter. There wasn't time to read it now, not with the Fast Dispatch Vessel already waiting beside the flagship. He stuffed it and the orders in his duffel, daring to hope he might actually have a little time to read them on the FDV, where he wasn't in command.

There was time.

His orders were an echo of Old Cuddy's comments yesterday. They appealed to him, mainly because he wasn't sentenced to more blockade tedium. The *Swallow* was to rove about the Mediterranean Sea. The orders came in formal Royal Navy diction, but he understood the underlying message: *Thrash any French or Spanish vessels that weren't sufficiently cowed at Trafalgar. Look about, see what the French might be up to, and keep an occasional eye on the Americans.* Fair enough; he could do that.

He worked up his courage to read Collingwood's letter, and learned something about that great, quiet man, who had willingly lived in the shadow of Horatio Nelson's genius. He had paid his own price, the price the entire Royal Navy had paid, from able-bodied seamen to admirals, which was time away from loved ones.

John read, blinking back tears:

I want you to have the chance denied to me. I know you have suffered loss. Find all the joy you can, John Beattie. Bring your boy and a bride back to the Mediterranean, if you can convince her. We'll think of something. Yours sincerely, Cuthbert.

There they were, official and highly unofficial orders. Of the two orders, he knew that sailing the Mediterranean with the bliss of unfettered command was a captain's dream. The second order, not so much. He doubted even Romeo could have convinced Juliet to get spliced and sail with him in a month or less, and more likely never.

During six days of sailing, Captain Beattie enjoyed the bliss of no command at all. The FDV was someone else's ship. His worry commenced again about three days out of Plymouth, when another dispatch vessel from Gibraltar hailed them and handed off an additional letter addressed to him.

Oh, no. Something else from Old Cuddy. He took it below deck and sat on his lightly swinging bed. What he read made his head ache:

If you are brave enough to attempt a marriage proposal, go to Portsmouth (not Plymouth) and then Winchester, to save time. You need a licence for a prompt wedding, something I doubt the Bishop of Exeter will issue, if that miserable worm of a curate has tattled to him. In Winchester Cathedral, hand Bishop North this note. I did him a great favour once. He will authorise a common licence, which will cost you two or three pounds. You can use it anywhere, even in Gibraltar or on my flagship, if you can convince Miss Fontaine to marry you. Godspeed, Cuddy.

Yea or nay? A coin toss sent him to Portsmouth instead of Plymouth, which meant a sleepless ride via post chaise to Winchester, stopping once so he could be sick. Odd how the rocking motion of a chaise set him off, when gale-force winds at sea never did.

Winchester exceeded his greatest dream, or maybe nightmare, since he had no idea what Anna would say. The Bishop of Winchester spent a moment in fond reminiscence of the favour Cuthbert Collingwood had rendered him, then issued the licence. The bishop even waved him off from the cathedral. Done and done and John had the licence to prove it.

He slept to Portsmouth, where another Fast Dispatch Vessel got him to Plymouth in mid-afternoon. He was no prize. He needed a bath in the worst way, except that he didn't care to drown in a tub when he fell asleep, despite the coffee. He reckoned he was a prime candidate for an insane asylum and every woman's worst nightmare.

He paused a moment before entering the Drake, nodding to a few friends outside, wondering if there was any other way he could ruin Anna's life. He decided there wasn't, and opened the door.

There she was at the front desk, smiling at a post captain and his wife, and indicating the ledger for a signature. He was struck by the fact that, despite their brief and harried acquaintance, he'd remembered so much about her, starting with her beautiful eyes, and moving down to her pleasant bosom and trim waist when she turned to get the keys. He noticed something else about her that he wasn't familiar with, a certain animation in her expression when she chatted and smiled. This was a woman in control of herself, despite all the misery he had heaped on her.

He took a deep breath, squared his shoulders and walked across the lobby, mere locomotion as terrifying as a fleet action. Anna had turned back to the desk where he knew Mrs Fillion kept the hotel's strongbox. He patted the common licence in his pocket, the frugal Scot in his head telling the one in his heart that he had wasted three pounds. Still, here he was, and he wanted, no, needed, to see Allan.

'Miss Fontaine?'

She looked around, gasped, and put her hand to her mouth.

He stood there and let his duffel drop from his shoulder. *What should I do?* ran through his mind. When Cathy had gasped, it was generally because she saw a mouse in the kitchen. To his utter astonishment, when he held out his arms to Anna, she ran into them with a velocity that made him take a step back.

The only logical thing to do was to hold her tight, which was so easy. She was exactly the right size to fit into his arms. He also knew that Anna could definitely do better than to affix herself to a sorry specimen like himself. And yet... She didn't seem inclined to release him, and there he was, still hanging onto her like a wet leaf plastered to her face.

'Miss Fontaine, I owe you an even larger apology for continuing to load my problems onto your shoulders. I...'

She stopped him with a fierce look, holding up her forefinger. She probably would have shaken it in his face, if she'd had enough room and they weren't still clinging to each other. He stepped back and released her, startled, yes, but suddenly energized. This was a woman to spar with. The mere idea woke up his tired brain and sent his thoughts in half-forgotten directions all at the same time.

'Don't you *dare* apologise again!' she declared.

'Well, I...'

She drew herself up, even though, with her small height, there wasn't much to draw up. 'Yes, we've had a little difficulty, but it's smoothed out now. We like living at the Drake.'

'I would call eviction, shame and fright more than a little difficulty.' He groaned inwardly. *Shut up, John. Listen to her, you dolt.* He tried something that had always worked when Cathy was in high dudgeon. He touched her cheek, almost a caress.

To his relief, her frown melted and her eyes softened. 'Until this happened, I never realised how boring my life was,' she told him frankly. 'I like being useful.'

He listened for anger, but heard none. After a glance around the lobby, and then at the room with the Perpetual Whist Game, where a grinning, appreciative crowd had gathered, she took his hand and towed him towards the stairs.

'Down you go, sir,' she commanded, but kindly. 'There's a fellow in the kitchen who will be overjoyed to see you.'

'Don't you mean "see your sorry carcass"?' he teased, because he'd heard that lift to her voice. He hoped it meant the worst was over.

Anna laughed. 'I admit I've thought something like that once or twice, but no, your life is not your own,' she said simply. 'If you stop apologising to me, we can possibly be friends, Captain Beattie.'

He plunged ahead. 'As to that, Admiral Collingwood has something else in mind.'

'Whatever it is couldn't possibly involve me,' Anna said. 'I'm not in the Royal Navy, and I doubt the Admiral thinks about anything except ships and war.'

He opened his mouth to say…what, he had no idea. Anna must be even more rare than he'd thought, a woman without guile.

She pointed down the corridor. 'The kitchen is just beyond. Allan and Pru like to help Pierre.' She nudged his shoulder in a conspiratorial way that somehow touched his heart. 'He spoils them with all kinds of pastries. Allan is not so thin now. If you were to stay awhile, you'd become a little less gaunt, too, Captain.'

'I wish I could,' he told her longingly.

'You're tired,' she said simply. 'I wish I could cure that.'

There are ways, he thought, but hadn't the temerity to say it. Just sharing space with her again told him forcefully that a few nights in Anna's bed would cure whatever ailed him. He knew that as firmly and solidly in this very moment as he knew anything.

This was obviously not the place for an intimate conversation, not with Mrs Fillion opening the kitchen door then exclaiming how good it was to see him. She turned her cheek for the traditional kiss.

'I'm going back to the desk,' Anna said. 'You're in for such a surprise when you see Allan.'

Don't go, he wanted to tell her, and nearly did, but Mrs Fillion was giving him the practised eye that she always fixed on lodgers at the Drake, assessing him in her discerning way. He didn't think she could read his thoughts, but felt his face grow warm at the possibility. Good Lord, when had he last blushed?

Allan saved him, turning around to see who had opened the door. 'Papa!' he exclaimed. 'Look what I can do!'

He knelt to hug his son, who was a far cry from the thin child with haunted eyes cowering behind Pru, who'd brandished a poker. And there was Pru, she of the thoughtful look, who still kept her eye on Allan. John hugged them both, admired the carrots chopped so fine, and nodded to Pierre.

'I put these little cherubs to work,' Mrs Fillion said simply. 'It's hard to dwell on terrible things with a carrot peeler in hand.'

He expected Allan to cling to him, but his boy had returned to chopping carrots, giving him a glance now and then, but busy with duties, and laughing with Pru.

'I almost feel abandoned,' he admitted to Mrs Fillion as she poured him a cup of coffee. 'He cried when I left.'

'He cried here, too,' she said. 'He was such a sad little boy. He clutched Anna's dress, but she was his solace. God bless her for turning to me.' She took a sip of tea. 'Quiet she may be, but she is far from helpless.'

'Her brother was cut from the same cloth. I never had a lieutenant so committed to duty.' He touched her hand. 'I will be forever grateful that you took them in.'

'It's been a blessing for all of us. How long are you here?'

'Admiral Collingwood told me I had a month, and that was two weeks ago. No time, as usual.' He told her of his trip to Winchester Cathedral and his admiral's near-order that he bring a wife to the Mediterranean.

He let that sink in. 'Does Anna have any idea about this?' Mrs Fillion asked.

'Not yet. I don't quite know how I feel about it,' he admitted. Might as well air all his dirty linen.

'I recall a sad widower for several years, who rarely said more than the barest minimum of words.' She took his hand. 'Everything changes, Captain Beattie.'

'I had a lovely wife I have never had time to mourn. I know I like and admire Anna. Who wouldn't?' He looked down. 'But will that be enough?'

'Look at me, Captain,' Grace Fillion commanded. He did. 'I think the person you need to trust is yourself.'

He thought about that as he watched his son. To his infinite delight, Allan left the prep table, curled up in his arms without a word and closed his eyes. John motioned Pru over, shifted Allan, and whispered, 'I have two knees, Pru.' The workhouse child sat on the unoccupied one and rested her head against his chest. He bowed his head over his dear ones, knowing full well there would be no Allan if Pru hadn't been there.

When he opened his eyes, Anna sat in the chair Mrs Fillion had vacated. He remained silent, watching her and thinking that everyone he wanted was within arm's reach. How to convince Anna, though? He shoved to the back of his brain the notion that he still needed to convince himself, too.

She spoke so softly. 'When that horrible man gave me six hours to leave, I knew Grace would take us in. Do you remember when you introduced me to her, she said to call on her if I ever needed anything?'

'Aye, but people say things like that all the time,' he

countered, as he wondered what this quiet woman was thinking.

'I never doubted her for a moment.' He watched as she took a deep breath and another. 'It was the same when you came to my door and asked if I could trust you.'

He didn't expect that. 'You can,' he managed.

'I knew that.'

'Will you trust me again?'

'Yes, certainly.'

'Why? Your life was regular and orderly before I bumbled into it.'

Her expression changed, becoming thoughtful, as though weighing him in a balance. 'My brother trusted you, Captain.'

He suddenly longed to hold her as close as he held the two children in his lap.

'If Will did, I can,' she said softly. 'What do you want from me now?'

Chapter Fifteen

It was a good question. Maybe it was forward of her, but Anna wanted to know, especially since she knew every moment counted with a man expected back on duty soon. She knew it had to wait as Grace joined them and gently patted the children. 'Up and about, you two. It's time to set the tables in the dining room.'

Allan and Pru perked up in that magical way of children revived by the smallest rest, and went to their next duty with no complaint.

What did Captain Beattie *want*? She knew he had no time to be a father, but here he was. Hopefully, she could convince him to let them stay precisely where they were. It was just the two of them now, something rare, Anna realised. She waited for the Captain to speak.

'I've found the perfect woman to care for my son.'

Anna had thought she was ready for such awful news, but she couldn't help her sudden intake of breath. He had found someone.

What to do with more bad news?

'How fortunate for you, sir,' she said, not daring to look at him, because that would make her sob out loud.

'I'm glad you feel that way. I'm relieved, there's no denying it.'

It was too hard. She stood up, eager to leave, even though that was bad manners.

'John Beattie, make sure she knows Allan likes to be read to at bedtime, and then sing a song, although he did recently hear a bawdy one by the wharf that made me wince. And...and he has a favourite spoon—don't ask me why. Hopefully, the woman you have chosen knows more about children than I do.'

'Miss Fontaine—'

She ignored him. This whole business, begun in such desperation a few months ago, had turned into something she was quite unprepared for, even though she'd known it was coming. How would Allan cope? More to the point, if she wanted to think of herself, how would she?

'I think Grace would let him take the spoon. Allan and Pru are thick as thieves, so this woman had better be prepared to take her, too.' She couldn't help herself, even if it sounded like whining. 'Drat you, Captain. We were rubbing along so well here.'

There weren't too many steps to the door leading above-stairs. She knew better than to make a scene in the lobby, but maybe there was somewhere in Plymouth that didn't remind her of the Royal Navy. *Now, where would that be, you nincompoop?* she asked herself. She crossed the room and put her hand on the doorknob, only to have the Captain put his hand against the door and keep it firmly shut.

'I don't work for you,' she said, staring straight ahead at the door. 'You can't stop me.'

'Look at me.'

Now *that* was a tone of voice she had never heard before from him. There was nothing of command, or frustration, or worry. If she hadn't known better, he sounded like a hopeful lover in one of those silly romances that she and Grace giggled over late at night when the lobby was empty.

To make certain, she looked. His face was the same, still giving off that air of capability. He had a little scar by his left eye. She was no expert, but she'd say he hadn't shaved in a day or two. Thank goodness women didn't need to shave. Nice blue eyes. And wouldn't you know it, eyelashes that she could probably envy, if she gave the matter any thought, which she resolved never to do, because he was taking away her lovely Allan.

'I'm sorry,' she whispered, 'You're only doing what you promised you would. I hope you found someone good.'

He rolled his eyes, something she was certain no one on any ship he'd captained had ever seen from this solemn man. 'Miss Fontaine, let us come to an understanding,' he began. 'You are looking at the most stupid man who ever lived.'

'I doubt that,' she said impulsively. 'You're forgetting that dreadful curate, may he rot in a leper colony somewhere, but he never will, because he would never volunteer to come within one hundred miles of one.'

He laughed. 'You're going to be a source of continual amusement,' he said, still sounding both proprietary and oddly loverlike. To her further surprise, Captain Beattie put his warm palm over her mouth to stop her. Oh, dear, she liked the feeling of it far too much.

'I obviously haven't a single brain in my head,' he whispered in her ear. '*You're* the woman I was talking about, Anna. *You're* the perfect woman. You think I'd be better at declaring myself, considering that I've done it once before, but I apparently haven't learned a thing.' He took his palm away and pulled her close.

'Let go of me, please,' she managed.

'I'd rather not,' he replied.

'My dress is riding up.'

'Doesn't bother me.'

'Grace will have something to say about this,' she tried.

'She'll go back upstairs.'

Captain Beattie grabbed her behind her knees and sat down with her in his lap. She gasped in surprise, but then tentatively leaned against his chest, which meant his arms went around her. She had convinced herself years ago that any lady over twenty was too old to cuddle. She had clearly been wrong.

He didn't seem to want to say anything more for the moment, and Anna didn't mind. She found herself enjoying the sound of his beating heart. Her practical brain reminded her that hearts beat. That was what they were supposed to do, or everyone would be a corpse. As she listened to someone else's heart, she knew she was never going to be alone again, not ever, provided this little event in the kitchen of the Drake went somewhere. With every fibre of her being, she realised she wanted that. So...

'John Beattie, what are you planning, if I am the perfect woman?'

'Up you get,' he said, making her wish she had said nothing.

He didn't go far, only to his duffel, where he pulled out an oilskin pouch. He sat down again and patted his lap. She knew what to do and did it; she was educable, after all.

'Admiral Collingwood summoned me from the blockade to his flagship to speak about my next assignment.' He held what looked like orders. 'Orders are usually boring. I'll condense it. For the first time in my life, I have dream orders that other captains would kill for.'

'Our side or their side?' she asked, which made him laugh.

'Probably both, if I am honest.'

'Is it dangerous, Captain?'

'Orders on an ocean in wartime?' he teased. 'I did have an inkling when I left here that such orders might be offered to me.'

She could joke, too. 'If you're so busy, why am I sitting on your lap?'

'It's the smartest thing you ever did. The Admiral was busy with correspondence, so I sat in the wardroom and opened my mail from Allan, Mrs Fillion, and you.'

He fell silent. She understood his feelings. 'We waited to write to you,' she told him gently. 'Allan was upset, and I even found our hardy Pru sniffling in the pantry.'

He took her hand. 'We wanted to have a good story to tell you. I… I suppose our letters broke your heart. We didn't mean to.'

'Aye, they did,' he said, and she heard his remorse. 'I'm still amazed at my sheer gall in foisting my troubles onto you. Ah, well. I handed Admiral Collingwood your letters when he saw how upset I was. He read them and told me his own story.'

She listened to Captain Beattie tell of a husband and father denied the chance to return home to his wife and young daughters, because of the need for vigilance in the Mediterranean Sea, Admiral Nelson's final command.

'Old Cuddy will likely never see his family again and he wants someone to be more lucky than he. I am to be the beneficiary.'

He found another paper, this one looking like parchment, and handed it to her. 'This is a common licence, signed by the Bishop of Winchester. I put you in a precarious position with my well-meaning hug. I cannot in good conscience leave you in ruin. Admiral Collingwood sees this as a convenient solution to our troubles and I cannot argue with him. It *is* convenient. Miss Fontaine, I am a gentleman. I do not ruin ladies.'

'I know you do not, Captain Beattie.'

She gave him a sideways look, feeling shy again, and wondering why, or even if, this excellent, harried, exhausted man cared anything about her, beyond his desire to do the right thing.

'These licences are for people in a hurry,' she said, and left unsaid, *Aren't they for people in love?* That question seemed out of place here. She wanted to assure him that she was not in a hurry, because she and the children had found a peaceful haven. Sitting on his lap, she decided that a lap might prove to be a peaceful haven, too.

'Aye, these licences are for those of us in a hurry. My ship is my parish, but it is not a place to cry the banns.' He rested his hands palms up in her lap. 'I have done nothing but disturb your peace, shame you and force you to...to...'

'Dig a little deeper and help someone in need?'

He took the licence from her. For one awful moment, Anna feared he was going to rip it into pieces. He tapped her hands with it. 'It's good for three months, ma'am, any morning between eight and noon, except Sundays. I must leave for Gibraltar tomorrow on another fast dispatch. Before I go, may I ask the harbourmaster to alert you when the next sloop of war or frigate is heading there?' He patted his chest and she heard paper crackle. 'Collingwood gave me a pass to do that. That is, if you are willing to bring along Allan and take a chance on me.'

'And Pru,' she added. 'I won't come without her, too.'

'Of course. Will *you* come?'

Under the quiet question, she heard all the uncertainty and worry that must keep such a father and captain awake at night. She had a practical mind and realised that this marriage would be extremely convenient for them both, removing her from the shame of her Plymouth circumstances, even though not of her doing, and providing both Allan and Pru with security.

'I believe I will come, Captain Beattie,' she said, her voice equally quiet. She had to say it. 'I promise not to make any particular demands on you. War is not the time for that.'

She saw relief on his face, which saddened her for a moment, until she reminded herself that they barely knew each other. And there was this: Anna Fontaine had learned since January that she was far stronger than she'd thought.

'I will come.'

'Done, madam. See you in the Mediterranean.'

Chapter Sixteen

After a sleepless night, Anna saw him to the dispatch vessel at dawn.

She rose to John's knock. 'See me to the ship,' he said through the door, and it was not a suggestion. She was ready in ten minutes, her hair tied back with a ribbon.

They walked into a day just waking. It touched her when he stood a moment, head up, gauging the wind. 'Do you always do that?' she asked curiously.

'Always. If peace ever breaks out, I will still do it.'

'What is it telling you this morning?'

'That coffee is brewing next door and I smell sausages.'

'Oh, you!'

'Miss Fontaine, it's fair winds to Gibraltar. I'd give a fast boat five days, ten days if we were dropping off orders and official mail. It is only I, this time.' He grinned, which, to her delight, threw off five or six years of marine warfare from a tired man. 'So I would split the difference, ma'am, and call it twelve days.'

She laughed at his calculations and swatted him with

a glove, causing vast consternation among a gaggle of midshipmen nearby.

'Be careful, Miss Fontaine. Pups like these think captains have no life off a quarterdeck,' he teased.

He walked in no particular hurry, duffel slung over one shoulder, and her drawn close to his other side. Anna noticed other men and women headed in the same direction.

'I never knew things were this busy so early,' she confided. 'I like my bed.'

'You might like mine better,' he said quietly, not looking at her, even as she watched a slow blush rise from his neck, confirming her suspicion that Captain Beattie was a modest man. She watched him swallow down some emotion, probably because they had arrived at the wharf and he had to be a captain again. *Or is he thinking of Cathy?* she wondered. *Stop it, Anna.*

Another thought from last night shoved its way closer: she kept picturing his relief at this solution to his current dilemma. After all, he'd never really proposed, but said, '*See you in the Mediterranean.*'

Don't overthink this, Anna, she told herself firmly. *Give the man some room. He said something about convenience.* She considered it, remembering, *And so did I.*

'Which ship?' she asked, almost overcome by the sudden reality that she couldn't bear to see him sail away. If she felt this way before even putting that common licence to good use, how would she feel after?

He pointed. 'The *Constant*.'

To her horror, it didn't look much larger than a toy in a bathtub. 'It's so small.'

'The better to move fast. You and the children will sail in a larger vessel.'

He kissed her cheek, gave her a long, silent appraisal, then turned and walked up the gangplank, not looking back. As she watched other men board the ship, none of them looked back, either. *Not because you don't want to*, she thought, suddenly understanding, *but because it is so hard to do.*

Anna and her children sailed two weeks later on the sloop of war *Jaunty*, glorying in a single gun deck and twelve carronades—which looked like pea-shooters—and bound for Gibraltar.

Packing was simple. Allan had little, Pru even less. Captain Beattie had already vetoed anything woollen in the Mediterranean, so that lightened her load but not by much, since most of her dresses were wool. Her flannel nightgowns needed to vanish, too, but she didn't have anything lighter. Mrs Fillion had solved her problem as she'd stood by, watching her pack.

'Grace, I have never lived in a warm climate,' Anna said, holding up her nightgown.

'Captain Beattie has been on short rations for a few years, my dear. Flannel will not deter him.'

I'm surprised I have a single blush left, Anna thought.

'One moment.' Grace left the room, returning with a blue cotton nightgown that looked almost transparent, to Anna's embarrassment. 'It packs small,' she said, smiling at Anna's big eyes.

People continued to surprise her. Anna had assumed

that Mrs Moore would come along, because her housekeeper and friend had willingly followed her from Papa's parish after his death, and then ruled supreme in Will's Plymouth kitchen. Still, it was good form to ask.

So she asked her old friend in the kitchen, where she spent most of her time. To Anna's astonishment, Pierre dropped his stirring spoon in the soup and clasped Mrs Moore to his ample chest. '*Mais non, mademoiselle, elle est à moi!*' was his fervent comment, which had turned Mrs Moore into a blushing young thing of forty-two.

'No, dearie, not this time,' had been her friend's reply. 'I'm staying here.' She giggled. 'P'raps because I love Plymouth so well.'

That last night in Plymouth, Anna had debated about confiding in Grace. Something propelled her out of bed and down the hall for a quiet tap on the door. 'Grace,' she said when the door opened, 'I have a dilemma.'

What a wise woman Grace was. 'Tell me your fear,' she said quietly.

'Can we really be happy in a convenient marriage such as this one will be? There is so much at stake, especially for the children.'

Grace raised her chin and gazed so kindly into her eyes. 'I know you have both chosen well. Marriages are just as likely to succeed for convenience as for love.'

'There isn't much time for love during war,' Anna pointed out.

'No, there isn't. However, you never knew his Cathy. She was a bonny lass and they were deep in love.'

'Do you think…?' She trailed off, not really wanting to finish her thought.

'Just be yourself,' Grace said gently.

'Lately, I've been wondering just who I am. I'm a little low on courage at the moment.'

Grace smiled. 'Low on courage? When you crossed the lobby and sought me out after that pernicious dealing with the estate agent, I saw something in your eyes.'

'Abject terror?'

'Far from it,' Grace said firmly. 'That day, I saw a little lady with the heart of a lion.' She chuckled. 'Since this is the Royal Navy we're talking about, perhaps a heart of oak.'

Chapter Seventeen

Some heart of oak. One day into the crossing of the English Channel, if Neptune himself had risen from the depths and stabbed her with his trusty trident, Anna would have considered it a blessing.

For two days she would have welcomed death. It passed on the third day because of a combination of things. The first was a gallon jug—so it seemed—of a liquid so evil that it could not have been devised by the hand of man, except that it was.

'Here you are, Miss Fontaine,' Captain Carlisle informed her sympathetically. 'The bosun's mate claims the recipe has been handed down from father to son since before the pharaohs. Drink it.'

She drank, amazed that it seemed to curl up in her stomach and purr.

The other matter might have been the real reason she decided to live. 'Allan is desperate with grief,' Captain Carlisle told her. 'He fears you are going to die and leave him and Pru alone.'

So, Anna appeared on deck in the early afternoon,

looked around and pronounced it good. The relief in Allan's eyes was even better than the Elixir from Hell. The Captain brought over a folding canvas chair and guided her into it. She held out her arms to Allan and tucked him close.

'I was just seasick,' she said soothingly. 'I wonder if your father ever gets seasick?'

'Surely not, Missy,' he said quickly.

'I will never be seasick again,' she promised him.

The sloop sailed down the length of the blockade of coastal France and Spain. As the weather warmed, Anna found herself on deck frequently, sitting in the canvas chair, her face to the sun. She felt all the tension and uncertainty of winter shrug philosophically and take leave. With Allan often asleep on her lap, she gave herself time to mourn the loss of her brother, and wonder what lay ahead with Captain Beattie.

Eight days out, an even smaller ship hailed them and hove to, a waterproof packet tossed aboard and delivered to Captain Carlisle.

The Captain spoke of the matter that evening after supper in the wardroom, where officers ate, and where they did, too. He tapped the side of his glass to get their attention. He held up the letter he had received. 'Apparently our old friend *La Guerre* is roving about, gentlemen,' he said.

'*La Guerre*?' she asked, confident enough among the officers to speak.

'She's a ship much like Captain Beattie's French-built

Swallow,' he explained. 'She roams the Mediterranean like a bully, but usually that area closer to France.'

'Now you see her, now you don't,' another officer said, too cheerfully to reassure Anna.

'There will be gunnery practice tomorrow morning first thing.' The Captain nodded to Anna and the children. 'It will be a little noisy.'

She was routed out early in the morning by the Captain himself. 'Dress quickly, Miss Fontaine,' he said. 'Follow me.'

He led her down a narrow ladder and into a tiny space at the bottom of the ship, where she felt the stronger motion of water against the hull. She looked around at barrels and crates.

'The bread room,' Captain Carlisle told them. 'If—and mind you, this is a big *if*—we find ourselves beset and under enemy fire, Miss Fontaine, I want you to hurry down here with the children.'

'Here?' She hoped she didn't sound dubious, but…

'We'll have target practice right after breakfast. The pitch and roll will probably frighten you more than the noise,' he told her. 'Remember this: if you hear a long drum roll, that is called Beat to Quarters. Get down here as fast as you can and stay here until we come for you.'

Anna nodded, well aware that he saw the fear in her eyes. Perhaps he had a daughter of his own, because he rested his hand on her shoulder.

'I will have some bandages put down here as well. We're too small for a surgeon. If I have any wounded, I will send them here, too.'

What could she do but nod again and declare, 'Aye aye, sir,' which made him smile.

'I wonder, Miss Fontaine, does our Captain Beattie have any idea how formidable you are?'

I am anything but that, she thought, then managed a smile. 'Does any future husband really know that much?'

'I know I didn't! Just remember that the *Jaunty* is fast and nimble.' He smiled. 'I would hate to anger Captain Beattie if something should go crossways.'

'We are at war,' she said simply. 'Don't worry about us, sir.'

He bowed. 'I'll get you to Gibraltar. Breakfast now.'

Anna wondered how she was supposed to eat, knowing that her still-recovering stomach was now tied into knots. As it turned out, it didn't matter.

They were barely seated at the table and Allan reaching to sugar his porridge when they heard someone on deck shout, 'Beat to Quarters! *La Guerre* on the starboard beam!' She held her breath at the sound of the continuous drum roll, which brought Captain Carlisle immediately to his feet.

He turned to her only long enough to shout, 'Bread room! Remember what I told you,' then ran from the wardroom. In mere seconds, only the three of them remained.

When the children looked at her with such trust, Anna knew the horrible responsibility of being the all-knowing adult, when the truth was that she knew nothing. She grabbed the lantern Captain Carlisle had hung on a hook. 'Follow me, my dears.'

They waited long enough for every man who wasn't already on deck to dash up the companionway, then took their turn, going down instead of up. Pru fell the last few rungs as the *Jaunty* started to dart about. It took no imagination to understand that the sloop of war was dodging and evading a more powerful enemy.

Bless the children. They were quiet and obedient. Anna hung the lantern on a hook above them and sat down. She gestured to Allan and Pru, who tumbled into her lap. She felt their shivering, and hugged them tight.

Pru, brave Pru, wet the front of Anna's dress with her tears. 'It's the noise!' she cried, as the carronades above them fired.

It *was* the noise, even though the rational part of her mind reminded Anna that noise itself wouldn't kill them. She longed to be on deck with the crew, able to see what was going on, and not down below, waiting for a cannonball from the *La Guerre* to blast them apart. She thought of Captain Beattie, who depended on her to guard his son. Even more than that, she wanted his arms around *her*. Up until now, war had been a distant distraction. The death of a much-beloved brother had brought it closer, and now she was in the middle of it. *John Beattie, where do you get your courage?* she asked, the air becoming heavy now with the smell of gunpowder. *Spare me a little, please, wherever you are.*

The *Jaunty* dodged nimbly again. One of the crates of bread tumbled down, cracking open and shooting out pilot bread. 'At least we won't starve,' Allan announced, which, God be thanked, made Anna smile.

Her smile lasted only until the hatch opened and a sailor pushed in a wounded man. 'Bandage him, miss,' he said, then left them.

With what? she asked herself, remembering Captain Carlisle's comment that he would provide bandages before their gunnery practice, which had suddenly turned into the real thing.

'Pru, you hold onto Allan,' she ordered, as she crawled the few feet to the wounded man, bleeding from a wound on his thigh. Drat him, if he didn't regard her as hopefully as Allan had looked at her earlier. *I don't know anything*, she wanted to tell him, obviously not what he wanted to hear, so she said nothing. *Think, Anna.*

Some god of wisdom must have taken her under his wing because she knew what she should do, the only thing. No time to be a baby about it. She stood up and braced herself against a keg.

'You're going to get an eyeful,' she warned the sailor, who clutched his thigh. She lifted her dress and untied her petticoat.

Wouldn't you know it; the wounded man was the embodiment of all those ribald jokes about sailors. 'I'll die a happy man, miss,' he managed to gasp, and then winked at her.

'For heaven's sake,' she scolded as she smoothed down her dress. She glared at him, then ripped her petticoat into strips as the guns roared and the *Jaunty* shuddered when a cannonball crashed into the ship somewhere.

Terrified, she mentally flogged her fear into a corner of the bread room and dared it to move. Ignoring the noise, she made a pad of one long strip. The sailor nodded and pulled apart his ripped trousers, giving her an eyeful, too. She pressed the pad against the jagged hole in his thigh and wound her petticoat strips tight around it.

'Looks good, miss,' he told her, shouting to be heard above the noise of battle. 'Knot it tight on top of the pad, there's a good girl.'

She did as he directed, then looked around for something to cover him. He pointed to a scrap of sailcloth. Pru tugged it out, and Anna placed it on his lap. She heard other men on the ladder, panicking to think of more wounded. They continued on by, running into the hold.

'What are they doing?'

'Listen,' he said. 'We've been hit twice. Hear it?'

She listened, then heard a rhythmic clank. 'What is it?'

'The pumps, ma'am,' he told her, sounding so matter-of-fact, when she wanted to run in circles like a crazy person. 'Getting t' water out.'

'What now?'

She didn't know how a wounded man could grin, but he did. 'We hope that Neptune likes the Royal Navy more than he likes the French.'

Chapter Eighteen

Anna motioned the children closer. 'I don't like this,' Allan told her.

'That makes four of us,' the sailor said cheerfully. 'Miss, you tie a right good bandage.'

'I'm discovering hidden talents,' she replied, heartened by his calmness.

She longed for silence, wondering how nice it might be, if she survived to see her wedding, to listen to John breathing that calm sleep of the content and satisfied person. Something deep in her heart told her she could provide him with restful slumber.

The nautical dance of death that was a ship-to-ship action continued: dodge and parry, fire, and dodge again on their nimble but wounded ship, well-captained. How long could they survive?

'Ah,' the sailor said, alert now. 'You hear that?'

'Something else? What?'

'There's another ship nearby,' he told her, listening intently.

'Theirs or ours?'

'We'll know soon enough.'

They waited. The sailor closed his eyes. It touched her heart to think that he had stayed awake, or maybe even conscious, because he felt they needed him.

He opened his eyes later when the bombardment stopped. 'We'll be all right now. Don't you worry,' he said, then closed his eyes again with a relieved sigh.

She heard someone on the ladder. His face blackened by smoke from the carronades, the first lieutenant opened the door, peered in and smiled, teeth so white in a darkened face. 'I'll get you topside,' he told Anna. 'And I'll get something better for Joey's bare bum.' He looked closer at her 'bandage' and grinned. 'I like the crocheted edging. Someone should suggest that to the Sick and Hurt Board.'

'Really, sir!' she exclaimed, but had to smile, despite all.

Topside was a tangle of rope and shell casings. To one side she saw a man covered entirely with bloody sailcloth, and looked away, saddened at the high cost of war.

'We had a time of it, Miss Fontaine,' Captain Carlisle said. He gestured to the tall man beside him, wearing an unfamiliar uniform. 'Miss Fontaine, let me introduce Captain Dan Tyler, US Navy.'

'How do ye, ma'am?'

'We owe you a debt, sir.'

'Indeed we do,' Captain Carlisle echoed. 'Miss Fontaine, if you will permit, I want you and the children on...on...'

'The *Hartford*,' Captain Tyler said. 'We harbour near Boston.' He nodded to his Royal Navy counterpart.

'Lately, we sail here, too.' There was no mistaking his good humour. 'Captain Carlisle, the Mediterranean does not belong to the Royal Navy.'

'Can we not continue to Gibraltar on the *Jaunty*?' she asked.

'Only if you wish to be towed behind her in our dinghy for safety,' Captain Carlisle said. 'Miss Fontaine, we're in precarious shape. I won't endanger you three by keeping you aboard.' He nodded to his fellow in rank, if not nation any more. 'Thank God Captain Tyler arrived to harry away the French.'

'Very well, sir,' she said, because there was no other answer.

'We should meet up with Admiral Collingwood's flagship along the way. I have asked Captain Tyler to leave you there with the sailor you so prettily bandaged.'

Anna couldn't help a sigh, nearly certain that the news of her bandage was going to follow her everywhere. 'Sir, it was all I had,' she reminded him patiently.

'Well, then... The *Hartford* will continue to shepherd us.' Anna heard the relief. 'For which I am grateful.' And this was for Captain Tyler. 'I owe peace of mind to you Yankees.'

She nodded. 'We'll get our luggage.'

'We'll help,' Captain Tyler said. 'Captain Carlisle is busy.'

He and two *Jaunty* crewmembers followed her down the companionway. 'It was a near-run thing, Miss Fontaine,' Captain Tyler said. '*La Guerre* seems not to have gotten the message of Trafalgar.'

'Which is...?' she asked, curious about an American opinion of the war with Napoleon.

'The Mediterranean doesn't belong to the French.'

Why are you here? she wanted to ask, but decided to leave those concerns to diplomats. It was enough to be saved from a possibly sinking ship.

Anna retrieved another petticoat then closed her trunk. No sense in being missish about the matter. 'Captain Tyler, since my patient is wearing my petticoat, look away, please.'

He took the hint, picked up her trunk and closed the door. She stepped into her petticoat as the *Jaunty* shifted in the water and then seemed to settle.

'Smartly now, Miss Fontaine. I don't like the way that felt,' she heard from the other side of the door.

Trunk on his shoulder, Captain Tyler led Anna and her little ones to the main deck and then to the ship's rail, where grappling hooks snugged the vessels together. His sailors carried their luggage across, then came back.

Anna turned to Captain Carlisle. 'Thank you, sir.'

He bowed. 'I wish I could have seen you to Gibraltar.'

'The French made that hard,' she replied. 'Safe sailing, Captain.'

'You, as well. Thank you again for doctoring my tar.'

Crossing from the *Jaunty* to the *Hartford* would have looked daunting to the Anna Fontaine of mere months ago; now, it was something she had to do, no argument. Captain Tyler went first. Allan followed, scrambling down over the *Hartford*'s railing. Pru proceeded more cautiously, but with the same result.

Anna came last, resolutely keeping her eyes on Captain Tyler. She hesitated at the railing, but his hands on her waist neatly carried her over, setting her on the deck. She nodded her thanks, and stared back at the *Jaunty*, sobered by the damage.

'I'm relieved we could render assistance,' Captain Tyler said. '*La Guerre* is here and there when we least expect her. Damn the French.'

Below-deck, he opened a door off a common area with a long table. 'This is the wardroom. Captain Carlisle gave me his last coordinates for Admiral Collingwood's flagship, which is closer than Gibraltar, if he is still there. We'll head that way first. Here's my cabin.' He smiled. 'I doubt you've slept much. Have a nap, courtesy of the US Navy.'

He lifted Allan and Pru into his hammock, and helped her to another foldaway canvas chair. Anna happily sank into it, thanked him, then closed her eyes.

She woke later to a light tap on the door. 'We've made Admiral Collingwood's flagship,' Captain Tyler said. 'Come up top.'

They followed Captain Tyler topside and looked up to see *HMS Queen*, gargantuan compared to *Hartford* and *Jaunty*. He took a speaking trumpet from his lieutenant. She scanned the officers on the quarterdeck and stopped, hand to her heart, to see Captain Beattie. He tipped his hat to her and blew her a kiss, which didn't go unnoticed by Captain Tyler.

'He's either a cheeky chap or your fiancé,' he said,

then raised the speaking trumpet. 'Captain Daniel Tyler, United States Navy, of the *Hartford* out of Boston, hailing His Majesty's Ship *Queen*. I request permission to discharge three English subjects.'

'For what purpose, sir?' came the reply from a man who looked infinitely grander than the Yankee captain.

'To render them useful to Captain John Beattie, sir.'

Her 'useful' Captain exchanged a few words with the *Queen*'s Captain. He bowed, took the speaking trumpet and raised it.

'Send them to us smartly. Where away then, Captain?'

'Sir, I will shadow *HMS Jaunty* to Gibraltar, if the *Queen* so desires. She was badly mauled in a fleet action by the French corvette *La Guerre*.'

The original captain took the speaking trumpet from John. 'You do not claim the *Jaunty* as a prize of war?'

'We are not at war, sir, not with you or the French. The Mediterranean is international water. My sole task is getting a pretty lady to a wedding.'

These Americans. Anna felt her face flame. She snatched the trumpet from him. 'I have been informed by Captain Beattie that wedding licences have a time limit. So does my patience.' She lowered the trumpet, wondering what she was turning into, in her brief association with two navies.

The laughter drifted across the water. 'Come alongside as close as you can.'

'Aye aye, Captain.' Captain Tyler turned to her. 'Ma'am, it's been a pleasure to have you aboard.'

'Now what?' she asked, not wanting to know.

'Watch.' He winked at her. 'I've never lost a soul yet.'

She held tight to Allan as Captain Tyler's helmsman expertly manoeuvred the smaller ship close to the *Queen*. Ropes flew, loosely connecting the two ships. In another moment, a series of ropes shaped somewhat like a chair dropped down, lowered from a spar.

'I can't possibly do this,' she whispered.

'Then *I'll* have to marry you,' Dan Tyler said.

She glared at him and he chuckled. 'Miss Fontaine, let me suggest that you put little Pru in first and seat Allan on her lap. I can guarantee you that my Royal Navy counterparts know what to do.'

Pru sat, even though her lip quivered. Anna kissed her cheek. 'My darling girl, trust a little longer.'

Pru nodded, looped her arms through the rope, then grabbed Allan and closed her eyes. 'You're squeezing me too tight,' he complained.

'Don't care,' she told him. 'I can't swim!'

Up they went, guided by two sailors at the ropes. Anna held her breath until they reached the *Queen's* railing above them, where practised hands pulled them up and over. She turned to Captain Tyler and held out her hand.

'Thank you, sir. If ever I can render you a favour…'

The rope seat came down again. She looped her arms as Pru had done, and let Dan Tyler adjust the restraining rope across her waist.

'I'm coming over, too, after they send the ropes back.' He gave the rope a tug. 'I want to meet your Captain Beattie.'

He signalled to the *Queen* and up Anna rose, too frightened to look down but determined not to embarrass the man who waited for her. She looked back at Dan Tyler, and saw him touch his hand to his heart.

Gazing back across the water to the mangled *Jaunty*, Anna bowed her head as the cost of war at sea settled into her heart and mind. She stared ahead at John.

'Convenient, eh?' she murmured.

Chapter Nineteen

Anna knew there wasn't a graceful way to land on the deck. It was a simple matter to release her death grip on the rope and lurch into John's embrace. 'Ah, such grace,' he whispered in her ear, which made her laugh.

He kissed her right there on the deck. Her nautical audience—*oh, the Navy!*—sighed in unison, which gave Anna the giggles, even though her face was red, her hair a mess and her dress rusty with dried blood from the wounded sailor. At least she was wearing a clean petticoat.

She thought Captain Beattie would make some comment to the bright-eyed rabble observing the whole scene with glee, but he merely turned to the other man with epaulettes on each shoulder and bowed.

'Your deck, Captain Thomas,' he said. 'Thank you for the loan of it. I'm taking this lady below.'

'Where is your ship?' Anna asked.

'This way, Miss Fontaine,' he said most formally, but with a smile. 'I'll show you my domain.'

With a nod to Captain Thomas, who wasted not a moment in shouting, 'As you were, men,' sending everyone back to their occupations, John took her hand and walked her across the deck.

He gestured. 'There she is, my *Swallow*.'

She heard the pride, and wondered about the *Swallow*, which she had naturally seen in Plymouth, but which looked so much smaller now as she stood on the much larger flagship.

John seemed to read her mind. 'Aye, *Swallow* is small, but she is quick, nimble and formidable.' He looked at her. 'Rather, I suspect, like you.'

She said something that she barely remembered after it left her mouth, because he kissed her again, quickly.

'We are now on the *Queen*, Admiral Collingwood's flagship.' He pointed up. 'The Admiral's flag.'

He rested his hands on her shoulders, all humour gone. 'What can I say? Thanks to the US Navy, you're here, too.' He turned to see the Yankee Captain hoisted on deck. 'And here is Captain Tyler.'

'He wanted to meet you.'

'I am in favour of meeting him, too,' John said. 'Not everyone aboard this ship will agree, but we need to know this new nation.' He went to the opposite railing to greet her rescuer and introduce himself. She joined the captains.

Captain Tyler nodded to her. 'Miss Fontaine, I have just informed Captain Beattie that I have something of interest to discuss, if Admiral Collingwood wishes to hear me.'

'I believe he will,' John said. 'Let us find out.'

He steered her towards a far grander companionway than on either the *Jaunty* or the *Hartford*. 'Collingwood already requested the children below-deck, where you will discover who really rules the waves.'

It was a hopeless matter, but she patted her hair anyway. 'I look a fright,' she protested.

'Then I've never seen a prettier fright. Here we are.'

She hesitated when they approached an ornate double door with a Royal Marine guard who snapped to attention. He ushered her and Captain Tyler through.

Anna knew that the stern of a ship, any ship, was the Captain's domain, but this was far grander, with a Turkish rug on the floor, and books held in place on shelves by strips of wood. A youngish man sat at a desk, writing.

'That can't be the Admiral,' she whispered to John.

'His secretary and gatekeeper to the inner sanctum,' John said. 'And here is the crew member I mentioned who really rules the waves.'

She stared at a pointy-eared brown and white dog who, with a composed air, regarded Allan and Pru watching him.

'He does rule the ocean waves,' Anna heard from another open door. 'My dog, Bounce, and his current entourage.'

That was her introduction to Admiral Collingwood, a tall man, taller than John, who probably had to duck below-deck. Leadership and dignity seemed stamped on his face, dress and bearing, but were overruled by the kindness in his eyes, especially when he regarded Bounce and the children.

Anna curtsied, and he bowed. 'Miss Fontaine, a wily post captain has lured you aboard my ship with the promise of matrimony. Come, come, lass, should you trust a Navy man? Ministers from pulpits everywhere counsel against it.'

'Admiral, you are not supporting my cause,' she heard beside her, which told her worlds about this august seaman's familiarity with his officers.

'On the contrary, Captain Beattie,' Collingwood said. 'I am delighted for you.' He came closer. 'As you were, Bounce.'

The dog gave a massive sigh and collapsed on his side, which was all the invitation Allan Beattie needed to flop down and cuddle close. Pru hesitated a moment, then sank down beside boy and dog.

There was something almost homelike about this room, with a well-used sofa decidedly rump-sprung and an equally ornate Turkish rug, where Allan and Pru now sprawled, at least until John held out his arms and Allan scrambled up and ran to him.

'I wanted to stay on the deck with you,' his son told him, 'but Admiral Cuddy wanted to give you a moment with Missy. Why do you need a moment with Missy? She is always around.'

'She is, thank God. As for why I need a moment with her, you'll understand when you're older.' John motioned to Pru. 'And you, miss, thank you again for watching out for my little rascal.'

'He's easy,' Pru replied, practical as always.

'I thank you all the same,' John said simply, and with a little bow that rendered Pru speechless.

'Come closer, my dear,' the Admiral said to Anna.

'Captain Beattie, perhaps it is not too late for both of us to remember formal introductions.' He bowed to her. 'I am certain this is Miss Fontaine.' He turned to the Yankee. 'And you, sir?'

John introduced Captain Tyler, who nodded to the Admiral. Anna didn't think Americans were interested in bowing.

'Admiral, it is an honour to meet you.'

'Captain Tyler's *Hartford* saved the *Jaunty*.' John took a deep breath and tightened his grip on her. 'And my dear ones.'

'For which we are all grateful, Captain Tyler,' the Admiral said. 'Welcome aboard. Yes, I am Collingwood, in charge of this pack of jackals.'

'It's a fine pack, sir,' Captain Tyler said. 'If I could have a moment of your time?'

'Aye, Captain Tyler.'

It was Anna's turn for a quiet sigh of relief. She was not one to seek out attention. Better let the men converse. She glanced at the children, suddenly wishing she was young enough to flop down beside them with Bounce, who groaned with the pleasure of two minions scratching his ears.

But no. Admiral Collingwood included her. 'Miss Fontaine, our American Captain tells me that you and the little ones had a time of it from a French rogue who obviously didn't get our distinct message at Trafalgar.' He turned to Captain Tyler. 'Now this Yankee tells me that he has appointed himself chief guardian of the *Jaunty*, on its way to the Rock.'

'With your permission, of course, Admiral Collingwood,' Dan Tyler said smoothly. 'I know it isn't far to Gibraltar, but his ship is not in trim. I would follow him for his safety's sake.'

'But *we* are the Royal Navy, sir, and you are not,' the Admiral said, not sharply to Anna's ears, but more with curiosity.

'The *Jaunty* was a ship in distress,' Tyler said simply. 'I defer to you, certainly, if you would rather one of your fleet escort her to Gibraltar, but I am willing.'

'Very well. You have my permission to give aid where needed,' the Admiral replied. He smiled. 'Captain Tyler, let me escort you topside and ask about *your* fleet in the Mediterranean.'

'Hardly mine, sir,' Tyler said as he followed the Admiral out of the door. 'We answer to President Thomas Jefferson.'

'Upstart,' Anna heard the Admiral say before the door closed, leaving her with John, the children and Bounce.

'At least we seamen have gone from fighting each other to teasing, instead. Come here, Anna Fontaine.' John said it gently, which was part of her wonderment about him. She had seen him at his most desperate, seen him coldly angry at a vile curate, seen him just now on the deck of a ship of the line, taking charge and then relinquishing it because he knew his place. She moved gladly into his arms.

'I have missed you,' she said, for his ears only. 'I was frightened on the *Jaunty*.'

'I can only imagine,' he whispered into her hair. 'Then

to physic a wounded man. Captain Tyler said something about a magnificent lady—I believe he means you?'

'Hardly that,' she told him, thinking of the fear and uncertainty she'd only admitted to herself and now to him. But did she have to blurt out, 'Here I am, sir. What now?'

It sounded like a jarring note to her ears, but John said nothing. *And you, what do you really think about this?* she wanted to ask.

'Admiral Collingwood is keeping you and Pru here tonight. I'm taking Allan with me to the *Swallow* for the night, some father and son time. I have had too few of those.' He touched her cheek. 'What say you to a flagship wedding the day after, and then sailing with me to Gibraltar? Aye or nay?'

'Aye,' she whispered shyly. 'I didn't get seasick and come all this way for nothing.'

He held her close, and she felt the laughter she did not hear. 'No, you did not. Anna Fontaine, you're a practical sort. Did you imagine any of this before I knocked on your door?'

Did you? she asked herself, and settled on, 'These are strange times.'

'I won't deny that,' he told her. He cupped gentle hands around her face. 'I do not know what lies ahead. Does anyone? Trust me.'

Chapter Twenty

'Our Navy is frustrating you, Miss Fontaine,' Admiral Collingwood said as they stood together on the deck of the *Queen* and watched John and Allan on the quarterdeck of the *Swallow*, following the struggling *Jaunty* and *Hartford*.

'Sir, I would have liked Captain Beattie to remain here,' she admitted.

He gave a heartfelt sigh. 'I have a confession, Miss Fontaine; if even the smallest occasion arises between now and his return tomorrow, I would like John to learn what he can about Captain Tyler and *his* Navy.'

'My life used to be simple,' Anna sighed.

'He will return tomorrow before noon for your wedding,' the Admiral reminded her, then laughed. 'My orders be damned, eh? Don't tell me you're not thinking that, pretty miss!'

'I'm no prevaricator,' she said.

'We have put you into an odd situation. Between you and me, Miss Fontaine…' What, he did not say, because his steward announced dinner. Anna wondered if she would ever know.

'There is this,' he told her over dinner in the elegant wardroom. 'My King has decreed that I will not return to England to see my wife and two daughters.' He sighed. 'I am needed here, commanding the Mediterranean Fleet.'

He seemed to want plain speaking, something Anna knew she possessed in great abundance—she was no diplomat. He also seemed not to want sympathy. She weighed both and let her heart decide.

'Dear sir, I always pray for the Royal Navy every night,' she told him. 'I have done that since my own late brother first sailed with Captain Beattie.'

'I imagine many ladies in England do precisely that.'

The Admiral dabbed his lips with his napkin and gave her his direct attention, an act which would have embarrassed her before John had arrived on her doorstep last January and practically demanded her help, his eyes equally determined. These were not men used to argument or dissension.

Admiral Collingwood wanted a comment? She had one just as frank as his. 'War has decreed a harsh sentence on you, sir. I will also pray for all of us who miss absent ones.'

'You touch my heart,' he said simply.

The strangeness of her situation receded as they adjourned to what would have been a sitting room on land, but which was here a clutter of charts and paperwork on desks overflowing in wire baskets. *All you want is your family*, she thought, and it saddened her.

'Are you dreadfully busy tonight?' she asked the Admiral, even as she wondered where her courage came from to so address him.

'I am always busy,' he said, but she heard no rebuke, just a lonely man stating a fact.

She knew what she wanted to do, but first there was Pru to consider. Pru sat on the floor by Bounce, her now-faithful servant, his eyes speaking volumes of his devotion to this new little human. Maybe her idea was presumptuous, but her woman's heart suggested otherwise.

'Admiral, at the risk of making a great fool of myself, do you have a basket of mending?' she asked. 'When my dear brother was in port, and pacing about the sitting room, I liked to spend quiet evenings darning his stockings and mending holes in his shirts.'

She had his attention. Admiral Collingwood quit pacing and stood there, so she babbled on. 'Sure enough, he would come and sit down, and I would tell him how my day had gone as I stitched.' *Please let this be right*, she thought. 'It helped him relax.' She couldn't help smiling at the memory, which had shifted from pain to a healing reminiscence. 'I was his little sister again, and I think—mind you, I am not certain—but I think he needed the homely reminder that a good portion of the world darns socks and carries on quietly.'

She stopped. *I have made a fool of myself*, she thought miserably as he stared at her. But no, it felt right. 'Do you have any mending, Admiral?'

He stared at her. To her relief, he smiled. 'You, madam, are the genuine article,' he said. 'Wait right here.'

She waited as he went into another room, leaving the door open. She heard him rummaging about and humming. He came out and handed her a basket with a courtly bow.

'Here you are, m'dear, my tattered clothes and a needle and thread. I hope it matches, but no one will see them. I am a sad case, Miss Fontaine. Darn away!'

Admiral Collingwood made himself comfortable on the sofa, shoes off, and told her about his wife Sarah—he called her Sal—and daughters Sarah and Mary Patience. 'Who is not patient,' he said, finger upraised. He laughed softly. 'She is not impressed by admirals, either!'

Soon enough, he reclined on the sofa, hands behind his head, looking for all the world like a man relaxing after a day at the office. He slept for an hour at least, which meant she had to put her finger to her lips several times when the door opened and some functionary or other peered in. Finally, they left her alone with the most powerful man in the Royal Navy, sound asleep as she darned his stockings.

She laughed inside at the crazy oddness of her situation, fairly certain this wasn't how most brides-to-be spent the night before their wedding. She watched Pru doze, too, leaning against the magisterial Bounce. *What should I be doing?* she asked herself. *I have no idea where I will be living, although I do not wish to be as far away from John as Admiral Collingwood is from his wife, even if I am currently a convenience.*

She finished her task, wondering how to wake up an admiral snoring on the sofa, when his eyes opened.

He looked about in alarm, as if uncertain why he was stretched out so comfortably and no one hurried about with papers to sign, or orders to issue, or whatever it was an admiral at war did.

'Do not fear, sir,' she said quietly. 'Some people looked in on you, and I made them go away.' She held up a handful of stockings. 'Now you have stockings without holes. Granted, some of the thread is colourful, but I work with what I have.'

He smiled at that. 'Miss Fontaine, you have just said something that I wish every man in the fleet understood. We work with what we have.' He sat up and gave her that piercing look she suspected had energised or intimidated many a seaman. 'You are a true original. I wonder if your lucky husband-to-be has any idea how fortunate he is.'

'I would like to see him now and then, but I've never been one to expect much.'

'My dear, it is past time for you to expect more,' he told her. He looked up from his contemplation of the pile of darned stockings when the door opened. 'Now the war intrudes again.' She saw his weariness, and knew the look was another glimpse at the high price of war.

The peace was over. The tired man snoring on the sofa turned into the Admiral of the Fleet again. He opened a door and beckoned her and Pru, now awake and rubbing her eyes.

'This is where I stow visiting dignitaries, you know, princes without countries, because this war tends to frown on the rule of headless kings; a pasha or bey from North Africa, or…' and here he bowed '…a lady on the verge of matrimony.' He chuckled. 'Of that category, you are the first. Sleep well, my dear.' Another laugh, this one more light-hearted, as if remembering earlier times, other tides, perhaps even his own wife. 'It might be your last good night's sleep for a few days.' Oh, yes, he was definitely a Navy man. 'Hah! How you can blush, Miss Proper!'

Chapter Twenty-One

With Pru sleeping soundly beside her, Anna woke to noise on deck. She moved away from Pru carefully, wanting a little space simply because she knew it would be her last waking time without a husband occupying that space.

She listened, dreading the sound of Beat to Quarters, but no drums came this time, only bells, the Navy's way of telling time. *There is so much I don't know*, she thought: Navy time, sleeping in a hammock, for heaven's sake, waiting for a husband to appear and, probably the biggest unknown of all, what to do with a man in her bed.

She had some idea. Even now, Anna smiled, remembering. Mama had been her usual forthright self, spelling everything out and offering reassurance, ending with her ringing endorsement of the married state: 'There now. You're of amiable disposition and should do quite well as the wife of a sober man.'

A sober man? Anna had been raised in a sober household of a conscientious, God-fearing and trustworthy clergyman, a vicar of rectitude, a man of good example.

'But Mama, tell me one thing,' she had asked. 'Is what you are telling me enjoyable?'

Then came Mama's never-to-be-forgotten smile. 'If you are most fortunate, you'll never regret a minute.'

That was the promise and hope she took with her, thinking of the adventure before her in this watery world of danger—she had seen it—and desperation—she had also seen this when she'd answered her door and her whole life had changed. *'Will you trust me...?'* rang in her ears and suddenly she wavered. *Do I know enough about you, or you about me, for us to trust one another and make this marriage a success?* she wondered. *Is this course of action wise when I have already lost so many people I care about?* Only time would tell, and it was past time for having any regrets over agreeing to this course of action. She had to focus instead on the practicalities of her situation.

Something else touched Anna's heart. You, sir, have also lost many people you care about: *My own brother, a wife you must have loved but rarely saw.* Anna also knew there had to be many more, considering how many men of the sea had died because one man tried to rule the world. 'What can I possibly mean to you?' she asked herself quietly. 'Do you even know? Do I?'

So many questions, but one thing heartened her: She knew Captain Beattie was a good man. Her own dear brother had told her that many times. She couldn't have explained it to anyone, but there it was. John Beattie was a good man living in hard times.

A practical woman, she needed to focus right now on

the events of the day. She had no wedding dress, only a simple sprigged muslin she had stuck in her trunk because it took up almost no space. As Pru watched from their shared bed, her eyes lively, Anna shook it out and despaired of the wrinkles. There was only one thing to do. She dressed in yesterday's dress, also wrinkled, but at least free from blood.

Sprigged muslin in hand, she opened the door to the main room to a hearty greeting from Admiral Collingwood, already seated at a desk drowning in documents. Bounce padded over for a pat on the head, quickly administered because she liked the dog with his pointy ears and expression of perpetual interest.

'Sir, is there anyone aboard who might press my dress?'

The Admiral tinkled a bell, which summoned the steward. 'Adams, Miss Fontaine could use a press.' And to her, 'Miss Fontaine, hand it over. The *Swallow* should be arriving soon, and I relish a wedding. Haven't seen one in years.'

Neither have I, she thought, *and this one is mine.*

'Papa, do you ever get tired of bobbing up and down?'

His son's announcement at the usual hurry-up morning meal in the *Swallow*'s cramped wardroom brought a general chuckle from the surgeon, the master, John's first lieutenant, a Royal Marine who was visiting, and the new second luff.

What a rare and wonderful moment it was to take his small son on his lap, feel him settle back as if it was his favourite place and tell him, 'Allan, there is an old story—

maybe it was on Noah's Ark—that when the bobbing of winds and waves stopped, everyone on board fell over in a heap.'

Allan considered the fact. 'I thought so,' he said, which resulted in more laughter from his officers. *We haven't been laughing much*, John thought. *I like this.*

'Do you like bobbing up and down?' his son persisted.

'I believe I do.'

'Will Missy and Pru?'

'Hard to say, but they won't be on the ship often,' he said, and didn't like the sudden hollow feeling from such a statement, one that would usually have troubled him not at all, except that he had met Anna Fontaine, and something had happened to him. Certainly, she would not be on the *Swallow*, and what a pity.

From the usual clatter of his brain at sea, another thought demanded attention: *I wasn't aboard either, John. Don't forget me, your own Cathy.*

'I won't,' he said softly, so his son could not hear.

'I like Missy and Pru,' Allan said.

'So do I, son,' he replied, even as Cathy remained in his mind.

He took that thought with him onto the quarterdeck, Allan tagging along, then standing still in imitation, legs wide, with one in front of the other, to the amusement of his crew on deck. John watched as the *Hartford* came alongside in early morning. Through a brass speaking trumpet he hailed Captain Tyler, who informed him in turn that the *Jaunty* had safely made port in Gibraltar.

'For which our Navy thanks you. Will you come with us back to the *Queen*?' John asked. 'There's a wedding.'

Captain Tyler must be the cheeky sort. 'If there is cake.' Would there be?

'I... I...do not know that myself,' he said, embarrassed how little he knew. He even wondered if Anna was having second thoughts. He'd be surprised if she wasn't. This was war, after all.

'P'raps I shall be there,' Tyler told him. 'I haven't kissed a bride in ages.'

Neither have I, John thought as more misgivings crowded in. *What in the world am I doing to such a kind lady?*

'Come if you wish, Captain Tyler,' he said and put down the trumpet.

He kept his own counsel on the return to the *Queen*, after suggesting to his sailing master, a man with children of his own, to find a patient sailor handy with knots, who might occupy Allan. Between the intricacies of a bowline and a handful of crispy salted potatoes from Cookie, his son was occupied, allowing John to wander below-deck. He stared at his sleeping platform, wondering how adept his bride would be in such a contraption, which was fine indeed, if a man held still in it. But holding still wasn't the usual marriage dance.

'This won't do,' he admitted to Adams, his steward, who handed him a tankard of grog, when he came into his cramped quarters and saw his captain contemplating the bed.

'Sir, you'll probably surprise yourself,' he heard in cheerful reply.

John thought of any number of colourful retorts of his own and discarded them all, preferring to spend time at his desk, contemplating a chart without seeing it.

He couldn't help remembering Cathy, daughter of the squire on the neighbouring estate—beautiful Cathy, with a mild temper and that bloom of colour in an otherwise pale complexion that had intrigued many would-be suitors, all of whom she'd dismissed in his favour.

'I loved you, Cathy,' he whispered as the *Swallow* made its way back the short distance to Collingwood's flagship. 'And you loved me, God only knows why.'

Seriously, what was the matter with women who loved seamen? He'd never forgotten Cathy's sad eyes and lovely face as he'd sailed away in a sloop of war, his first command. There she was at the wharf on his return five months later, softly round with child, her smile as pretty as ever, with one difference: that rosy bloom on her cheeks was permanent now, the deadly bloom of consumption. Thank God their baby had never contracted that feared ailment.

Two more sailings—one to the blockade for several months and the other to the Battle of Aboukir Bay—with a small son at the first return, and then a three-year-old held by his nanny as Cathy had struggled to appear healthy.

He'd learned of her death while he was on Gibraltar. Her last letter to him had been dictated to her mother. She spoke of love and regret and having failed him somehow, when he knew the failure was his, because he and other men like him were duty-bound with no choice.

I could have run a counting house, or been called to the Bar as a barrister, he told himself after reading that regrettable letter. *I should have been there for her.* That was three years ago. Surely it was time to move on. Logic told him that even had he chosen a landlocked occupation, Cathy would still have died. Still, there seemed to be no logic to love.

Now he sat in his cabin, rethinking the last few months. Should he despise himself for dumping his troubles upon his dead lieutenant's sister? The answer was a resounding no, because at the time he'd had no idea what else to do. When she'd opened the door that evening, took in the sight of a desperate father with nowhere else to turn, he'd known something unexpected, right down to the marrow of his bones: this woman was going to be important to him. Some sense he had either never paid attention to or recently acquired told him so.

He knew he had changed Anna Fontaine's life and altered everything about her orderly existence. That she bore it with uncommon grace was not lost on him. He knew without a doubt there was a deep well of courage inside this woman he dared to marry in this age of revolution and war.

He took that thought on deck, admiring the knots Allan produced, and nodding his appreciation to the seaman-teacher beside his son. 'MacNeish, you are an excellent instructor,' he told his patient deckhand. 'Thank you for teaching Allan, my little sailor.'

'Sail ahead. Ahoy to the *Queen*!' John heard from the crow's nest. He became all business then, signalling to his first luff to bring the *Swallow* alongside.

'Mr Marsing, the speaking trumpet, if you please.'

'Aye, sir.'

At the usual distance, John hailed the *Queen*. 'Requesting permission to come aboard,' he shouted into the brass tube.

'State your business, Captain Beattie,' he heard, aware of the barely stifled amusement. Trust Captain Thomas's bosun, a cheeky fellow, to enjoy this hugely. Oh, hell, everyone was grinning down at him. Could a man have no dignity?

'A wedding is my business, you black dogs,' he said and laughed, which made his own listening crew grin and look at each other. Had they never heard him laugh before? Maybe it was time to make some changes on the good ship *Swallow*.

First things first.

I want a wife, John thought as the larger flagship sent down a ladder. *I need a wife for Allan and Pru, if not for myself.*

He turned to his first luff. 'Mr Marsing, I will be returning with a wife and we will sail back to Gibraltar, briefly,' he said. 'The deck is yours.'

Chapter Twenty-Two

Captain Beattie knew his wedding could only be a modest affair, which he felt would suit Anna, who was not an ostentatious lady. What he was unprepared for was how lovely she looked, and what the simple sight of her did to his sorely tried body.

Aboard the *Queen*, he saluted, then shook hands with Captain Thomas. Whatever wedding dignity there was blew away when Allan ran ahead with Pru, who was waiting on deck, then tore down the companionway with her.

Allan was back in a moment, eyes wide, so excited. 'Papa, you should see Missy. She is beautiful.'

Allan was right. Anna met him at the bottom of the steps, eyes bright, smile genuine. He knew he looked upon a healthy woman, which soothed his soul. He took her hand and leaned close enough to be private.

'Not too many months ago, I insisted upon a hug,' he said. 'It got us both into trouble, but I must insist again.'

They embraced, which, for some reason, meant it was Bounce's cue to bark.

'She looks pretty as a picture,' the Admiral said as he watched from the door of the wardroom.

From her light blue dress to the little seed beads woven through the dark mass of hair wound into a knot at the nape of her neck, to what adorned her throat... John looked closer. Always happy to admire her handsome bosom, its splendour was overshadowed by an amazing necklace of intricate gold chain that resembled lace. A row of emeralds twinkled even in the low light below-deck.

Admiral Collingwood smiled like a proud papa. 'Captain, she's wearing a blue dress. This necklace of mine—spoils of war from the battle of the Nile—is both old and borrowed. I was at a loss for something new until this arrived. Hand it over, Wolfe.'

As if on cue, the *Queen*'s lieutenant of the lowest grade stepped forward with a smile and a sealed envelope. He handed it to Anna. Admiral Collingwood rubbed his hands together. 'Where would the navy be without exquisite timing? Let's call it new.'

John knew what orders looked like. 'Old, new, borrowed and blue,' he reminded Anna when she looked at the envelope rather suspiciously. 'It's my next orders. How bad can it be? I already know I am to rove the Mediterranean.'

Anna accepted the news serenely. 'Too bad there are not orders for a wife and children,' she commented, but he didn't hear any anguish in her tone. *Why would there be, when this is a marriage of convenience*, he chided himself.

'Orders will keep until tomorrow, even if they are something new,' Collingwood said. 'Tuck them away for now.' He gestured towards the wardroom. 'Come, come, my dears. Between eight and noon, you say, Captain Beattie, according to my friend the Archbishop of Winchester? Please tell me that you have the licence.'

And so they were married. John handed the common licence to the *Queen*'s chaplain, a rare bird in a fleet of often profane men. It touched his heart as his little son, eyes lively, escorted Miss Anna Fontaine across the wardroom, with the chairs lined along one wall under a massive chart of the Mediterranean. Officers took their seats. Soon, Pru stood alone, the only other female in the gathering except for his bride.

It touched his heart when Anna gestured to the child. 'You're my maid of honour,' she announced. 'If I had a bouquet, you could hold it. Come close, my dear.'

'Who giveth this woman to be married?' the chaplain asked as the ceremony started.

'I do!' Admiral Collingwood boomed out. 'She's a bonny lass.' John heard laughter in the room from the men of the *Queen* and the *Swallow*, and even Captain Tyler of the *Hartford*, who stood back to one side, as if in doubt of his reception.

Indeed she is a bonny lass, John Beattie thought as he took her hand. When the chaplain asked if there were any objections to this union, he thought of many that a sensible woman could raise, and end this odd business. All this sensible woman did was listen with interest, a lurking smile on her face. She said yes in all the right places, and he said aye when called upon.

He must have been a real pup at his first wedding, also in time of war. This time, the gravity of the words came home to roost on his shoulder like a vulture, when the chaplain asked him, 'Wilt thou love her, comfort her, honour and keep her, in sickness and in health? And forsaking all others, keep thee only unto her as long as ye both shall live?'

He looked at the woman beside him, amazed she had even followed him to this ship in the Mediterranean. Her beautiful eyes welled with tears, but he saw no sadness. 'Aye,' he answered, even as his conscience flared once again.

Aye. He knew he would say it and everyone expected it, but he hesitated for a fleeting moment, thinking of Cathy's sickness and Anna's health. And as long as you both shall live? They were in a war zone! How naïve he had been the first time. Maybe that had been easier then, because he knew less.

'Aye,' he said firmly, wondering if he knew any more.

In turn, she said, 'Yes,' her voice softer, but no less determined. He closed his eyes and thanked God—sometimes a distant fellow to him—she had opened the door that awful night.

Cherish. For better. For worse. Richer. Poorer. Love. Cherish. Cherish—what a lovely word. *Breathe, John.*

There was no ring. 'Later,' he whispered. What mattered now were his words, 'With this ring I thee wed, with my body I thee worship,' then something about worldly goods. The power and majesty stunned him, almost as though he had never heard them before. Perhaps he hadn't. Perhaps he was paying better attention this time.

There was so much more. He listened carefully, gripping Anna's hand, her squeezing back, then kneeling together for the Lord's Prayer, and rising united. The final responses tore at his heart in this time of war and uncertainty: 'And evermore defend them from the face of their enemy. O Lord, hear our prayer.'

He gathered her close. The wardroom rang with cheers. Bounce wagged his tail with supreme velocity. An uncommonly fine Madeira went around, and from somewhere, the *Queen*'s cook had engineered a cake. '…t'would have been taller, sir, but the sea was rough yesterday morning. The last layer sailed right off, it did.'

Now, their departure. Allan seemed happy to remain aboard the *Queen* with Pru while his father and Missy left for a few nights and days. 'Your father says he has some business in Gibraltar,' the Admiral told him, 'and I say that Bounce needs your company here, you two.'

To cheers and the inevitable ribald comments the Navy was fond of, the crew of the *Queen* saw them over the side and onto the *Swallow*, where another reception waited, this one not fuelled by Madeira but something else, that undefinable union of shared battle and victory. He told his new second lieutenant to authorise a tot of rum for everyone, and not grog. 'I won't water down a wedding toast,' he declared. That meant three cheers, and another three, and then his own, 'As you were, men, and thank you.'

Here it was. He turned formally to his first luff. 'Mr Marsing, you have the deck.' Then, softer, 'Only call for me in extreme emergency, as in the Second Coming of our Lord, or Napoleon himself. Do I make myself clear?'

'Aye, sir, you do,' said his lieutenant with a smile. 'We'll steer a course towards Gibraltar.'

Holding tight to Anna's hand, John led her to the companionway. 'Well, madam wife, shall we?'

Down the companionway, they passed through the wardroom and stopped only because he heard someone clear his throat. He turned to see his carpenter, a long-married man with a wife and children in Portsmouth. 'Yes, Brownlow?'

'Over here, sir, if ye don't mind,' he said softly. 'My Betsy would skin me alive if I embarrassed your lady wife.'

'Yes?' he asked when they stood on the steps of the companionway.

'I made an adjustment in your cabin, sir. I mean, in case you were wondering what to do.'

John smiled inside, thinking of the times when his fellow commanders had twitted him about being too easy on his crew. He'd mostly ignored them. His years at sea had schooled him in the art of finesse. 'Brownlow, I think I get your drift.'

'I thought you might, Captain. Sweet dreams, if I may be so bold.'

He couldn't help a blush, but below-deck was usually in a half light and he doubted Anna would notice. From the thoughtful expression on her face, he suspected she had ideas of her own.

'Well, madam wife, I should probably carry you over the threshold, but...oh, why not?'

He opened the door to his quarters, that compact space across the aft of the ship with his desk, a few chairs and a regrettable pile of charts in one corner. Time to tidy this, but maybe not right now. He picked up his wife and stepped into his little domain, that place where he read, charted courses, thought, paced about, questioned his decisions, and hoped for the best.

So far so good. He set her down, kissed her soundly, then opened the door to his sleeping quarters and grinned. 'I'll be damned, Mrs Beattie, if I don't have the best crew on any ocean,' he told her.

Anna's eyes were wide. She put her hand over her mouth and she smiled, too, thank God.

Brownlow had disconnected the ropes that kept his sleeping platform in motion. The bed frame was now anchored on the deck, held in place by marlinspikes. It wasn't going anywhere. No one was going to be dumped from this bed, not tonight.

'My dear, turn around,' he said. 'I recall buttoning two of your buttons several months ago. I intend to unbutton them all now. You know, in the interest of finding out if you have more freckles than those on your nose, which, by the way, I've been wanting to kiss.'

'I understand, Captain,' she said. 'You'll probably discover—since you are the observant type—that they match the ones on my front.'

A wife in a million. If that was so, then why this odd sense of restraint between them, suddenly? He hadn't planned on that.

He hesitated.

Chapter Twenty-Three

Anna knew herself well. As possible marriage alliances never materialised, her practical side had assumed command. As the years marched on, she'd accepted the reality of her single state.

Everything had changed with that knock on her door, and the first sight of this man who was now her husband. Always a quick assessor of people, she saw distraction, misery and worry, coupled with the most exhaustion she had ever seen in a person. It almost seemed to seep out of his pores.

She recognised that exhaustion, because her brother Will had brought it home with him after every voyage. She'd quickly learned to help Will out of his cloak and offer food, which he always ate like a starving man, with glances of apology at her.

At first, Will used to think he needed to go with her to the sitting room and talk about his latest voyage, whether it be to the distant Azores, the feverish Caribbean or, in more recent years, to the tedious, mind-numbing blockade of Spain and France.

She remembered the night she had been making some comment, then looked over at her brother sitting beside her to see a man sound asleep. She had wakened him gently, told him to go to bed and, for heaven's sake, sleep around the clock. After that, his return from duty never bothered them, because they knew what he needed most.

This was different. She was now married to Captain John Beattie, an association so intimate and unexpected that even now, seeing him standing there by that amusing bed, she wanted to push him down and command him to go to sleep, that this would certainly keep until they knew each other a little better.

But she was no fool. Anna also saw a man with desire in his eyes. She knew little about such longing, but some instinct told her that John Beattie needed her right now. Yet his own hesitation had opened a small window on the dilemma she thought he struggled with.

How to play this hand? She could think of nothing but plain speaking, even though it would probably toss both of them into great chasms of embarrassment.

She saw him frowning at her. *Come on, Anna, say the right thing*, she told herself. *There is a man's dignity at stake.*

She sat down on the funny bed and patted the space beside her. She took his hand and rested it against her thigh. She turned slightly to look into his eyes. Ah, yes, the exhaustion. And more. She addressed the more.

'I believe, dear man, that you're wondering what we just did in marrying so hastily.' There. That was a simple start.

Better and better. She let herself breathe a little when he smiled and shook his head.

'Madam wife, I believe you might be the smartest person in this room,' he said, which made her laugh.

She nodded. 'If it's any consolation, it takes a smart person to see that.'

That brought another genuine smile to his face. Goodness, but he was a handsome man when he smiled. *Lucky me*, she thought. *Onward, Anna.*

'I did you a huge service by solving your problem so conveniently, didn't I?' she asked.

'Aye, you did. I will be forever in your debt,' he told her, then looked away. 'I ruined you in society's eyes, and gave you no choice but to marry me.'

'John, don't be too determined to make me better than I am,' she said, warming to the issue. 'You're a man of honour and you had no choice in the matter, either.'

He seemed to think about that, which to her delight meant a comradely arm around her shoulder. It didn't feel like a lover's grasp, but she relished the friendliness of the gesture. Maybe it was a small building block from which to create an actual marriage, if they had the time, in this time of war, to proceed slowly.

'You're right, oh, Anna the Wise. You are an amazing lady. I'm wondering at my good fortune, even as I feel a little ashamed to have brought you to this. I had no choice but to marry you, and you had no choice but to accept.'

Somehow, she wasn't entirely surprised when he added, 'Pardon my frankness, Anna, but it has been a long time since I experienced the pleasures of the bedchamber.' He sighed. 'Does that make me a complete ogre?'

'Not at all,' she assured him, and felt something that might have sent her into maidenly blushes only minutes ago: they might even understand each other. 'Captain Beattie, why is it that men think they are the only creatures on the earth with such feelings?'

'Well, I… Hmm.'

'Captain, I am nearly thirty. Thirty! Frankly, sir, I never thought I would know what it feels like to be married. It made me sad to think I would go to my grave untouched.'

He gave her a long look. 'Anna Beattie, you're blushing.'

She dared to lean forward and kiss his cheek. 'So are you.'

He tightened his grip on her. 'Now that we are speaking so frankly, there's one other matter,' he said softly. 'You know I had another wife. There might always be a part of me that misses her.'

'I can understand that,' Anna said slowly. 'She was your first love, and the mother of your son.' *And you still love her*, she thought, waiting for the knowledge to hurt. To her relief, it did not. Again, that practical side of her nature understood.

'Would you…would you mind if I talked about her now and then, or told Allan about his mother?'

She heard the earnest note in his words and knew she couldn't deny him that request, nor would she want to.

'Mind? Never.'

There they sat. The mattress did feel good, and the

last few days had been trying in the extreme. She patted his hand. 'John, I'm tired, and if I am tired, you must be exhausted. Unbutton my back buttons. I already know you're a handy sort to have around. I'm going to find my nightgown—actually it's Grace's.'

'You're serious?'

'Yes. Everything else is practical flannel because I have lived in chilly, draughty Plymouth for some years. Apparently, Grace has a past I did not question.'

'You're amusing,' he said as he got up. She heard the relief in his voice. 'Turn around. I am a button expert, as you know.'

He was. She felt not a qualm in the universe about stripping right there and putting on said nightgown—*Watch if you want, husband*, she thought a little wickedly, then crawled into the wonderful bed. 'Do you have a preferred side?'

'By the door,' he said. 'Get in, madam wife, and move over.'

Anna did. He joined her, stretching out, yawning hugely, then speaking softly but with a certain contentment that touched her heart. 'Mrs Beattie, I remember I was five days after Trafalgar standing up, ordering my crew about, making decisions, second-guessing myself and worrying—always worrying.'

'I am happy not to be a captain,' she told him. 'That would make me grouchy.'

He chuckled. 'I was a bear!' He yawned again, then touched her shoulder. 'I'll be asleep in minutes, but you are right: I need you.'

'I'll be here when you're ready,' she told him gently. 'We are both practical sorts, are we not? War has robbed us of time and leisure. We are both on an uncertain path.'

'Aye, we are,' he said, and was silent. In mere moments she heard his even breathing.

She slept then, too, feeling herself relax and nearly melt into the mattress. She was warm from John's warmth. This body next to hers was not a captain with a fearsome reputation, but a man next to a woman. There was nothing new about this in the great scheme of the universe, but it was new to her, and it excited her.

The warmth of a grown body next to hers was soothing and even soft. She felt herself sinking into the mattress. True, the bed moved from side to side, but what of it? My, but these last few weeks *had* been exhausting.

She didn't know how long they slept against each other, but some time as morning approached, she woke to his hand on her back, rubbing it gently. *Now he needs me*, she thought, not John Beattie perhaps, but a man living under a mountain of unrelenting warfare and stress she could not even imagine, and she had a good imagination.

She sighed when his hand cupped her breast, then smiled when he seemed to weigh it in his grasp, and whispered, 'I do like a substantial handful.'

He caressed her breast, then turned her on her back and rolled on top of her.

This was new and strange, but she did not feel shy. 'What do I do?' she whispered back.

'Whatever you feel like,' he said. 'I know my business, madam wife. Relax and trust me.'

At a time like this? To her delight, she discovered she did trust him. She let herself relax and enjoyed the feel of his kisses and caresses, which meant his entry was simple and easier than she would have thought. Perhaps she was more ready for this than she'd imagined.

He began a gentle rhythm, which increased in tempo when she abandoned every caution to the wind and added her rhythm to his. She thought her legs might be better across his back, which made him mutter something that sounded like, 'Good instincts,' which, under any other circumstance, would have made her laugh.

She felt his excitement mount, then fill her. He groaned but kept his lips between her breasts to muffle himself. She caressed his back, savouring the peace that came as his heartbeat slowed until it matched hers. He kissed her ear and whispered, 'You are legally my wife now.' Again, that low laugh, and another whisper, 'Next time, I promise I'll return the favour.'

He cuddled her close, then relaxed in sleep. She didn't think he was worn out from the actual exertion, which had certainly roused every nerve in *her* body. She ran her hand lightly over the contours of his face and saw a man of war, an anxious father and a grieving widower lying there without a care, for once. *I did that*, she thought. The notion humbled her.

She knew this was a rare opportunity to personally assess this man she had married. She had him to herself, this handsome fellow with reddish-blondish hair, a straight nose, the thin lips of a Scot and his own freckles here and there.

She enjoyed watching the gentle rise and fall of his chest, deeply aware now how fast a man's heart could beat when he was intent upon a woman. *My heart, too*, she thought. *Goodness.*

It was almost light in his quarters when she woke to John kissing her bare shoulder. She rolled over and looked into warm, appreciative male eyes.

'It's your turn,' he said, and she knew precisely what he meant. She gave herself over to him entirely, abandoning herself completely: no war, no worries, no what-to-do-with-the-children, no conscious thought except his pleasure—and now hers as well.

When she cried out, he put a gentle hand over her mouth. 'Shh, shh. It's a small ship. Can't have my crew too envious.'

'I had no idea. I would urge you even deeper, if I thought I could.'

'You can't,' he replied practically, because he was John Beattie. 'This is as close as anyone gets, ever.'

'I like it.'

'Thought you might.' She felt his chuckle. 'Anna Beattie, if I show up on deck—and I must, soon—I should make sure I'm not smiling too widely. They'll throw me overboard for shark bait, otherwise.'

What an odd time to get the giggles. When he rose up a little so she could breathe, she asked, ever practical, 'Has anyone else in the world ever had this much fun?'

'Countless millions,' he replied, 'but right now, only us.'

He got up then, carefully balancing on the deck. She

watched as he seemed to feel the motion with his feet. 'What?' she asked.

'We're nearly to Gibraltar. The current changes. Up you get, madam wife. There's something else we have to do after we tidy up a bit.'

Easier said than done, especially since her man thought she needed his help with the washcloth. 'Mrs Beattie, you're a menace to rational thought,' he said finally. 'I suppose you're going to tell me to put my clothes on now.'

'You'll look more professional on deck if you do.'

He got as far as his smallclothes, then pulled her down onto the sleeping platform again, this time with Admiral Collingwood's letter in hand, the 'something new' of the wedding. He waved it around.

'It's time,' he said. 'I can't ignore orders.' He cracked the seal. He held it a little away to read. 'My God, Anna,' he said finally. 'My God.'

Her first instinct was fear, which faded quickly. She heard only awe in his voice.

'What?' she asked, hoping she sounded calm. She knew the Navy was a hard life and they were at war. She and the children had nowhere to live while he continued in the Mediterranean, as he already knew would be his lot. '*What?*'

'The kindest thing imaginable,' he said. She heard the emotion. 'Anna, our dear Admiral wants to loan us his house on Menorca. I... I...thought it was only rumour that he had a house there.'

Had she even heard him right?

'He...he has a *house*?' She looked at her husband, who

seemed to be having trouble drawing a decent breath. It brought home forcefully to her the agony of men condemned to the sea during war, iron men in wooden ships who yearned for the comforts of home and family, like normal beings. 'Breathe,' she whispered. 'In and out.'

'We've been doing the in-and-out,' he teased, which relieved her, because his ribald Navy humour hadn't deserted him. He held his orders closer to her. 'Right there, third paragraph.'

She read silently, then gasped and read it out loud, the better to believe it. *'And tell your lovely wife that she and the children have my permission to take up residence in my little place. I'll take you there myself when you return from Gibraltar. Move your return along smartly, too. I need you and the Swallow patrolling.'*

She put down the letter and nestled closer. 'Did you have any inkling of this?'

'Collingwood had mentioned Menorca was a possibility. I was hoping to find quarters in Gibraltar for you and maybe see you and the little ones occasionally.' He kissed the top of her head. 'I know the Admiral wishes his wife and daughters could come to him. The Admiralty has decreed him too valuable to be anywhere but watching the French.' He tapped the letter. 'Now he is helping us.' He lay back and stared at the ceiling. 'The very idea of sailing into Port Mahon and finding you there… I never imagined staying in his house!'

Chapter Twenty-Four

Oh, the curse of the practical mind. Anna knew it was time to re-enter the real world. 'Up we get,' she announced. 'I am counting on you to button up my dress and not kiss my freckles. I promise not to stare at your trousers and wonder how everything fits in there.'

He laughed at that. 'It's a deal, Mrs Beattie. I'm the Captain and you are my crew.'

'Just as I want it,' she said simply.

He was ready quickly. 'I'll be in the wardroom,' he told her, after he combed his hair at the mirror in his narrow closet. He stood there a moment, staring at something. She didn't think he was being vain.

She brushed her hair after he'd left. Knowing it needed more attention, she opened his closet to see the mirror. Next to the mirror was a drawing of a pretty lady who resembled Allan Beattie. *So, there you are*, she thought, then frowned. She almost felt jealous then. But what she and John had was purely based on convenience, nothing else. Wasn't it?

She made a parting and braided her hair low against her neck, all the while eyeing Cathy Beattie.

'Whether it's convenient or not, I'll take good care of him for you,' she said softly, and closed the door.

John took her hand in the wardroom, where his steward waited, as well as the man in a plain uniform she knew as his sailing master, plus a Marine in red and gilt. Another man in a plain uniform with the caduceus on each side of his collar was the surgeon. They bowed and she curtsied, hoping no one had any idea what had been going on in the Captain's quarters for most of the night.

Anna accepted a cup of coffee from the steward. *Give yourself a few days and you will no longer be a novelty*, she thought. She created a homely egg sandwich from the egg and toast on her plate, which made the Marine smile. 'My little son does that, Mrs Beattie,' he said.

'Then I am in good company, sir,' Anna told him.

'Men, I have our Admiral's orders,' John said. Omitting the part about the house soon to be loaned, he read them word for word. 'We are on patrol. The Mediterranean is ours to sail freely, to harry the French however we can and, most important, learn what they are up to. We will have a home port.' He looked at them. 'Gentlemen, we are to be based in Port Mahon, that jewel of the Balearics. Mr Lynch,' he ordered his second lieutenant, 'please inform Mr Marsing on the quarterdeck. Let us proceed to Rosia Bay.'

Mr Lynch nodded. 'Aye, sir. Will we tarry long?'

'Long enough to take on supplies that should be waiting for us.' He turned his attention to the surgeon. 'Mr

Coles, you have the Admiral's permission for everything you can beg, borrow or steal from hospital stores.'

Anna listened as orders went around, hearing not a sound of uncertainty, and knew she sailed on a well-captained ship. The other side of this man she now called husband was hers, alone. It both humbled and excited her.

He kissed her hand with a loud smack, to everyone's smiles. 'Come along, Mrs Beattie,' he teased. 'I expect there will be a resounding hip-hip hoorah from the deck when you show your pretty face. Right, men?'

To a man, they all stood and raised their coffee cups. She dipped another curtsy, playful this time, and let her husband steady her against the motion of a ship on the tack, bound for shore.

It was as John had predicted. As soon as a grinning Marine guard opened the companionway hatch and Anna stepped through, her husband gave a high sign of some sort and the bosun piped her on deck.

'John, do not even try to tell me there is a special call for a captain's bride,' she said, trying to be heard above the applause and whistles.

'No, Mrs Beattie. This one is more along the lines of "Hail the Monarch" and they don't mean me. Up you go to the quarterdeck. Take a seat in the marvellous deck chair, and watch my good crew bring us in.' He knelt beside the chair after she sat. 'This will be short, but you're coming ashore with me now. We have something to see.'

An hour later, they made it to the Rock and sailed smoothly into Rosia Bay, with its hotch-potch of buildings cobbled together and general ragtag air. 'This is where we docked after Trafalgar,' he said, standing next to the railing with her. 'We limped in.' She covered his hand with hers.

The *Swallow* docked at the wharf, with waiting supplies ready. 'You and I have another place to visit.'

It was a short walk, made longer because as soon as they were out of sight of the port, John stopped and kissed her, holding her close. He held her off a little, searching her face. 'I just realised something, Mrs Beattie.'

'What might that be?' she teased. 'You are a student of my face? I think it's rather ordinary.'

'Not at all. You're a lovely woman.'

She blushed at the sincerity in his voice.

'I believe, after our wedding night, that I am finally… starting to exhale.' The humour left again, and she saw a man exposing his vulnerabilities. 'Believe me, it is relief unimaginable. Oh, this is hardly loverlike, but…'

Anna smiled, resolutely pushing away the image of the woman next to his shaving mirror. The wife he'd loved. 'I believe you,' she said simply. 'We'll take our time.'

Another kiss, and then a laugh. He whispered in her ear, 'If you turn around slowly, you'll see that we are being watched.'

'I earnestly hope not,' she whispered back, then turned, started, stared and laughed. 'That is a monkey! One, two, three of them.'

'Rock apes,' he said. 'I hope they were entertained.'

He led her to a raw-looking cemetery, and stopped at the entrance. 'Our Admiral says it will be called Trafalgar Cemetery.' He looked down. 'Too many good men gone. Some day I predict it will be green, with flowers. What a battle that was!'

She kissed his hand, realising something more about her husband: *No matter how long I know him, I will never know how terrible that day was.* She glanced at his face. *He will never tell me all of it. I will not pry.*

She saw bare graves of heaped-up dirt, and here and there a headstone. 'These are some of our Trafalgar dead, and those who survived the battle, only to die later, like your William.' He looked across the rows, seeing something beyond her vision.

Down one row, and then another. He held her hand in a firm grip, keeping her close. She knew who he was looking for, and thanked the Almighty again that John Beattie had pounded on her door in Plymouth that cold night.

'Here he is,' he said reverently. 'I could not bring myself to consign Will to the deep. We were so close to Gibraltar, so close.' He removed his hat. 'I gave Mr Marsing funds for a marker, and told him what I wanted cut into the stone. I had no idea at the time how…how true the words would be.'

Anna put her arm around her husband, this stalwart captain made of iron, like all the other men in the fleet. She knew him now as he really was, a man with doubts and fears of his own.

'*Lieutenant William Fontaine, RN. 1772-1805,*' she read out loud. Only thirty-three years? Too short, too short. '*Exemplary Officer. Devoted Brother. Friend.*' She faltered, then continued. '*Greater love hath no man than this…*'

This had been such a day of surprise and revelation. Now, looking at this memorial to her brother, who lay close by, she knew that other special love of family.

'I will miss you, Will,' she said softly. 'We could easily have grown old together, dear brother.'

War had changed all that. She patted the headstone, deeply aware that she had so much more than a watery grave known only by its latitude and longitude; Will was *here*. This rough cemetery would grow in size as war dragged on, but also in beauty, as mourners honoured their dead. She owed the man beside her, who had brought her brother to shore.

'Captain, I know you did not have to bring him here,' she said. 'I will be forever in your debt that you did.'

'He was an excellent first officer and a good friend,' John replied. She heard all the strain and took his hand. 'I had no idea at the time how you would figure in my life, Mrs Beattie.'

Call me Anna again, she wanted to tell him, but refrained, thinking of that lovely picture of Cathy in his quarters.

She had her own surprise for him, earlier doubting the wisdom of it, but confirmed now in this sacred place. She thought again of Cathy, but knew this was *her* choice and her moment. From her reticule, Anna pulled out the ring box found among Will's effects. She opened it and they both looked at the intricate filigreed golden mesh, intended for an unknown person. She held it out to her husband.

'I think this is the perfect place and the perfect ring. Do you?'

He took it from her, his tears unmistakable, then acknowledged her emotion. 'Two watering pots. Will would have laughed at us.' He held up the ring. 'This is right, I agree. Thank you, my dear. And thank you, Will Fontaine.'

He slid it onto her finger, saying again those timeless words from their wedding. 'With this ring I thee wed, with my body I thee worship, and with all my worldly goods I thee endow.'

She let him pull her to his body, his hand on her hair. She closed her eyes with the pleasure of something that simple. Her arms went around him, aware as never before of herself bound to another in every way possible, no matter what lay ahead.

Dear man, she thought, *I could quite possibly love you some day. Stranger things have happened. Could you ever love me, too?*

She shivered suddenly, as a cool breeze swirled around them. His arm tightened around her, but this time, for some unaccountable reason, she wasn't comforted. *Love takes time*, she thought, and heard the gods of war laughing at her. *Did they laugh at you, too, Cathy?*

Chapter Twenty-Five

With this ring, I thee wed.

John's own words seemed to resound in his heart that night aboard the *Swallow*, ship resupplied and ready to sail. They rested in his sleeping platform on the floor, exhausted in a pleasing fashion after another round of mutual satisfaction, he who had lain for years on a fallow field, she relishing the newness.

'Moderation, moderation,' his Presbyterian minister had preached in faraway Kirkcudbright, his ancestral home. 'The Lord God Almighty loves effort and hard work. Pleasures are fleeting.'

After this night with Anna in his arms, he couldn't disagree more. Pleasure was here to stay, and high time. How could he ever explain to this dear creature, sleeping beside him, that he had been so tired since Trafalgar? It was exhaustion of the soul, made worse on shore by the guilt of finding his son nearly abandoned.

His thoughts turned melancholy. *What if I hadn't knocked on her door?* he asked himself. No, it was best to dismiss that thought. He knew how, and he tried it, with Anna so close, her leg thrown over his. He put his hands over his own eyes, something done before to him, years ago.

He hadn't meant to waken his sleeping wife. 'John, is something the matter?' she asked. 'A nightmare?'

'Oh, no, I...'

What was there about this calm lady he had married because he'd had to? Even now, her hair a mess and her nightgown somewhere else, she radiated serenity where none was to be had, not with their nation at war.

'Tell me, please.'

He did, making it a brief story of his ship in the South Pacific coming across the foundering wreck of another frigate. He'd still been a midshipman, unused to the sight of so much death, rendered even more sad in such a lonely spot with no help in sight.

In the telling, Anna moved closer, her flesh warm and comforting. Bolstered by her kindness, he told her how his captain had put his own hands over his weeping midshipman's eyes.

John took a deep breath and another. 'I was so embarrassed, wondering what my captain thought of me. He told me, "Sometimes this is all you can do, and then you must forget, or it will destroy you".'

Why did he have to tell Anna *that*? She was silent, and he wondered if she had changed her opinion of him, whatever that was. How would he know? He might as well spill it all.

'So many times...too many times...in the last ten years, I have put my hands over my own eyes.'

He held his breath and then nearly died from delight when she firmly pressed her hands over his eyes. 'Do you not remember that I did this to you that night you knocked on my door?'

Oh, God, she had. 'How could I have forgotten that?'

She took her hands away. 'What a night that was! Only ask, John. Or don't ask. I will know. I trust you will, too, if ever I need your hands over my eyes.'

He slept in her arms most soundly until morning and eight bells. He wanted her again, but he knew duty called. She only smiled at him. 'We'll keep. Go and be a captain.'

They sailed from Gibraltar on good winds. Anna knew now to ask permission to come onto the quarterdeck, which her husband gladly gave. He seated her in the wonderful canvas chair and she promptly fell asleep, worn out from little sleep.

The blast of the bosun's pipe jerked her wide awake. She looked around, frightened, then relaxed as Mr Marsing gave her a hands-down sign. Where was John?

'Ma'am, he just had the bosun pipe Assembly,' the lieutenant said.

'Assembly?'

'Ma'am, he does something I've never seen another captain do.' He looked skyward, perhaps wondering if he was betraying a confidence, then plunged ahead. 'Some day if I ever captain a ship, I will do the same thing.'

'Which is…'

'He's going to read Admiral Collingwood's orders out

loud, so everyone knows what we will be doing on the *Swallow*.'

'Don't all captains do that?'

'Precious few. I know other officers and crew who would happily sail on the *Swallow*, simply because of him. He treats us as equals,' he said, his voice soft, almost in awe. 'Some things must remain secret, but he has an instinct about what can be said for the benefit of all.'

'I believe I would do that, too,' she told him, then felt the warmth rising from her neck. 'As if we ladies would ever command anything. Maybe when Hades becomes the North Pole.'

Mr Marsing laughed, which made a deckhand stare in awe. 'Aha, ma'am! You're a plain speaker like the Old Ma… Captain Beattie.'

'So was my brother,' she said softly. 'Will was just as bad.'

'I remember,' Mr Marsing said, at ease now. 'I miss him, too. I have big shoes to fill, ma'am.'

I expect you are filling them very well, she thought, but knew better than to say that out loud, considering that he would get all rosy again, which couldn't help the dignity an officer needed, especially as sailors were now assembling below the quarterdeck.

John joined them, with a smile for her and a nod to Mr Marsing. He walked to the rail, balancing nicely, as in charge as if he were the Lord God Almighty. *What is it about these men?* she asked herself.

'Thank you for assembling, men,' he said, his voice carrying. He held up Admiral Collingwood's orders. 'Would you like to know what we'll be doing out here in this marvellous sea...um...besides amusing me?'

She blushed when the men laughed, then found herself laughing, too. This was no time or place to be a reticent, superior ogre in skirts. To her amazement and humility, she felt a sudden bond with the crew, something she'd never anticipated. It might have been there all along, considering her brother's connection to the *Swallow*.

'Let me be clear about these orders,' John continued, his voice firm. 'They are not repeated ashore. Our duty is to hunt down *La Guerre*, a French sloop of war labouring under the misapprehension that the French still rule *our* sea!'

He bowed when they cheered at that. Anna sat back, stirred to her heart.

'Men, *La Guerre* is a pest, a nuisance and a disruption, diligently involved in bullying smaller ships, especially our Fast Dispatch Vessels, and the sorely tried *Jaunty*. It must stop.'

He looked around, gesturing large. 'Crew, I call this a plum assignment. We can rove at will in search of the foe, who might be planning other surprises for us. Admiral Collingwood states in his orders that we will be based at Port Mahon on Menorca, where we *will* conduct ourselves like gentlemen when ashore.'

Anna smiled at that, noticing the grins. She also noticed several nods of agreement at his next words. 'I wish to forge a working relationship with the *Hartford*, a nimble ship like ours. The Yankees have taken a liking to

North Africa—you know of the treaty they recently made with those Tripolitan scoundrels.'

He turned to Anna and doffed his hat in salute. She inclined her head, reluctant to be noticed, but aware how hard she was to overlook, the sole female aboard.

'As you know, my lady wife sailed on the *Jaunty*, which was attacked by *La Guerre*, and saved from destruction by the *Hartford*. As for the Yankees, let us be aware who our friends might be.' He gestured to the sailing master, standing near the railing. 'Master Lyon, resume our course for the *Queen*, and then Port Mahon. That is all, men. As you were.'

Chapter Twenty-Six

Much later—why did the officers drag out dinner in the wardroom?—they were finally about to make love when someone knocked at the door from the wardroom. 'Ahoy, Captain! Captain Tyler is on deck.'

'I could grumble,' Anna's husband said quietly. 'I swear I could.' He raised his voice. 'Coming.'

'I'll be here when you return,' she said, starting to rise. He stopped her. 'Don't do a thing,' he said. 'I have a robe somewhere. Ah.' He stood by the sleeping platform, looking down at himself. 'Calm down, John,' he muttered. After a minute, he put on his robe and padded from the cabin, looking as well-dressed as if he was.

She wished amnesia on any impressionable midshipmen standing the watch. She lay there, thinking of stories she would *never* share with anyone about her watery honeymoon.

She thought of that house waiting for her in Port Mahon, one where Admiral Collingwood had told her he seldom visited, wishing it were a second home for his family. So many hopes dashed, thanks to Napoleon and his imperial aspirations.

It didn't bear thinking on, especially since John returned soon enough. He shrugged off his robe and sank down onto the sleeping platform again, gathering her close. 'Let's see, where were we?' he asked in the dark.

I wish I knew, she thought. *I am a convenience. I believe I want to be more. How?*

Anna couldn't fault his husbandly instincts. His own satisfaction meant hers as well. Later, as he drowsed beside her, his arms around her, she touched his face, which made him turn and kiss her fingers. 'Mrs Beattie, thank you,' he said.

She smiled to herself. It wasn't a loverlike remark, but she was nothing if not an optimist. 'You're welcome, Captain Beattie,' she teased, which made him laugh.

'Am I insufferable?' he asked.

'Only a little. I want to know more about Port Mahon.' Interesting how bedtime talk was so beguiling. She never would have expected that. 'Will I like it?' She chuckled. 'Have I any choice?'

'Spoken like a true Navy wife,' he murmured, his voice sleepy. 'A house on Menorca? Who knows?'

'*Was* that Captain Tyler?'

'Aye. He wanted to warn me that *La Guerre* was seen sailing east towards Menorca. I thanked him nicely and reminded him that I have a new wife aboard.'

'You didn't!'

'Certainly I did, madam.' His voice changed, and she heard the captain in there somewhere. 'He still gave me a lecture, telling me that Menorca is famous for many inlets and bays. I took his warning seriously. We'll be watching for *La Guerre*. Hush now.' He yawned. 'I am tired.'

'I can give you a little space, John.'

'No. I like to hold you close. You don't mind, do you?'

'No,' she said softly.

He sighed, and she smiled, knowing a contented sigh. In a moment his breathing was deep and regular. The *Swallow* might have been a sloop of war, but Anna Beattie felt only peace and rejoiced.

Morning came at six bells, which she decided was her favourite time of day, at least at sea. No one seemed to want Captain Beattie right then except her, and he required little persuasion beyond a leg thrown over him. How simple was man.

Breakfast in their quarters was boiled eggs and Madeira, of all things. 'It's the bottom of the bottle,' he told her. 'Cookie said the rum was gone, and who wants rum for breakfast anyway?'

Even Anna could tell something was going on outside their haven on the *Swallow*, with its row of little windows. 'Duty calls?'

'Aye, Mrs Beattie. I'll shave now, and I won't slit my throat because the sea is calm. You'll come along to the *Queen*? I'm eager to see our children.'

I wonder if you know what you just said, she asked herself, charmed by the simple way he included her. She observed him as he shaved, relaxed and humming, eons away from the desperate father of last January. *Thank you, Admiral Collingwood*, she thought as she dressed. *A house on Menorca? My goodness but you are kind.*

Another hour, and there was the *Queen*. Her heart lifted to see Allan and Pru, both of them beaming, far removed from last winter's terrified children. *We're having an adventure*, she thought as she hugged them.

Bounce came next for a scratch and a pat from her, and the same from Captain Beattie. 'Admiral Collingwood says we are feeding him too much,' Allan announced, 'but he leaves choice bits around for us to feed him anyway. And do you know? The Admiral reads to us at night like you.'

She smiled at that, and turned her attention to her husband and the admiral, deep in conversation, aware how this powerful man missed his own children. *Sir, you are blessing my life and my husband's, but I am sad for you.*

She sat with the children, amused when Bounce rested his head in her lap and looked at her with soulful eyes. 'You, sir, are a blatant hound in search of pats and rubs,' she declared, and administered both, which meant high-pitched yips that attracted his master's attention.

'Mrs Beattie, you should consider yourself highly favoured,' Collingwood's deck-voice boomed out. 'A year ago, I was declared Baron of Chelford. Bounce assumed at least half of my title and demands proper obeisance. You should see how he struts the deck!'

He turned his attention to Allan, who leaned against his father's knee. 'Midshipman Beattie—I've been calling your son that, Captain—we are requested and required to take Bounce to the gun deck for his walk.'

'Aye aye, sir!' the little boy responded. He put two fingers to his lips and whistled. 'Is that right, sir?'

'Perfectly fine,' Collingwood agreed. 'I couldn't have done it better myself. Excuse us for a moment.' The admiral held out his hand to Allan and nodded to Pru, who took his other hand. With Bounce leading the way, the unlikely group left the ostentation of Collingwood's flagship quarters. The secretary seated nearby resumed his sorting of papers.

She came closer to her husband and lowered her voice. 'Do you know anything about the house in Port Mahon?'

'Only that you and the little ones will live there while the *Swallow* keeps an eye on the French. I cannot fathom my good fortune.' His comments were quiet, but she heard their sincerity. 'Let's walk the deck, too. I asked the bosun to pipe Mr Marsing aboard. I want him to hear the admiral's orders.'

On deck, he strolled with her as though they walked in a park, past coiled rope and sailors mending sails, and others on hands and knees, scraping a more distant part of the deck with pumice stones. A group of boys barely older than Allan sat before a blackboard where the sailing master wrote equations. There beside the *Queen* bobbed the *Swallow*, looking so small.

It was a world she had never imagined until a mere week ago when she'd stared in awe at the Rock that was Gibraltar. 'John, I never thought this would be my life.'

He smiled down at her. 'This is what you get for answering my knock in January.' The smile left his face. 'I don't know what I would have done if you hadn't opened your door.'

Her heart and soul absorbed the bleakness. On tiptoe, she put her hands over his eyes for a brief moment, because they were on deck with others around. It was enough.

He blinked when she took her hands away. 'Let's see what Port Mahon has to offer,' he said. 'I doubt it will be boring.'

Chapter Twenty-Seven

Boring? Hardly, not with Admiral Collingwood himself signing on as crew on the *Swallow*, with Bounce as his companion. Collingwood's flagship remained at anchor near Gibraltar. 'You'll never know I am here, Captain Beattie,' he said, which made the admiral and captain both laugh. To Anna's relief, none of it bordered on the hysterical.

Collingwood was a good companion for the sail to Menorca, the smaller of the four Balearic Islands and possessing the best harbour at Port Mahon, with its deep inlet, so he told them. To Anna's delight, the admiral sat beside her on the quarterdeck in another canvas chair, commenting on seabirds, and admonishing Bounce not to think about trying to catch one.

That night under sail, Anna brought out a basket of her husband's overused socks and darned them in the wardroom, with the admiral comfortable on that same canvas chair, moved below-deck. He watched her homely housewifery, peace in his eyes. It took only minor urging on John's part to encourage a few sea yarns from Collingwood to his ever-attentive audience in Allan and Pru. He pronounced himself rejuvenated by this small snatch of leisure.

'My dears, I have not looked at a chart or a letter of complaint in a whole twenty-four hours,' he said before retiring for the night in the Captain's quarters—the best *Swallow* had to offer—where the swinging platform had been hastily restored to its proper function.

'Where are we sleeping?' she whispered to John.

'Quietly and properly in the Purser's quarters,' he whispered back. 'He stayed behind on the *Queen* to subdue his own paperwork. Allan and Pru will be on pallets here in the wardroom.'

She was dubious about the Purser's sleeping platform, but they were at tight quarters. John helped her in, only smiling a little when she clutched him in fright, and settled herself for actual sleep.

'See there? It's a nice motion,' he assured her as they swung to the rhythm of the wind and waves. 'By God, all additional shenanigans aside, you are a pleasant little bundle to cuddle, Mrs Beattie.'

They were wakened early by Admiral Collingwood's cheerful halloo and a light tapping on the door, which he opened. 'Captain Beattie, let us take a turn about the deck,' he ordered. 'I must know more about your suggestion to work in tandem with the Yankee captain.'

'Aye, sir. Let me extricate myself carefully without dumping out my wife. I'd like her to still enjoy Navy life. Give us a moment.'

Collingwood laughed. 'Mrs Beattie, you should have

been more wary when the Navy came to call,' he said, and added, 'I have the utmost respect for a lady who is so kind to provide aid and comfort to that sorry carcass beside you. Accept my great admiration, dear madam.'

Who could object to that? 'He'll be on deck in a minute,' she said.

It was more than a minute as her husband carefully climbed from the platform and she hung onto the sides. When the motion stopped, he lifted her out and kissed her. 'You'll be in a bed tonight that doesn't move, unless we want it to.'

'You're a rascal, John Beattie. Go on deck and walk with the other rascal on board.'

She enjoyed the private time of washing and dressing, then walking into the wardroom to see Allan and Pru playing cat's cradle, while John's steward whistled and set the table for breakfast.

'Missy, where are we going?' Allan asked. 'Is there a house somewhere?'

She took him on her lap, enjoying the fragrance of little boy, even as she wondered at the trust of children, who, as far as she could tell, seemed to think that adults knew what they were doing. She understood how easy it was to love a child, especially one who had been set adrift by people who should have provided for his welfare. He was *her* Allan now; she knew it.

She looked at Pru, watchful Pru, who had saved John's son. She gestured her closer. 'I have room for you on my lap, too,' she told the girl with the too-old eyes. 'I always will.'

To both her delight and her deep compassion, she watched those eyes change a little, just a little, almost to a child's eyes.

'I do not know what our life will be like in Port Mahon,' she told them. 'I've never been there, either, but the admiral wants us to reside in his house. That way, Allan, when your father makes port, we will be there waiting for him.'

'I wondered what was going to happen to us,' the boy said, cuddling close.

'It's hard not to know, isn't it? There's a war, and I sometimes wonder if any of us knows what will happen.'

'Even grown-ups?' Allan asked. 'Grown-ups know everything.'

'I wish we did.' Anna kissed his head, then Pru's. 'I do know this, though: we will do our best in Port Mahon and…' It struck her with that same force that had told her John Beattie might be an easy man to fall in love with if she wasn't careful. 'We will do our best together, because I love you.' Oh, Pru's watchful eyes. 'Allan, I love you *and* Pru.'

'Me too, Missy?'

'Yes, my darling girl, yes,' Anna said softly, wanting nothing to break the charm of the moment.

When John returned from his walk on deck with Admiral Collingwood and Bounce, she quietly delighted in his gentle embrace, in its own way as exciting as his passion.

'Anna, here we are. Admiral Collingwood's generosity to us is our first home. In the whole horrific jumble of events that is war, I never expected this.'

What could she say to that? A kiss sufficed.

Admiral Collingwood stood on the quarterdeck, hands clasped behind his back, looking up and up at the village of white stone, interspersed with pastel-painted structures and lush Mediterranean greenery, perched so high above the bay.

'It's enchanting,' Anna said, 'More a painting than reality.'

'Should I pinch you, Mrs Beattie?'

'Don't you dare!'

'Bring us in, Mr Marsing,' Captain Beattie said, and stood beside the admiral.

Anna clasped hands with her children, in perfect accord with Pru's gasp, 'Gor, Missy, it's splendid!' and Allan's, 'It's not like Plymouth!' There they were, the five of them plus Bounce, lining the railing.

Since it was a deep-water harbour, Mr Marsing directed the crew to snub the *Swallow* right to the wharf. She counted eighteen guns on a larger frigate anchored offshore, and multiplied by two. 'That's the *Reliant*,' John said. 'A thirty-six.' She heard the fondness in his voice as he spoke to Allan. 'Son, I was a midshipman aboard her, seven years older than you are, and scared out of my wits.'

'You weren't always a captain?'

'Nay, lad, nay.'

'I could do that, too?'

'If ye have a mind to, and if Missy doesn't object.'

Anna listened to them, hearing no stilted conversation because they knew each other now. She recalled awkward conversations with Will after he returned from a year at sea, as they reacquainted themselves with each other's habits and minor eccentricities. She watched husband and son, and gestured Pru closer. Her arms encircled the ever-watchful girl.

Soon the sails were furled and the gangplank lowered. The bosun piped over the admiral first, then Allan and Pru—properly impressed—with Bounce skipping around them and nearly tumbling overboard.

Anna followed on Captain Beattie's arm. He turned and lifted his hat to his crew. 'Mr Marsing, release them in timely fashion. Men, don't embarrass me or the *Swallow*. We sail tomorrow with the tide.'

Too soon, Anna thought sadly, *too soon*. But this was not the time to mourn something she had no control over, not when there was a new world open to her view unlike anything she had ever seen.

'Here I am,' she said. It sounded foolish.

'And I am beyond grateful,' her husband said. 'Speaking of which, look at that climb ahead.'

There, directly ahead, she stared at a formidable rank of steps to the town high above. 'How many?'

'I counted them once, when I was a midshipman. One hundred and fifty, if you are sober,' he said as they began the climb. 'Thousands more if you are drunk on Madeira.' He laughed. 'Or perhaps two steps and a lengthy roll, which would bring you to the attention of the surgeon.'

The children raced ahead, Allan stopping only to stare at darting green lizards then trying to catch one. Anna appreciated John's slow, deliberate pace, probably for her benefit. She turned to watch Admiral Collingwood and his entourage of junior officers behind them. When she paused, the admiral cupped his hands around his mouth. 'Go on, my dears, save yourselves,' he shouted.

'They're called the Pigtail Steps,' John said, after the laughter subsided. 'You know, after many a sailor and his pigtail.'

'Did you ever...'

'No, madam,' he replied. 'I look silly in a pigtail. Tried once, though, in the South Pacific.'

And that was enough conversation until they reached the top, and Port Mahon proper. 'We'll wait for the admiral,' he said, when he could speak.

Luckily, it was a comment that required no reply. He turned her around for a look back to the bay.

'Oh, my,' she said softly. 'Oh, my.'

'There are inlets all around Menorca,' he said. 'This is the deepest, but a hard one to leave when winds are unfavourable.' He tightened his grip on her waist. 'With you and our children here, it might always be a hard one to leave.'

Our children, she thought in delight. It sounded so lovely.

He drew her close, which earned them both a 'Huzzah' from Admiral Collingwood, who'd finally reached the top and couldn't utter anything else. They guided him to a convenient stone bench, probably placed there to show mercy to newcomers.

When he could speak, the admiral nodded to one of the younger officers who had gone ahead, apparently bargaining with a Menorcan sitting atop a wagon pulled by two donkeys. 'It's not a coach and four, but it will take us to my house.'

'Which is where, sir?' Anna asked.

He gestured along the shore. 'Not far. There's an inlet closer to where Menorca meets the Mediterranean. It commands a view of the harbour's entrance. Strategy, my boy,' he said to John, then turned to Anna. 'On the beach below my house I can see everything coming and going. My dear, *you* could be the first to see Captain Beattie when he pulls into port.'

'I expect I will be,' she said softly, feeling no urge to look away like a maiden. 'I will watch,' she said to John alone, when the admiral stood up to wait for the now-approaching cart.

The children joined them. John's arm went around his son's shoulders automatically, and Pru sat next to her, not presuming. She smiled when Anna put her arm around her, too.

'Papa, is this place going to be our home?'

'For a while.'

'Will you be here?'

It was a good question. Anna listened for his answer. She heard John's struggle, and the almost imperceptible way he moved closer to her until they were hip to hip.

'As often as the *Swallow* and I can sail into port,' he replied finally. 'I have no control over the French, and they are the enemy. Son, you saw them in action firsthand.'

Allan was the logical sort. 'We were downstairs…'

'Below-deck…'

'Below-deck in that little ship, and we were afraid.'

Allan amended himself. '*I* was. Dunno about Missy and Pru.' He looked at his father. 'Do you ever get afraid?'

'All the time,' John said, which touched Anna deep in that place only he had reached inside her.

'Then how…'

Yes, how? I want to know, too, Anna thought. She hesitated, then put her hand on his leg.

He was silent for a long moment, this husband of hers, silent until he looked up at Admiral Collingwood's 'Hello!' across the little commons ground, where he stood by the donkey and cart, their luggage already loaded. John raised his hand in acknowledgement.

He looked at her, so serious, then down at Allan. 'I do it for you, son, and Missy and Pru. It is my duty to swallow my fear and protect those I love and our nation, God save it.'

His smile was for Anna alone. 'Let's go and see our new home. Allan, I'll wager you can outrun Pru.'

The children took off towards the admiral and Bounce.

'Was I wrong to say that?'

It was her turn to think of some way to express how she felt to this man she admired more every moment. She thought of the grinding war that had been going on for more than a decade now.

'You were perfectly right,' she said softly, for his ears only. 'Counting the cost is more mathematics than I can do. I will never know your sort of courage.'

He kissed her hand. 'Though painful at times, it's also easy when you consider the alternative. As for your courage, don't underestimate yourself. I shan't.'

Chapter Twenty-Eight

Exploring a new house, more exotic and grand than she ever could have imagined—hers was a logical mind—convinced Anna that she could overlook those little green lizards that even invaded houses. She clapped her hands with pleasure to see an actual bed.

Evidently Allan had a logical mind, too. 'Missy, it's only a bed. Pru and I have already found two more rooms with beds just down the hall.' He grinned at his father, who listened to this whole exchange with something more than glee, if the slow wink he gave Anna was any indication.

When the children raced after Admiral Collingwood, her husband sat her down on the bed. 'Will it work? We could try it out right now.'

'You are absurd,' she countered, then smiled at his Navy humour. 'Very well, let's close the door, but if one of those lizards I see on the balcony decides to land on us, one of us—I volunteer—will scream and the children will be back here. Care to explain that?'

'Mrs Beattie, *you* are the rascal,' he said. 'I can wait.'

And he did, happy to explore the house with her, starting with its amazing view from their second-floor balcony, once he'd evicted the lizards. 'What a sight. I can't see the bay from here, but I am certain we can from the beach, as the admiral said. Perfect.'

After a long look, they followed the children down the corridor. She watched Allan and Pru, hand in hand with the admiral. 'John, it's heartbreaking; all he wants is his family with him.'

'I know.'

'He's been so kind to us,' she said simply, not wanting to consider even a month without her husband but knowing she'd have to.

'Aye, Mrs Beattie. I can give you no guarantee how often I can drag myself up the Pigtail Steps to…um… test the bed.'

'Then we will leave it in God's hands,' she told him. 'And you're still a rascal.'

Where was this silliness of hers coming from? She asked herself that as she adjusted her tattered cloak of dignity around her and was all politeness when the admiral introduced them to Hector and Hermione Durand, the house's caretaker and cook. They were an older couple. Anna smiled to see one friendly face, and a pretty one. Hector Durand appeared to possess a permanent frown. He was mannerly enough, doffing his frowsy cap but replacing it immediately. She sniffed. And where had that cape been?

Maybe it was John's guarded expression that the admiral noticed. 'Come, come, John. Aye, the Durands are French in origin—I was aware of that when I hired them—but they hate the turmoil of revolution as much as we do! All Menorca does. What say you, Hector?'

The glum-looking caretaker was in no hurry to reply. Finally, he put his hand to his heart. 'Capitaine Beattie, you may repose all faith and trust in us. Our names are French; we are not, after a lifetime on both Mallorca and Menorca.'

'Good to know,' John replied, equally formal. 'This lady is my new bride, and I rely on you to treat her well.'

The caretaker smiled at Anna, or at least as much of a smile as he could muster, apparently. 'We are here to serve, *madame*. Hermione will sit with you soon and you will plan meals together. We will never disappoint you.'

The Durands bowed and returned to the kitchen. Admiral Collingwood watched them, then whispered, 'Hector is a bit of an eccentric. He never takes off that ugly cape and cap, so don't stand downwind of him if you can help it.'

'Please tell me Madame Durand has redeeming qualities,' John said.

'Indeed she does,' Collingwood said. 'She makes up for her husband's faults by cooking excellent meals. You'll never starve in this house.'

'We should manage quite well,' John said. 'Admiral, I am…we are…forever in your debt for your great kindness to us.'

The admiral became their tour guide. 'There are four bedchambers on this floor,' he explained. 'Yours is the grandest. Allan and Pru seem to have commandeered two of the other rooms. On the ground floor, you saw the sitting room, library and dining room.' He looked around conspiratorially. 'The kitchen is the Durands' domain. Invade it only on pain of death.'

'We will happily leave that part of the house to them alone,' John said. 'As for me, I will be content to eat whatever comes out of the kitchen, and enjoy the view from these magnificent windows in the sitting room.'

'And the verandah beyond,' Collingwood said, sounding wistful to Anna. He brightened. 'Actually, I would like to install a telescope on your bedchamber balcony above us. Think of what I could see!'

Downstairs again, while the men kept their heads together in the business of war, Anna found herself at home in the dining room as Hermione explained the workings of the house, women's business.

'We have been practically idle here,' the chatty woman said as she poured tea. 'It is a bore to merely keep the place tidy. I am glad of your company.' She leaned closer. 'There are two maids in a house nearby, lazy but amiable. They live with their mama and papa. I use them occasionally.' She looked around. 'Their papa is a smuggler, so if you need anything, only say the word.'

'The Captain tells me that the islands are in Spanish hands after years of English rule, and here you are of French extraction. Smugglers, too?'

'But of course! Don't tell me that no one smuggles in your England.'

'If they do, I don't know them,' Anna replied, feeling out of her depth and more naïve than usual, aware she had been sheltered from so much.

'No fear, Madame Beattie. You need only to remember this: we are Menorcans first. French, Spanish? Bah! Who cares? Not we of the islands.'

As she spoke, she rattled the keys on the chatelaine around her waist, then looked down, as if noticing them for the first time. 'Madame Beattie, do you wish to wear the household keys?'

Anna happily begged off that responsibility. 'No, *madame*. I consider myself a guest in the admiral's house. You are the housekeeper, not I.'

'You do not know how long you will be here?'

'I have no idea.' She stopped, knowing better than to say anything about John's purpose here. 'My husband is subject to the demands of the service, and that is that.'

If dinner was any test of Madame Durand's ability to concoct a highly edible meal at short notice, Anna felt herself relaxing, even in this strange environment she never could have imagined herself living in, until John had knocked on her door. The admiral ate with them, beaming at the children, pleased with himself, which pleased her. Allan ate everything in sight, which made Madame Durand smile. Pru watched them all in her careful way that touched Anna's heart.

'Pru watches over all of us,' she told John later that night after he came out of Allan's room, and she said goodnight to Pru in her room. 'She reminds me of Madame Durand.'

'Turn around. I know my duty and your dress needs unbuttoning.' He chuckled. 'Madame Durand does watch. She insisted on remaining in the dining room after the admiral cleared all of you out because he wanted some time alone with me. "But you might need something," she insisted.' Another laugh. 'He assured Madame Durand that he outranked her and was perfectly capable of spelling out war plans without her help.'

'I believe we are in good hands here,' she said, her breath coming faster, because John Beattie had a way with not only buttons but her petticoat, too. Since she had already decided that drawers were optional—Menorca was warm—matters moved along quickly.

His clothing might have come off fast, but John took his time, exploring her thoroughly with kisses until she took matters into her own hands—so to speak—and guided him where she wanted him. He appeared to be of the same opinion, and she swiftly found herself enveloped by a man as eager as she was. He didn't object when she pressed her hands so hard against his back and they moved in rhythm that she remembered from aboard the *Swallow*, a sweet-sailing ship.

Once was good, and a little later, after some conversation that she found almost as pleasant as love-making, so was twice. She sank into that wonderful mattress, since her bones had turned to jelly. She slept well then, and so did he.

Morning came and with it the pleasure of more love-making, but this time accompanied by the reality of parting soon. He lay beside her so peacefully that her mind wandered to Shakespeare's *Romeo and Juliet* and that stupid line about parting being such sweet sorrow. Nonsense. Tears welled in her eyes at the thought of days ahead with no warm spot in the bed beside hers and, even worse, the fear that she might never see him again. There was no sweetness to this sorrow.

'No tears, Mrs Beattie,' she heard in the depth of her misery. 'You're sending me off whole and hearty. It's been years since I've been this contented.'

'I wish I could come along,' she said, then remembered she was a practical woman. 'No. That would be folly. I know better than to ask what you will be doing. Will taught me that.'

'You read my orders. The *Swallow* is to rove and see what we can find out in this part of the Mediterranean. We'll report to Admiral Collingwood as appropriate.' He pulled her close, tucking her head against his chest, where she heard his steady heartbeat. 'I will anchor here whenever possible. I've showed you where the strongbox is, so you will never want for money. Madame Durand told me there is an Anglican parish. The Reverend is an old dear, she says, and he recently acquired a schoolmaster mere weeks ago. Madame Durand said she will see that you meet the teacher. Apparently, he lives there at the church.'

She nodded, pleased at the idea of school. 'I'll see that both Allan and Pru attend.'

'That's my girl. The Durands seem solid.' He smiled. 'I must warn you: Admiral Collingwood said something last night about possible guests here. It seems that the French have played merry hell among some of the Italian houses of nobility. You might end up hosting Italians. My experience says they are a noisy and dramatic bunch who might drive you crazy.'

She raised up on her elbow to give him the full benefit of her stare. 'You realise that before I met you, my life was orderly and tidy?'

'What a bore.' He cocked his head. 'I hear children. I wish the war would wait, but war waits no better than tides do.'

He dressed and went down the hall, calling to Allan. Anna took her time, making the bed, then shaking out John's nightshirt and hanging it in the side of the closet he'd claimed. She stopped to see that drawing of Cathy she had noticed first on the *Swallow*.

'You were a lovely lady,' she said. 'And look, your husband takes you with him wherever he goes. Some day, maybe I will have a portrait, too.'

Parting turned into something immeasurably difficult. She had said goodbye to John before, but never after marriage, no matter how 'convenient' both of them had decided it was. She noticed his glances at his timepiece, and saw a man either steeling himself for goodbye or eager to leave.

She heard it in the advice he gave Allan over breakfast to do whatever Missy told him, and find ways to help her in Admiral Collingwood's wonderful home. 'Beattie is a name well-known in the fleet, son, and here at home now. Remember that.'

Admiral Collingwood had his own announcements. 'Mrs Beattie, yesterday I sent Hector Durand to buy a horse and cart, which he found and will keep here—you may have noticed the stable. It's a little less than half a mile from Port Mahon to my house. You need only tell him when you wish to go to the port, or that Anglican church and school, and he will oblige.'

'Thank you, Admiral,' John said. 'What do I owe...'

Collingwood held up his hand. 'This is my idea and my expense. No argument, captain, and that is an order! Alas, you and I must leave as soon as he pulls up in the driveway.' He looked around at them all, his gaze resting on Anna with sympathy. 'It's never easy to say goodbye.' He smiled. 'Better to practice it in a sweet place like Menorca, my dear.'

What could she do but agree? Anna clasped her hands together. 'Admiral, tell me: is the first goodbye the hardest?'

To her chagrin, his eyes misted over. 'None are easy. We do this for England, don't we, John?'

'Aye, sir. Don't see me off, you three,' John said in turn. 'I'm curious about something.'

Anna let herself be folded into her husband's generous embrace. 'This is never easy,' he whispered into her hair.

She did not doubt him. 'What are you curious about?'

He gestured to the children. 'Allan, yesterday I noticed steps leading down from the edge of the property. I imagine they lead to the beach below the house.'

Allan nodded, his eyes bright, ready for an adventure, when only months ago he had been a sad little fellow, hungry and clinging to Pru. 'I can go down the steps.'

'How about the three of you get yourselves to that beach?' John asked. 'I think the land slopes more there, so it isn't like that dreaded climb from the dock to Port Mahon proper.'

'Why do you want us to do that?' Anna asked. 'I like an adventure, but I'm curious, too.'

John shrugged. 'No particular reason. I wonder what our own inlet looks like, that's all.' He gave Allan a man-to-man look. 'I will appoint you as temporary leader of this expedition, son.' He pointed to Anna. 'Mind you, temporary. Missy is the head of the house when I am away. If she declares the steps unsafe, you will not take them. That is an order.'

Then she had to wonder if maybe her husband was the wisest man she knew, especially when the little fellow sniffing back tears at yet another farewell turned into a boy ready for an adventure on the steps.

'You're a wise husband,' she told him.

'Just a practical one. It gives me a chance to kiss you.'

They kissed and he shouldered his duffel. 'Admiral Collingwood and I are on our way.'

'Will you and the *Swallow* take him back to the *Queen*?'

'Nay, lass. The *Swallow* is bound on a fishing expedition, first to find the *Hartford*. We two ships will scout between Mallorca and France, not sailing too close together, but close enough for mutual aid, if needed.'

'Admiral Collingwood is going to swim to his flagship?' she teased.

He laughed. 'Remember the *Reliant* in Mahon's harbour? The frigate will take him back to his flagship.' He kissed her again. 'Beware of possible Italian guests.'

'I will,' she whispered, wanting to say so much more as he left, but contented herself with, 'Be safe.'

'I promise I will, but, like you, I face the truth. This is war. Stay out of trouble, if you can.'

She waved from the porch, then wandered upstairs to straighten things. From the balcony she saw the children heading towards the steps and went into the closet for better shoes. She looked at John's side and noticed that Cathy's picture wasn't there any more.

She leaned against the door, telling herself to be patient.

'I know you need Cathy with you,' she said out loud. 'But I wonder, will it ever be my turn some day?'

Chapter Twenty-Nine

Anna hurried downstairs to follow the children. When the horse and trap were out of sight, she rounded the corner in time to watch Allan and Pru start down the stone steps, narrow and steep and a far cry from the Pigtail Steps. They bounded down with no regard for danger or sprains or any other imaginary ills that a mother might fear.

That was it. She stopped, aware as never before that these were her children now, since she wanted to scold them to be mindful, take care and not frighten her. *You might not have started life as mine*, she thought, *but, by all that's holy, you're not going down these steps without me right behind, sounding like your mother, because I am in every way that counts.* She thought of Cathy's picture again and sighed.

John was right. The distance from the admiral's house to the small beach below was less vertical than from Port Mahon's dock up to the village proper. She descended cautiously, raising her skirt to avoid tripping. At least there wasn't anyone to stare at her legs except Allan and Pru.

Pru steadied her when she neared the bottom. Anna put her hand to her heart and admired the view of the deep blue inlet, every underwater rock and plant so visible, so foreign to someone used to the cold and damp of England. They were in another inlet, more narrow than the one at Port Mahon, where many ships could anchor, but cutting further into the island. Seabirds wheeled on the air currents and swooped down to check them out. The effect was both charming and enchanting.

'If it were easier to get here, I could envisage a picnic,' she said.

'Pirates, even?' Allan asked hopefully.

She laughed. 'No pirates! I am taking my shoes off. Footwear is highly overrated on sandy beaches.'

Everyone's shoes came off and, by common consent, were left at the foot of the steps.

It wasn't much of a walk because it wasn't much of a beach. Anna stood a long time at the water's edge, looking out to sea, wondering when the tides actually changed, amazed at her nautical ignorance. She wondered if the *Swallow* had already sailed.

'Missy, is that the *Swallow*?'

She looked where Allan pointed, hopeful, because it mattered to her that John might be looking for them, too. She had reasoned he was too busy now to watch the shore, but she waved anyway, just as Allan and Pru did as they ran towards her, waving as they came.

To her heart's delight, it was the *Swallow*, with its gunports closed and the smaller guns he called bow-chasers at the front. Not front, fore. And this was starboard and not port. She knew so little. 'But I care so much,' she whispered to the wind as she waved.

'Look!' Allan said, pointing again. 'Do you think…'

They gazed, open-mouthed, as the *Swallow* tacked towards shore. 'What's he doing…' Pru asked '…there?'

They saw a sailor toss a line into the water. He pulled it out, measured, and called out to the helmsman at the wheel.

'He's measuring the depth of the water,' Anna said. 'Look! The ship's coming closer.'

'Papa might call this a good anchorage for smugglers,' Allan told her, his eyes lively. 'Let's name it Smugglers Cove.' He shrugged. 'You know, people claim things in the name of Spain. We can, too.'

'Smugglers Cove it is. I think that is as close as *Swallow* is going to come.'

They watched. Anna put her hand to her heart when she saw John descend from the quarterdeck and come to the gundeck rail. He blew her a kiss, doffed his hat, then shouted, 'Home soon, you rascals!'

Anna blew him a kiss back, then laughed as all the crew on that side of the ship did the same. She blinked back tears when his hand went to his heart.

She heard a shouted command from Mr Marsing on the quarterdeck. As they watched, the ship altered course and sailed from the inlet and into the sea, with all its danger.

They stood close together until the *Swallow* was out of sight, then stayed a little longer when the *Reliant* came next. 'Admiral Collingwood and Bounce are aboard this ship,' she told them. 'Let's wave to them, too.'

Smaller ships sailed after the *Reliant*. They watched from their marvellous vantage point, then turned towards the steps. The children climbed with an agility she could only envy, hampered as she was by a long dress and petticoat.

As she climbed higher, Anna saw something she hadn't noticed on the way down. It looked like a torch of some sort, stuck in the sand. No, it was two torches. 'Interesting,' she said out loud. Maybe this really was a smugglers' cove. She looked back at the sea, impressed with the idea. It was perfect. Anything sailing by this little inlet before entering the larger inlet of Port Mahon would see a torch burning. Hadn't John said there were many such inlets on Menorca?

Don't let your imagination run away with you, Anna, or you'll start believing in Allan's pirates, she told herself as she hitched up her skirt again and climbed the steps, wishing for a handrail. The children—her children— helped her from the last step to the back lawn.

She stood with them, then admired again the view of inlet and ocean. 'We live in a beautiful place, my dears,' she said and clapped her hands. 'Now we must be practical and see if Port Mahon has a seamstress for you and me, Pru, and yes, there is a school for both of you.'

'Me, too, Mama?' Pru asked, her eyes not so much watchful as hopeful.

Mama!

'Yes, my dear, you, too. Make no mistake: it will always be the two of you.' What would a mother say now?

That was simple. She held up a warning finger. 'Neither of you two, singly or together, will ever go to…to…'

'Smugglers Cove?' Pru asked helpfully, her eyes lively.

'Yes, indeed, unless you tell me first. Is that understood?'

'Aye, Missy,' they both said.

'Good!' She decided that was enough. The torches didn't look recently used, but still… As they walked to the house, she decided to mention the matter to John, when next she saw him.

Chapter Thirty

During the next two weeks, Anna reminded herself that yes, John had given her permission to use the money in the strongbox. The first time she opened it she gasped at the amount, then blinked back tears because he had left her so much, as if anticipating his own death or capture.

The thought stayed with her all that day, prompting her to arrange his pillow next to her body in their bed. *For someone used to sleeping alone for years and years, you are a ninny*, she scolded herself as she faced that first night in a solitary bed since their marriage. *There are going to be many such nights, Anna Beattie, thanks to Napoleon, wretched man.*

Madame Durand proved to be helpful in diversion. Anna's admiration for Admiral Collingwood's housekeeper grew daily, although Hector was silent and seldom about. Madame had a ready answer to Anna's question about a seamstress, which meant a visit soon from a woman with a tape measure around her neck and a determined look on her face. Her name was Clotilde Gomez, her name illustrating again to Anna the diversity on Menorca, with its French and Spanish inhabitants.

And British, too, Clotilde reminded her, when Anna asked about the Anglican church. 'Only recently, the Rector agreed to allow a Mr Hal Brown to teach the children of the small English community here. Mr Brown is from England, I believe.' Madame Gomez thought a moment. 'Someone did tell me his mother is from Mallorca.'

'That is the bigger island next to this one,' Madame Durand said. 'Clotilde, I doubt he has a mother there.'

'Well, I...'

'Rumour and speculation.'

'Mallorca, Menorca...' Anna couldn't help her laugh, and didn't mind admitting to both women, 'You are all so interesting here.'

'We Menorcans are a *ragout* of this and that,' Clotilde assured her. 'Hold still. Let me measure from your waist to your ankles. My husband likes the stern English sermons from the Rector, so we attend St Matthew's. That is how we heard of Mr Brown. Your country only returned our islands to Spain two years ago.' She shook her head. 'And now Spain and France are allies? This would confuse anyone except a Menorcan.'

'I am surprised there is an English teacher,' Anna said.

'He has been here for a short time, it is true,' Clotilde told her, then leaned closer, confidential. 'He must be persuasive. He convinced the old Rector to let him live at St Matthew's, since the classroom is there. The Rector is so particular, but he is getting old, and agreed.'

Anna considered her feelings about rectors, grateful

that Mr Brown wasn't one. *I have had enough of those*, she thought. *I could become a heathen*. The thought made her, the daughter of a vicar, smile inside.

Once Anna had chosen material for cotton dresses from Clotilde's supply, the seamstress came with them to Port Mahon in Hector's new pony cart.

'Here it is, St Matthew's,' the seamstress said, pointing to a church overlooking the inlet, seeming small and dowdy compared to the Catholic church in the more elegant plaza. And was that a mosque with a minaret?

'I am certainly not in England,' Anna murmured to Madame Durand, who had accompanied them. Indeed, the housekeeper liked to come along on errands. Her husband had little to say, beyond chirruping the pony and humming tunelessly. Anna had no objections to the Durands. Menorcans seemed to speak an odd conglomeration of French and Spanish—or was it Catalan?—with the occasional English word. Hector and Hermione, fluent in French, knew the local *patois*.

Her introduction to Hal Brown was more than she'd expected. He was a tall man with handsome auburn hair, and a capable air about him. *Such a strange island this is*, she thought, as he listed his modest but adequate credentials. *Clotilde is right; Menorca is a ragout of all sorts of people lucky enough to find it*. She felt herself relax. If discovering exotic places and kind people was to be her own lot with the Royal Navy, she pronounced herself fortunate.

'Indeed, I will be pleased to educate your children,' Mr Brown told Anna, when Clotilde left them after her introduction. 'Your husband is based here on Port Mahon? I did notice a French-looking ship but with Royal Navy flags docked here.'

'Currently,' Anna said, mindful of John's admonition not to say too much. 'You know the Royal Navy: things can always change.' *Like this subject*, she reminded herself. 'You were clever to notice the *Swallow* as French-built.'

He smiled at her and the children. 'Life moves slowly here, Mrs Beattie. We take an interest in many things, perhaps out of boredom.' He opened a ledger, where she noticed English names. 'I have a small class, but I have not been teaching long. Bring your little scholars here on Monday, Wednesday and Friday. I teach from eight until eleven of the clock. Two shillings a month. Their names?'

'Allan and Pru Beattie,' Anna said promptly, then reached for her purse. 'This will do for three months, sir.'

He nodded, put her money on his desk and wrote in their names. As he wrote, Anna felt Pru leaning close. When the teacher rose to put away the money, Anna touched her shoulder. 'What is the matter, my dear?'

'I have a last name now and it is yours,' the child said. 'Will the Captain mind?'

'You *are* ours,' she whispered back, nearly overcome with a feeling unlike any other.

'I thought…' Madame Durand began, when they were seated in the pony trap again. 'Pru is also yours?'

'We are an interesting family, *madame*,' Anna hedged, keeping her voice low, unwilling to embarrass Pru. What to tell her? 'The Captain was a widower with a son. Pru came along, too. She's Pru. We love her.' *I've said enough*, Anna thought.

'She seems poorly dressed, and I wondered what she was doing with you,' Madame Durand persisted.

'Clotilde is sewing for her as well, *madame*,' Anna said firmly. 'She is now family.'

Madame was finally silent, to Anna's relief. What could it matter to her? She hoped Hermione Durand did not think her impolite. The woman was a wondrous cook, and Anna knew *she* was not.

Pru stayed close to her that day. After Allan was tucked into bed and sleeping, she sat beside Anna on the balcony in the room Anna shared with the Captain. It had become their favourite place, perhaps because it overlooked the sea. Pru looked at her now with a different expression, less solemn, far less wary. Anna thought she understood and it touched her heart.

'We will never change our minds, my dear,' she said quietly. 'The Captain owes you an enormous debt, and so do I. You and Allan and I all needed each other at Mrs Fillion's. That was a hard time, wasn't it?'

Pru nodded. 'I was afraid.'

'So was I.'

She looked in surprise at Anna. '*You* were afraid, too?'

'My goodness, yes, my dear. I was terrified.'

'I didn't know…' Pru hesitated.

'Yes?'

'…that grown-ups feared anything.'

'We do,' Anna said simply. Should she? Yes. 'Even the

Captain has confided in me that he is afraid at times. It's part of being human.'

Pru sighed. Was it disappointment? Was it relief? *I know so little about children*, Anna thought, then took another chance, since she had been taking chances ever since she'd opened her door to John.

'Pru, I have never put myself forward, but the times seem to require it now, wouldn't you agree?' To her relief, Pru nodded, giving Anna the courage to continue. 'I'd say we make a good crew on land, fears and all. Now we're in another strange place, but we are together—you, me, Allan—and will remain so. The Captain will join us when he can.'

Pru rested her head against Anna's shoulder. Anna put her arm around the child grown too old too fast, and kissed her hair, which smelled of Menorcan sunshine. Pru sighed and closed her eyes, and somehow, in some way, grew a little younger. *Trust me*, Anna thought.

The day when Anna, disgusted with herself, realised that waiting for John and the *Swallow* to reappear was a senseless waste of time was the day she heard the door open and that longed-for, 'Ahoy, you lubbers! Give me a kiss!'

Me first, me first! she thought as she hurried to the hall, and she was first. John tossed off his fore and aft hat and grabbed her, pulling her close. He smelled of brine and a little bay rum. He could have smelled like a kitchen midden and it wouldn't have mattered. He kissed her soundly, held her off and joked, 'Oh, it's you,' and kissed her soundly again before she even had time to laugh and swat him.

When he picked her up to hold her even closer—grateful no one else was in the hall—Anna *did* see someone over his shoulder, a wide-eyed young woman standing by the door John had flung open.

'John, put me down,' she whispered into his ear. 'Who...who...'

'My wife, the owl,' he teased, but set her down. 'Mrs Beattie, I completely forgot my manners.'

'Indeed you did,' she said, happy to have his arms around her, even if her skirt needed adjusting.

By now, Allan had hurled himself down the stairs and into John's arms, with Pru close behind, to stand there until Anna beckoned her forward.

'We have a visitor,' she said. 'John, mind your manners.'

He gave her a kindly smile. 'You're a good woman, Mrs Beattie,' he said. 'Let me introduce you to a princess, or something like that.'

She came closer most regally, in Anna's eyes, but when had she ever seen a real princess before? There was a superior expression on her face, as if the last place *she* ever wanted to be was on Menorca, or in a house with an obvious commoner who kissed a man so brazenly.

She came a few steps closer and no more, as if it were the commoners' turn to do the honours.

'She's a little particular,' John whispered. 'I didn't bow to her on our first encounter and she still holds that against me.'

'You plebian,' Anna whispered back and moved towards her, because she saw something else in the young lady's eyes. Maybe it was the weariness of someone out of her depth and desperate not to show it, or someone tossed about by the fortunes of war, even as they were.

'I am Mrs Beattie, wife of Captain Beattie,' Anna said, hesitant to extend her hand, which she suspected would receive a rebuff. At the same time, she didn't feel inclined to curtsy. 'Do you…do you speak any English?'

'I should hope so,' the young lady replied most properly. 'I am Sofia Callona, daughter of the Count of Callona. My mother is Lady Cynthia Pruitt of the Kent Pruitts. Surely you have heard of *them*.'

Well, no, she had not. Still, this was a guest.

'We're delighted to have you here,' Anna said. 'This is Allan Beattie and Pru Beattie. We are houseguests of Admiral Collingwood. You are our guest, and you are welcome.'

There was a long pause, and Anna wondered if she had said something wrong. 'Princess?' she asked.

For the first time, the young lady seemed less assured. She waved her hand. 'As I said, my father is Conte de Callona, near Modena. You may call me Signorina Sofia.'

'So we shall, *signorina*,' Anna said.

That's not quite so grand as a princess, she thought. *At least I needn't genuflect.*

'I am so tired,' *la signorina* said simply, then seemed to visibly rally. She held out a folded page. 'These are my needs. See to them. Show me to your sitting room and I will wait there.'

John rolled his eyes, but thank goodness Signorina Sofia was looking at her, and not him.

'Come with me and make yourself comfortable. I will inform our housekeeper that you are here.' She took the paper and led her into the sitting room, with its huge windows overlooking the back lawn and its slope to their own inlet.

When the *signorina* was seated and studiously ignoring them, John took Anna's arm as she started towards the Durands' kitchen domain. 'Admiral Collingwood sent her to me via Fast Dispatch Vessel. Someone will meet her here in a few days and escort her by private yacht to England. Let's see her list of demands.'

He looked over his shoulder. 'Allan and Pru, please take my hat and duffel upstairs to my room. Thank you, dears.'

When they were out of sight, he sank into a hall chair and pulled Anna onto his lap. 'I confess to growling at my crew and looking all squinty-eyed until Mr Marsing—imagine this—told me to stop acting like a surly idiot.'

'He couldn't possibly have said that.'

'It was more like, "Sir, we'll tie up in Port Mahon as soon as possible".'

'Serves you right,' she teased, then unfolded the paper as he read over her shoulder. She read it again, amazed at its contents. 'John, according to this…this missive, she must have an airy bed chamber that overlooks the sea, sheets changed daily, a bath every morning, absolute quiet until eleven of the clock each morning, and a maid to brush her hair and dress her. And she must approve of the daily menu.'

'P'raps no one told her there is a war on?' He sighed. 'Let's break the bad news to the Durands.'

Madame took the news with a sigh probably heard on neighbouring Mallorca. 'Please assure me this is only a short stay.'

'That is what the Admiral's note said,' John assured her. 'Three days, maybe four.'

Madame thawed enough to tease, 'And the bedchamber? I trust you will be giving up yours, as it is the only one that overlooks the sea?'

He chuckled. 'Alas, Mrs Beattie and I had other plans...'

Anna felt her face grow warm, but Madame laughed. 'Captain Beattie, I suspect that men are the same the world over.'

'We must be.' He had the continued good grace to give the housekeeper a courtly bow. 'Anna and I will find a bed in a closet if we must!'

'A closet?' Madame Durand scoffed, then smiled. 'I have a better idea. Come with me.'

Chapter Thirty-One

It wasn't a closet. It wasn't even unpleasant. Madame Durand asked Anna and John to follow her through the kitchen and past the garden. She pointed to what Anna had thought was a gardener's shed, next to where the beans were already vining.

'You may have noticed that Hector can be morose at times. When he gets that way, I banish *myself* here.'

She opened the door with a flourish. Anna put her hand to her mouth in amazement. 'Madame, this is… Words fail me!'

Madame Durand's eyes sparkled, as though she had just pulled off the greatest surprise since the invention of surprises. 'Even Admiral Collingwood has no idea. It is yours for as long as the ooh-la-la *signorina* demands your bedchamber.'

John picked Anna up and carried her over the threshold. 'Madame Durand, I echo my wife's sentiments,' he said. 'We will be the envy of nations out here in the… ahem…gardener's shed.'

Madame allowed herself a smile, then gave them a

more pointed look. 'You may tell this guest that yes, I will have a bath drawn for her daily, and yes, I will see to her sheets.' She raised one finger and her expression grew militant. 'But no one, not even the daughter of a count, will tamper with the menu in this house, as long as I draw breath! That is all.' She made her stately way back to the house, posture impeccable.

'I'd like an early start,' John said. 'No, no. No alarm from you, or "What will the children say?"' He closed the door with his foot. 'Just a really good kiss. For now.'

It was an excellent kiss, starting at her forehead and ending about where the cleavage began in her dress. She clung to him, then released him reluctantly and surveyed the room, nodding her approval of thick curtains. She sniffed the pillows. Ah, yes, lavender. The bed was ample. She sat down then lay back and sighed blissfully.

'Mrs Beattie, don't tempt me,' he said, and made a gesture towards his trouser buttons. 'I don't generally stand the watch on the *Swallow*, but I keep odd hours alone on the quarterdeck. You can't fathom how many times I've undone your buttons and counted those freckles on your shoulders.' He looked at the ceiling. 'And other ones.' He put a gentle hand on her cheek. 'I'm only here for tonight.'

'I hope you'll have time to tell me about your sailing, too,' she said as they returned to the house arm in arm.

'A little, but you must promise never to divulge anything to agents of the French lurking about,' he teased, 'or anyone else, for that matter. Captain Tyler and I are sailing between Mallorca just west of us, and north towards France, Toulon in particular. I must say we are seeing troop movement—' he held up a placating hand '—through the glass. We're not close to shore. We're still figuring out how to stay within helpful distance of each other without being obvious, with an eye out for *La Guerre*. We're about as sly as two ships can be.' He kissed her. 'Don't look so sceptical! I prefer that look where you admire my prowess.'

'You are hopeless!' she teased, enjoying this captain, pleased to see he was more relaxed, less strained. *Is this what it means to be a Navy family?* she asked herself. *I like it.*

He went upstairs to retrieve his duffel that the children had been last seen hauling up the steps. Anna straightened her dress, patted her hair and nerved herself for a visit to the sitting room.

What she found touched her heart. Sofia Callona lay curled up on the sofa, hands pressed together under her cheek, asleep. *She feels safe here, the same way I feel*, Anna thought, surprised, but upon consideration, not surprised. By the never-used fireplace, Allen and Pru were going through their shell collection, talking softly. She smiled when Pru put her finger to her lips, her eyes kind. Anna blew her a kiss, picked up her mending and seated herself close by. She had gone through John's stockings and was working on his shirts now.

She looked up later when Sofia started, as if in fright. Anna went to her, debating only for a second before resting her hand on her shoulder. 'Shh, shh,' she crooned. 'Go back to sleep.'

Sofia closed her eyes. When Anna saw her tears, she

wiped them away with John's shirt. 'Don't worry,' she said softly, as she'd spoken to Allan mere months ago, when every sound had made him jump. 'You're in a safe place.'

Anna debated only a second, and sat on the sofa. Without a word, Sofia moved closer. 'I was so worried when Mamma and Papá had to flee from Callona.'

'Why didn't you go with them?'

'I have been in Roma in a convent school. Callona seemed so far away, especially when armies and intriguers are between you and home…'

I feel sorry for you, Anna thought. Still, 'I thought, well, isn't Napoleon an Italian?'

'No, no,' Sofia said impatiently. 'The French remain in control, but Callona is an Italian city-state, one of many. Who knows if that will ever change? Pardon me, Mrs Beattie, but between the two of us, Italians do fly off the handle and bicker among themselves, one city against another.' She might have been part English, but her hand gesture was all Italian. 'Bah! How did the Romans ever conquer the known world? Why couldn't Napoleon leave us alone?'

'Life's a mystery,' Anna said, wondering that same question. 'Your parents fled to England and worry about you, I am certain.'

'They are in Kent, where Mamma was born. At least, I hope they are in Kent.'

She looked down at her hands, and Anna noticed her nails were bitten to the quick. *Poor girl*, she thought. *Poor little one*. She took a chance, and decided to overlook Sofia's imperious air. This was a frightened child. 'These are hard times, aren't they? How old are you, my dear?'

Sofia looked almost gratefully at her, the veneer of superiority tucked away, at least for the moment. 'I am almost seventeen. I am counting the days until I see my parents.'

'The Captain told me someone would be here in a few days for you. He has a yacht.'

'Luigi,' she said. Anna heard her relief. 'My uncle said he would send someone named Luigi. From there, I will go to England.' Her sigh echoed in Anna's heart. 'All because someone thinks ruling the world is a good idea. Maybe for him. Not for me.'

Anna thought of her brother resting eternally now on Gibraltar, and her constant silent prayer that no one would injure her husband, all because one man wanted more and didn't care how he got it.

'I believe I would give the earth to have my husband come home every day from work, sit as we are sitting and chat with me,' she said. 'That would be enough.' She almost patted Sofia, then reconsidered. Perhaps that would be rude. 'We wait and hope. Let's go upstairs. I'll show you your room. It does have a lovely view of the sea.'

I suppose rank hath its privileges, Anna thought hours later after a more congenial supper than she would have thought possible, considering Sofia's earlier haughty air. All the same, Sofia didn't seem to mind usurping her hosts from their bedchamber, which made Anna smile to herself and think, *She is still the daughter of a count.*

John delighted her by usurping *her* role as bedtime

reader to the children in Pru's room. Anna watched from the doorway as Pru and Allan fell under the spell of the Scot's charming accent. He was a far cry from being that desperate father, which warmed her very soul.

When he'd finished, they both kissed Pru goodnight. John swung Allan into his arms and carried his son to the other bedchamber. He winked at Anna. 'And you, Mrs Beattie, can make your way to the gardener's shed.'

'Why there, Papa?' Allan asked.

'That is where we are sleeping tonight. I promised the Durands I would do an inventory of what I find in there,' John teased. 'You know: rakes and shovels. Maybe a wench. Go to sleep, son.'

Anna smiled all the way to the shed. She was climbing into Madame Durand's soft bed when John opened the door.

'I believe you have the best-looking bottom of any woman I ever saw.'

'And you would know this how?'

'The usual way. You don't mind if I show off my wares? Standard issue.'

If he could joke, she could, too. 'I wouldn't know standard issue from any other. You're my only source of information.'

Oh, John. 'In that case, I am well above standard issue,' he told her as he stripped and tossed his clothes towards hers. 'I dislike braggadocio, but the word *prodigious* comes to mind.' No other word came to *her* mind, certainly. He lay down beside her. 'This is turning into a delightful habit,' he said.

She was more practised now, enjoying the slow rhythm, happy with how well he fitted, prodigious or otherwise. He was in no hurry, even as she felt her own desire grow. No stranger to suggestion, he increased the tempo, then fulfilled her every need as she gasped and clung to him. Then it was his turn, as she caressed his back then pressed down hard, hearing his groan of satisfaction.

'Mrs Beattie…'

'Yes?'

'That's all. Mrs Beattie.'

She enjoyed his weight, so nicely distributed above her. 'I feel safe like this,' she whispered finally. 'Why is that? I mean, here we are in a garden shed, for heaven's sake.'

'It is because we are, at this moment, the only two people in the entire universe. Remember?' He chuckled. 'The garden shed is a new one for me, too.'

He kept her so close, her head on his chest now. Then began that wondrous part of marriage that probably no one ever tried to explain, but was, in its own way, pure joy: idle bedchamber chat.

She learned about how good the coffee was on *Swallow*, and the letter from a Fast Dispatch Vessel to the *Swallow*'s surgeon, announcing he was the father of twin boys, as of six weeks ago. 'We teased him about that,' John said, his hand gentle in her hair. 'The sailing master wanted to know if they were called Pete and Repeat. I like that dress you abandoned a little while ago. You found a Port Mahon dressmaker?'

'She made Pru two dresses as well, my love. Do you

know, Madame Durand has a wonderful egg source. I've never seen yolks so yellow.'

'The yolk's on you, eh?'

And so on until she slept, content knowing they would do this all over again, until dawn turned them into rational human beings. The war would pick up where it had so mercifully left off. The difference? She knew she wanted more.

'I treasure this,' he told her after their second round of lovemaking, simply because who knew when they would have this chance again?

Still, she could try. 'Do you have any idea when...'

'I'll be back? I never know. Up we get.'

He looked around for his smallclothes. She watched from the bed as he dressed, admiring this captain of hers.

'Captain Tyler—Dan and I—have been keeping an eye out for each other,' he told her. 'I don't want to be in port long, because *La Guerre* knows the *Hartford* is a small ship and as nimble as *Swallow*, but without the firepower.'

'I saw that, too,' she said, remembering that frightening time in *Jaunty*'s hold. 'When *La Guerre* attacked *Jaunty* as we were making our way to Admiral Collingwood, the French backed away when *Hartford* showed up.'

'Exactly. The bully is less brave when it's two against one.'

He buttoned his trousers, mind obviously on business of a nautical nature again. 'The man on the yacht said you can expect someone to fetch Sofia Callona soon. I hope she is not a trial to you.'

'Under the noble mantle, she's just a frightened girl,' she said. 'We will manage well for a few days.'

'Good. You know, sometimes I feel sorry for the petty princes, dukes and counts of Italy, with their little city-states and puffed-up importance. Quarrelling, always quarrelling. If they ever unite into one country, I'll be astounded. Hand me my neckcloth, oh, Port Mahon wench.'

They teased each other as they walked hand in hand to the house, Anna certain that to do anything else might bring tears. Breakfast was a feast of bacon and eggs, toast and spicier Port Mahon delicacies that made Allan hesitate. Anna watched Pru eat everything without complaint as she always did, knowing she watched a child used to deprivation and too wise to leave anything uneaten.

Sofia Callona picked at her food, then put down her fork. 'I am desperate to see my parents,' she admitted, and bowed her head.

Anna half rose in her chair, but Allan reached Sofia first. Anna watched, her heart full, as the child patted her shoulder. 'You'll see them soon,' he said in his earnest way. 'There was a time I didn't think I would see Papa again, and here he is.'

Anna held her breath, hoping Sofia responded kindly to this child who still stayed close to her and spent a lot of time watching the water, waiting and hoping for his father's return. She let her breath out slowly when Sofia turned sympathetic eyes on him.

'If you can wait, I can, too.'

Allan nodded, so serious. '"Time and tides" is what my papa says. Isn't that it?' he asked John.

'Aye, laddie. Time and tides, Signorina Sofia, and one thing more: we are doing our best to get you to safety.'

'I thank you,' Sofia said.

Anna saw the sympathy in his eyes. So much for Royal Navy captains being made of iron. She took Sofia's hand and gave it a squeeze, touched by answering pressure from a young lady made old too soon, another child of war.

John rose. 'I must take my leave.' He turned to Madame Durand, who had brought in more toast. 'Did Hector arrange for that pony trap?'

'*Oui, Capitaine*,' she said. 'Will you return soon?'

'I never know, *madame*, but I do know someone will be here soon for our lovely guest.' He nodded to Sofia, his eyes kind.

'Thank you for bringing me here, Captain Beattie,' Sofia said. 'I promise to be a good guest.' Her expression was a curious blend of apology and good will. 'I probably didn't need my list of demands.'

'You shouldn't need them where you are going,' he said. 'I hope you won't be seasick on the yacht. I didn't see anything on your list about *mal de mer*.' He turned to Anna. 'Kiss me quick, Mrs Beattie.'

And he was gone again. Madame Durand gave a piece of toast to Allan, and he piled on the marmalade. Sofia took another sip of her tea. Pru left the room, saying something about making her bed. Dame Routine had reasserted herself. Now it was time to miss the Captain all over again.

But there he was at the door. He motioned her outside.

'Did you forget something?' she asked.

'I did indeed. Something I was going to show you.'

He handed her a picture of herself, the drawing done by a child, but the artist had captured her big eyes. She smiled, guessing who had drawn it.

'Admiral Collingwood told me Allan sketched this when you and I were in Gibraltar,' he said. 'He gave Allan a box of coloured chalk he had been saving for his girls.'

'I had no idea. How kind. You know, Allan is rather talented,' she replied, touched and delighted at the same time. 'Thank you.'

He took it back. 'I want it. I have a place for it on the *Swallow*.' He took a deep breath. 'I have a picture of Cathy.'

'I know,' she said quietly.

'Be patient with me,' he said, his voice soft, too. He kissed her and closed the door.

Anna returned to the gardener's shed to gather the sheets and empty the night jar, homely tasks that reordered her world again. She noticed Pru walking up from the steps to their inlet. Pru hurried to her, eyes wide.

'Where were you?' Anna asked.

'I don't like it when Captain Beattie leaves. I… I wanted to see the *Swallow* one more time, you know, from our own little inlet.'

Anna held up a finger. 'I did ask you to tell me before you went down there, do you remember?'

She nodded, her eyes troubled. 'I'm sorry, I won't do

it again.' Then Pru came closer and whispered, as if conspirators lurked. 'There was a flaming torch. What does that mean?'

Chapter Thirty-Two

What, indeed? Anna knew she could brush it off with a laugh, but this was Pru, who watched over them all. She knelt beside the child. 'Perhaps someone is interested in us.'

She knew she could not say something like that to Allan, but Pru was older than her years. Her reply gave voice to Anna's fear. 'More like the Captain's business.'

'More like,' Anna agreed. 'Say nothing of this to anyone, my dear.'

'Can you… Is there any way to tell the Captain?'

'Only if we lived in a magical world far different from this one,' she said frankly. 'We must wait until he returns.' She managed a smile. 'You and I are good at waiting. We are also good at saying little to others.'

She could tell Pru was mulling over that comment.

'Yes, Pru?' she asked gently.

Pru sank down lower in the grass, her head bowed. *John, I wish I knew what to do*, Anna thought. *I am so ill-prepared. I am also afraid.*

She sank down on the grass, too. 'Tell me,' she said

simply, holding out her arms for Pru, who didn't hesitate to sit on her lap.

'Wh...when those women left us in Plymouth, I almost ran away and left Allan there alone,' Pru said finally, as if pincers pulled the words from her throat.

'But you didn't.'

'I wanted to run.'

'You didn't,' Anna repeated firmly. 'Pru, it's hard to do the right thing sometimes, and it is permissible to be afraid. What matters is that you did the right thing.'

'We were so hungry. I had to decide to stay and not look outside for food, or...or run away. It is a lonely feeling!'

The words sounded torn from her whole body and Anna held her closer. *I know the lonely feeling*, she thought, then knew what to do. She put her hands over Pru's eyes for a brief moment. 'It's done now, dearest, and you did not fail anyone. Sometimes this feels good, too. There now. We'll sit here a moment, then go back to the house. We'll sit here as long as you want.'

The child relaxed in her arms. They stayed that way long enough for the warmth to seep more than skin-deep, into some place Pru needed.

When Pru sat up, her eyes were bright again, hopeful. 'We'll be sure to tell the Captain,' she said.

'We will.'

'I wish we knew when he will return.'

'So do I, but in the meantime we will take care of our guest and keep ourselves busy. Let's not mention the torch to anyone,' Anna said.

'Our secret?'

'Only until we can tell Captain Beattie.'

Silence was less of a trial than Anna feared, thanks to Sofia's demands, which, as demands went, were not onerous, but distracting enough to suit her. Pru and Allan had already weathered their first week of parish education at St Matthew's in Port Mahon. The church had none of the beautiful stonework of the Catholic church in the village centre, and the more distant mosque. A good Anglican, Anna dubbed St Matthew's serviceable.

The children seemed content with Mr Brown. 'He's not too patient, but I think we are bright enough,' Allan assured her. Anna wanted to laugh out loud at his solemn assessment, considering that whatever instruction the young teacher gave them was their first brush with education.

Pru had her own observation about their teacher. 'Mr Brown spends a lot of time staring out of the window,' she said, then shrugged. 'It is a lovely view.' She brightened. 'P'raps he has a sweetheart in the port.'

Allan pooh-poohed that. 'Pru, he's too old for a sweetheart.'

With what she thought was masterful control, Anna managed to remain straight-faced, thinking of her husband, even as she wondered what John really thought of her. Either time would tell or it wouldn't.

It took no convincing to get Sofia to accompany her and the children to Port Mahon in the pony trap, loins girded for another morning of school. Even Madame Durand wanted to come along this time, chatting with Sofia about her plans, a far cry from the housekeeper with raised eyebrows over their guest's list of demands.

'Madame Beattie, you could take *la signorina* to Clotilde and have her measured for dresses,' Hermione suggested. 'Not that what you are wearing isn't lovely, but…'

La signorina dismissed that suggestion with a withering glance. 'Convent clothes, eh? I don't mind. I will only be here for a few days, then to England. Papá thought it prudent to leave Italia, you know, where one scarcely knows who is friend or foe.'

Madame Durand nodded. 'It is that way everywhere,' she said with a sigh. 'Madame Beattie, you at least will be with us for a while, *oui*?' She smiled behind her hand. 'The Captain does like to come into port as often as possible, does he not?'

Why does it matter how often he is here? Anna asked herself. Since Pru and Allan sat by Hector in the pony cart, she nearly said it. Instead, she asked herself the question beyond the question: *Why should it matter to you, Hermione Durand, how often John comes into port?*

'I have no idea when he will return.' She changed the subject. 'Sofia, when I married Captain Beattie, I brought along dresses better suited to the English climate. Shall we take out those hems and start you a wardrobe for Kent?'

Madame Durand, I dare you to change the subject, she told herself as she made small talk about English customs as they wandered along to Port Mahon. She waved goodbye to Pru and Allan at St Matthew's, then dutifully followed the Durands into the marketplace for some haggling over melons and other Mediterranean delicacies. In the market, she saw Hector huddle with men his age, then walk away quickly.

He stood at the pony cart when they returned carrying baskets of food, and helped them in. 'He will return to collect the children,' Madame Durand said. 'You will be busy sewing.'

So it went for the next four days, hemming and creating as English a wardrobe as Anna could muster, all the while praying for John to return, because something was different, now that they knew...what?

Rather than continue sleeping in the gardener's shed, Anna easily convinced Pru to share her room. By unspoken consent, neither mentioned the one torch burning, as though not speaking of it made it go away.

At least Sofia had mellowed from the imperious *signorina* with a list of demands. She showed a thoughtful side, which relieved Anna as nothing else could have. 'There is something about the mirrors in this house,' Sofia said one morning after she'd tried on Anna's favourite blue wool dress.

'I know the mirrors are clean, because Madame Durand is a far better housekeeper than I,' Anna said. 'Is the glass too wavy? Does someone unfamiliar stare back at you?' she teased.

'I believe that is the case,' Sofia said seriously. '*This* Sofia's shoulders aren't held so high. She seems more relaxed. Mrs Beattie, is this house magic, or are you?'

'I am no sorcerer,' Anna told her, both amused and

touched. 'We're ordinary here, and war and its attendant discomforts seem far away. Perhaps that is it.'

'It is more, and you are part of it,' Sofia insisted softly. 'I am at home here.' She leaned forward, her eyes kind. 'Mrs Beattie, that is your special gift. Do you think Captain Beattie knows that, too?'

'I hope he does, dear child.'

'I am at peace here,' Sofia said simply.

A week passed, an uneventful week, the sort of week that might have bored Anna in England, but which let the sweetness of Port Mahon, this house, these children, their guest, fill her heart. *I am needed*, she told the mirror that night.

So it happened that when Sofia's rescuer finally arrived on Saturday—an older gentleman with an air of nobility—Anna knew she would miss the guest who had gone from burden to friend.

He arrived after breakfast. Madame Durand knocked on the library door where Anna sat listening to Pru read aloud, with appreciative applause from Sofia and Allan.

'Come in, Madame Durand,' Anna said. 'We're just enjoy…'

'*Zio!*'

Sofia ran to the door, throwing herself into her uncle's arms. She spoke in rapid Italian, her eyes happy. She took his hand as Anna rose from the sofa. 'Mrs Beattie, this is Conte Emilio Callona, my uncle from near Modena. You are to be my escort to England instead of Luigi? Papá will be delighted!'

Anna gave the best curtsy she knew and was rewarded

with a bow from a gentleman who obviously inhabited a more exalted world than hers. He held out a note, and his English was beautiful. 'I was told to present this to the mistress of the house—' he made a modest gesture '—in case you did not feel inclined to relinquish this priceless pearl to me, my own niece.'

She knew without opening the letter that even in trying times matters often resolved themselves precisely as planned. She noted the expensive paper, and the stamp and seal at the bottom next to an elaborate signature.

'We will miss her,' she said simply.

Even Madame Durand looked sad. '*Conte*, when must you take this jewel?'

'Now,' he said, perhaps unaware that, except for Sofia, his audience was obviously not as pleased. 'Her parents will be delighted to see her.'

Sofia left them at midday, after hugs and more tears. 'I promise I will write to you from Kent,' she said. 'Mrs Beattie, perhaps you will visit me when you are next in England.'

Anna assured her she would. She walked her to the pony cart, Hector his usual morose and silent self as he held the reins. Another hug from Sofia, another courtly bow from her uncle, and they left, Sofia turning around to wave, handkerchief at the ready.

'I don't like saying goodbye to people,' Pru told her as Anna walked hand in hand with her to the house. Trust Pru; by the time they were in the foyer, she'd reminded Anna that now she had her bedchamber back.

Madame Durand was changing the bedlinen as Anna

dragged herself upstairs for a private sulk. 'There now,' the housekeeper said, patting the pillow. She looked closely at Anna. 'My dear, such puffy eyes! Come down to the kitchen and I will put some sliced cucumbers on them.'

Just leave me alone, she wanted to say, but that would be rude. She saw the folded note by her side of the bed and opened it to read Sofia's original list of rules and requirements. Her now-friend had written across the bottom in her neat script:

My English mother would have said, 'A friend in need is a friend indeed'. I never understood that before, but I do now. Love, your friend in need and deed, Sofia.

Now, where was that other friend? Anna asked herself the next morning, and the morning after. *If you don't think about him, he will show up*, she told herself, which didn't prove helpful. Neither did, *You're a grown woman, Anna Beattie, and too old to mope about like this*.

The Durands had taken the children to the parish school. In fact, they insisted, even usually silent Hector telling her gently that she needed time alone. As penance for her grouchy mood, she put herself to the task she liked the least, organising the linen closet. She was deep in refolding pillowslips when she heard a familiar voice in the hall below, calling her name. She smiled, then her smile vanished, because the tone of John's voice yanked her back to January and desperation.

'God, please don't let him be wounded,' she whispered as she dropped the pillowslip, which suddenly felt as heavy as a lead bar.

'I'm upstairs, John. Wh...what is the matter?'

She met him on the landing. He grabbed her by the shoulders.

'We're fine,' she assured him, frightened now.

'Where is Signorina Callona?' he demanded, his eyes boring into hers, captain's eyes, and not the eager husband she wanted to see.

'Good news, my love,' she said, relieved. He must not know; he would be pleased. 'Imagine this: her uncle arrived a few days ago and...'

He pulled her close. 'Anna, that *is* her uncle, but the uncle who loves Napoleon, damn him. Her other uncle, her real rescuer, is dead aboard a yacht we found drifting north of these islands. Anna, she is in enemy hands.'

Her dear brother, lying in his Gibraltar grave, had once called her the stalwart member of the family. '*Nothing seems to faze you, sis,*' he'd teased once. '*A million ladies would collapse in a heap before you would even blink.*'

A million ladies must have collapsed. Anna stared at her husband, watching him turn into three men before her eyes. The room whirled them all around and she fainted.

Chapter Thirty-Three

She woke, lying on her bed, to the horrible odour of burned feathers waved under her nose by Madame Durand.

'That will do, *madame*,' John said. 'Leave us.' The door closed behind her.

She tried to sit up, but the room still revolved. John held her close as she sobbed. 'There is the letter,' she managed to say, 'over there.' He ignored the letter, then lay down beside her. She clung to his hand. 'I never would have let her go, but he was her uncle and…and… You see that official letter. What have I *done*?'

He held her close as she tried to burrow inside him, anything to be swallowed up and disappear. 'You did what anyone would have done. My God, *I* would have done the same thing, had I been here with you. Shh, shh, no tears.'

That was easy to say, she thought as she wept. She heard John's low voice: 'Pru, Allan, I'll speak to you soon. Give us a moment.' The door closed.

'They're back from the parish school. They need me,'

she said, rubbing her eyes because they hurt from so many tears.

'They can wait. Hear me out.'

She lay in his arms, desperate to find out what he knew. She hoped it would make her feel better, but knew it wouldn't because Sofia was gone.

'Captain Tyler and the *Hartford* were sailing in tandem with us. We're doing that more and more. We came across a yacht drifting, and boarded her.' He paused and she saw the pain in his eyes. 'The crew was dead, and so was an old gentleman.'

'Sofia's uncle,' she whispered, anticipating his answer.

'We only knew that because the yacht's captain, a man named Luigi, lay there beside him, barely alive.'

She shuddered, and he held her tighter.

'What he managed to say before he died was that they had been boarded by a French ship—probably *La Guerre*—carrying Sofia Callona's uncle, the one you met.'

'She...she knew him. She was so pleased to see him. She thought... Oh, John, he was to take her to England!'

'Wrong brother, and how would she have known? She was distanced from the whole business because she was in that convent school in Rome.'

'Such a nice man,' Anna said softly. 'So courtly, so dignified.'

'So traitorous. Mr Marsing and I pieced the story together from what Luigi managed to tell us. There were two uncles, one loyal to Napoleon, an *afrancesado*, as the

Spanish would say—oh, don't get me started on the Spanish, who can't decide whose side they are on!'

'John,' she said quietly, as calm reason began to peep out from wherever it had fled in terror.

'Aye. The other uncle was opposed to our despot from Corsica, that damned Bonaparte.'

'What else?'

'That's all we know. Luigi died.' He held up the letter. 'The count *you* saw obviously confiscated this from the yacht. He killed his own brother.' He shook his head. 'The things people do for a little power…'

They lay there in silence. She wondered if he slept now, imagining that once this long war ended he would probably sleep for a week, perhaps hibernate for a winter.

'John, you need to know something else. It may not matter, but it might.'

'Tell me.' He sighed. 'If you could make it good news, I'd be grateful.'

'I don't know what it is. After you sailed last time, Pru went down those steps again. You remember, the ones down to the inlet.'

He smiled at that. 'What a delight! I have to admit it was grand of you to give us a send-off from our own private inlet last time. All the same, better tell Pru not to do that again by herself. Those steps look risky.'

'I've already mentioned it to her. But you might find this useful,' she told him. 'She went down near dusk after you'd left this last time, and discovered a torch burning. There were two torches by the rope ladder. Do you think…?'

She knew her man. He raised up on one elbow to look at her.

'We have wondered how someone always seems to know when we are in port. One torch? That might be the signal for the *Swallow* leaving port.' He lay back and stared at the ceiling. 'Two torches probably mean our arrival.'

He pulled her close this time, as if wanting to burrow inside her for *his* comfort. 'This changes everything. We have to be certain, Anna. Up you get. God forgive me, but I am about to tell a monumental lie to our children.'

She heard *our children* the loudest and longest, until *monumental lie* pushed its way through, shouldering aside the sweetness. He opened the door, stepping back in surprise because the children still waited there. Anna watched John kneeling down to gather Pru and Allan close.

'We heard Missy crying,' Allan said, his expression troubled.

'She was overjoyed to see me, laddie. That is all,' her generally truthful husband said, and then, 'I'll admit I was near tears of joy myself, to learn that Sofia is now in the care of her uncle, who will see her to a better place.'

You can be a shrewd liar, she thought. *She is certainly in the care of her uncle. As for a better place? Unlikely.* Still, it sounded true enough to satisfy the children. She glanced at Pru watching, not wary now but considering. Maybe she would always be that way.

Anna exchanged glances with her husband. 'You or me, dear?' she asked.

She was right. 'Me,' he said, then smiled at his son. 'Allan, I have something for you in my duffel. It's right on top.'

Allan brightened. 'Where?'

'I left it inside the front door.'

When Allan hurried off, John held out his arms to Pru. 'We haven't much time, but Allan is too young to hear this. Come here, Pru.'

She settled on his lap.

'Pru, I didn't want to tell you what really happened, but I know you are more aware than I have given you credit for.' Another breath. 'The man who came for Sofia was her uncle, aye, but let me tell you what happened to her other uncle. It's not a pretty story.'

He was economical with his words. Anna watched Pru's face and saw the sadness.

'I was hoping it would be different,' she said at last, then half turned on John's lap to look at his face. 'You told Allan and me that Sofia was in safe hands. You're not really very good at lying, Captain Beattie.'

'Maybe I don't do it enough,' he replied, which made Pru shake her head.

Anna took Pru's hands in her own. 'Tell us how you knew he was lying.'

'Your voice changed, sir. You looked at me then looked away.'

'You've had too many people tell you one thing and do another, haven't you?' he asked. 'I won't do that again.'

'I would know if you did,' Pru said. 'What is *really* in your duffel?'

'It really is a sack of lemon drops. I know Allan likes them. Do you like lemon drops?'

'I've never tried one,' she said longingly.

'Tell Allan to share, Captain's orders.'

'Aye, sir,' she said, and darted away.

'You are amazing,' Anna said.

'I'm an idiot for trying to fool a wise child,' he said frankly. 'Now, what should I do?'

'Kiss me and then we'll have dinner.'

'That's hardly a punishment.'

'It isn't meant to be. I think that men usually underestimate the fairer sex,' she said, then kissed him. 'Don't do that again.'

'I won't. Promise.' He kissed her back. 'Mrs Beattie, this could become a habit.'

Dinner was a hurried affair, after John announced to Madame Durand that he was returning to the *Swallow* to get the ship to sea as soon as possible. 'Do tell Hector to have the pony trap ready after dark. We'll get a better wind then.'

He was quiet through dinner, his thoughts miles away.

What are you thinking? Anna asked herself, wanting to ask him out loud, but not with the children there. There was a set look to his jaw, a resolve. She watched his face through two courses of Madame Durand's delicious meal—amazing how proficient she was on short notice—and to the three cheeses dipped in *mahonnaise*, invented in Port Mahon, some said.

He spoke to Madame Durand. 'Dear lady, would you let the children help you clear the table? I'd like a moment alone with my wife.' He shook his head. 'This is a short visit. We'll be outside the sitting room. I like those canvas chairs on the veranda. If I fall asleep and start to snore, Mrs Beattie will nudge me.'

Madame Durand nodded. 'I could do with their help.' She leaned closer and spoke softly. 'I can distract them far longer, *Capitaine*.'

'No need. Let them help you in a leisurely fashion, then send them here. We'll all enjoy the sunset.'

'*Mais oui*.' Madame marshalled her forces. 'Come, children, you may eat the leftover titbits if you are efficient.'

When they left the dining room bearing dishes, John moved his chair closer. 'I have a bold idea, one which I doubt you will approve of, but which I need done most particularly.'

'That's a little mysterious,' she said.

He kept his hand on her thigh, as if drawing comfort from touch alone. 'Needs must, Anna, needs must,' he said finally, sounding tired.

They walked from the dining room to the sitting room, then through the glass doors onto the veranda, where he sank into a canvas chair. She pulled her chair closer, craving every second in his orbit. There was a chill in the evening air, which surprised her, considering that it was June in a warm spot in the universe, a beautiful island with seabirds quarrelling on the air currents and nesting birds rustling nearby, tending to little ones of their own.

'I like it here,' he said. 'I do wish Admiral Collingwood could know the peace that I feel right now.'

'He would if he had his wife and children near as you do, my love.'

He smiled at *my love*, and she wondered, slightly panicked, if she had said that before. 'I'm probably the envy of the fleet, except…'

She did not know what he would have said because Allan sneaked up behind him and covered his eyes, with Pru smiling beside him.

How many days like this is my husband permitted? she thought, hoping for many, but aware, as never before, of the cost of command.

'I have a task for you, Pru,' he said. 'I wouldn't ask it, but I am curious about something.'

'Please, no,' Anna whispered, suddenly knowing.

John touched her leg. 'Trust me.'

Her mind raced back to the first time she had heard those words from him, a different man, a desperate man with no choice.

'You still have no choice, do you?' she said, her voice gentle because she truly understood him. 'I do trust you.'

After a long look, her husband turned his attention to the matter at hand.

'Pru, please satisfy my curiosity,' he said. 'I have been informed by my superior officer sitting here beside me that I am probably asking too much.'

'What is it, sir?'

'I am curious about those torches you saw at the bottom of the steps, there in our secret inlet.'

'I could check easier in daylight,' Pru suggested. 'And safer.'

You could, Anna thought, aware what John needed to know to confirm his suspicions.

'I must know if both those torches are lit,' John told Pru. 'And a child playing will be overlooked. If you would rather not go, tell me. I will not love you any less.'

Anna watched Pru's face as the child considered the request. She saw no fear, only a stalwart girl measuring out the task.

'If I move carefully, I can do it.'

'You only need to go down far enough to see the torches.'

'I will come, too,' Allan said.

Anna held her breath as Pru leaned towards the boy. 'I have a better idea. Let us take a rope between us. You go part way down. When I go the rest of the way, I will tug twice on the rope for two torches lit. You can run back here and tell your father. He'll know sooner that way.'

Allan didn't like the idea and told her, but Pru was masterful. Anna realised she was watching the two children they'd been last November and December, trying to stay alive in an empty house, with Pru in charge, so young herself.

'You did what I asked when it was just the two of us,' Pru said quietly. 'Allan, do that again for me.'

Silence, then, 'I will do it for you,' Allan told her. He looked at his father. 'We will be ever so quiet and careful, Papa.'

'That's all I ask,' the Captain said, after a visible struggle that tore at Anna's heart. 'Pru, if I am asking too much…'

'You're not, sir,' she said, and shyly touched his shoulder. 'I am having the best time of my life. We'll take care. There's rope by the shed.'

Hand in hand, without a backward glance, they walked across the lawn, stopping at the gardener's shed for rope.

Anna and her Captain stood on the veranda, watching in the growing darkness as the children approached the steps, then disappeared. John tightened his grip until she wanted to cry out, but didn't.

'They're taking forever,' he said after mere minutes.

She could not have agreed more.

The sky turned from grey to ink. When it felt like midnight in the next century, she heard scrabbling on stone. They hurried to the edge to see Allan waving the rope like a talisman. 'Two burning torches, Papa!' he declared. 'Pru tugged.'

Pru followed soon after. Anna grabbed her and held on tight, while Allan started to protest at his father's own strong grip.

'I saw two torches brightly lit,' Pru told him. 'What does it mean?'

Anna glanced at John. She knew what he would say, and she dreaded it.

'It means that someone in Port Mahon wants to know when *Swallow* is docked at the wharf. Two torches must mean we are here. When it is one torch, *Swallow* is heading back to sea.'

'I don't understand, Papa,' Allan said. 'Couldn't they just ask you?'

Thank you, Allan, she thought as the captain started to laugh, a genuine belly-laugh with no panic in it.

'Allan, that makes perfect sense,' he said when he could speak. 'When I find out who it is, I'll ask them.'

Allan nodded. 'I would, Papa. Wouldn't you, Pru?'

Pru looked down at her lap and smiled. 'I might.'

John gave the children what Anna knew was a captain's look. He put his finger to his lips. 'Consider yourselves my crew. I order you to tell no one. Promise me.'

They understood. He kissed them.

'It's bedtime for you two,' Anna said, keeping her voice light after such solemnity. 'Allan, I found your favourite soap when I was cleaning out the linen closet. Would you find me another bar in there? I like it, too.'

Allan ran ahead, but Pru walked sedately between them. 'If I could give you a medal, brave girl, I would,' John told her when Allan was out of earshot. 'Thank you.'

She took their hands. 'Captain, you gave me something better than a medal: a home. Thank you and goodnight! I can read to Allan tonight.'

She skipped ahead, too, a child and no conspirator. John put his arm around Anna.

'I am leaving as soon as I can, but I need to lie down for a few minutes at least,' he told her, his lips close to her ear. 'It might be wild surmise, but making sure I am in port means they can harass the *Hartford*. It chafes me. Together, we two ships can keep *La Guerre* at bay. Separate, the smaller *Hartford* is fair game.'

'I know I'm sounding like Allan…'

'But why?' he teased, finishing her question. 'This is

for you only: Captain Tyler thinks *La Guerre* is landing French troops on Mallorca. Just a few at a time, so as not to arouse suspicion.'

'Why these islands?'

'If he can't conquer England—Trafalgar and our blockade have stopped him—Napoleon wants to control the Mediterranean. Maybe he has designs on Egypt again. Men like Napoleon are never satisfied. He wants the Royal Navy gone. What better start than to take Menorca and fortify it for France?'

'And here you are in a small ship,' she said.

'Two ships,' he corrected. 'Anna, I am going to make a leap of logic and assume two torches mean what we think. I will alert Captain Tyler. We will formulate a plan. I don't know what it will look like, but trust me.' His smile was genuine and comforting; she knew it. 'I have asked that of you again and again.'

'I trust you, dear man,' she said simply. 'I always will.'

You are dear to me, she thought, and not for the first time. Maybe she was admitting it to herself at last.

'Keep that in mind,' he told her, his voice just as soft.

They stood in their bedchamber then. Was this the moment she'd wanted? Who knew when a time would ever be right? They were but two puny people in the middle of constant, grinding war. What she wanted to know mattered to no one except her.

'Before you leave, tell me about Cathy. I know you treasure her portrait. I want to know her a little.'

She heard his involuntary catch of breath, then a sigh that sounded like relief. Maybe he had been wanting to speak about her, but didn't think it a kind subject for his new wife. Or she could be horribly, terribly wrong.

Trust me, she thought, as though willing the words into his very soul. *Trust me.*

He made himself comfortable, settling into their bed, pulling her down beside him, his grip loose.

'She was my dear love,' he said. 'I can't recall a time I didn't love her.' He chuckled, which relieved her heart. 'I didn't even propose. I came back from the Indies, held her close and asked, "Should we spend three weeks crying the banns, or get a special licence and marry fast?" Anna, I paid a fortune for a special licence. And look, I did it again for you!'

She attempted a smile, feeling a pang as she considered how different the circumstances were. He rested her head against his chest, maybe as if she were Cathy. His voice turned serious then.

'She knew even then she had consumption. She didn't tell me until I returned from the Nile. I didn't know what to say. She told me she yearned for a child, which could have been a death sentence. Allan was born nine months later, when I was in the Caribbean.'

He stood suddenly and paced the room. She said nothing that might stop the flow of words. He sat down again, cross-legged on their bed, and stared at her.

'Her skin was so pale and she had no energy. Thank God we could afford a wet nurse and nanny. Every exertion exhausted her.'

Anna leaned forward and put her hand on his knee. He covered it with his hand, then got up again and picked up his uniform coat, rummaging. He returned to bed with a folded note.

'Light the lamp.'

She did so.

He handed the paper to her. 'Her original letter faded with time and brine. I've copied it several times since. Please read it.'

She felt his eyes on her as she read silently, her heart going out to this couple she didn't know, because this was a different husband from the man beside her.

Dearest, I knew. Don't despise me for that, Johnny. I wanted to know the delight of you, and if God was benevolent, I wanted the blessing of our baby.

Anna looked at him, seeing his anguish as if the note was only hours old.

'I could never have despised her, and never had the chance to tell her,' he said. 'I have read and reread this. I have memorised it. Keep reading.'

She did as he said.

Please remarry, Johnny, please. Love, Cathy.

What was there to say? Her logical brain did not fail her. He either would or wouldn't come around to the marriage she now knew she wanted, that of a dear heart in tune with hers, generous in love. They were married and would likely stay that way. Whether it was mere words on a document, or the kind of love that sank deep into the heart and body, she did not yet know.

She folded the note and handed it back to him, then leaned closer and covered his eyes with her hands.

'Dear man, when she told you to please remarry, didn't you believe her?' Who was brave enough to say *that*? Only her.

She expected no answer and didn't get one. She took her hands away and looked into his eyes. *Are you in love with me?* she wanted to ask, but Anna Beattie was no fool. That question could wait; she doubted he even knew himself. She knew her answer, but it could wait, perhaps forever.

Instead, she lay down and pulled the sheet to her shoulder. To her delight, he lay down beside her and pulled her close.

'I am a work in progress,' he whispered in her ear.

Chapter Thirty-Four

He left two hours later, after holding her close in their bed as she cried again over Sofia, still blaming herself. She also wept for young Cathy and young John Beattie, but he didn't need to know that. 'None of what happened to Sofia was your fault, Anna. None of us knew of two brothers, their treachery and hatred of each other. If you want to blame someone, blame Napoleon.'

She had to ask. 'Do you think… Sofia is dead?'

'Dead? No,' he replied. 'I'm not saying that to make you feel better, although, God knows, I want to. I think she is more useful to France as a bargaining chip of some sort. Go to sleep, Mrs Beattie.' He rested his cheek against hers for a brief moment. 'I am no fool, either. Maybe this wasn't the time or the place to show you Cathy's letter, but I have no way of knowing what will happen to me even tomorrow, or the day after.' He kissed her forehead. 'The wondrous part of all this is that you are here with me.'

Was this the time for a light comment? Anna didn't think she possessed one. Well, maybe one.

'And I haven't yet run screaming into the night, do you mean? I can't imagine a worse time to think about love, Captain John Beattie. Can you imagine two more stupid people?'

'No, I can't,' he said, and she heard the humour.

'Seriously, when might you return?' She knew this mundane question might restore his equilibrium.

It did. 'That depends on our next move. The *Hartford* was weakened by her last single encounter with *La Guerre*. Thanks to Pru's discovery and your surmise, I harbour no illusions that when I sail, someone on this island will alert *La Guerre* with one burning torch that *Swallow* is out and roaming. Somehow, I must find a way to get close to *Hartford* before *La Guerre* knows I am there, too.'

'And fight?'

'That's what we do, my love. Hush now; rest a bit.'

It was strange to say goodbye to John in the middle of the night, children asleep and the house quiet. Sure enough, Hector, hunched over and muttering something, was there with his pony trap.

Anna walked John to the front door, where he enveloped them both in his cloak, seeking one last moment of privacy. John glanced at Hector and spoke softly to her. 'Trust no one here.'

Her voice was equally soft. 'Be careful.'

'If I can be.'

'I mean it, John.'

'So do I. Remember my profession.'

How can I forget? she asked herself after they kissed.

She watched until the pony trap was out of sight, then turned around and nearly bumped into Madame Durand. 'Oh!'

'He's sailed already? Doesn't he usually stay a few days?'

'Duty calls,' Anna said, unnerved that someone could move through the house so silently. *You know the captain's habits as well as I do*, she thought. 'Goodnight,' she said, startled when the housekeeper took her arm.

'Madame Beattie, it's already morning.'

'So it is.' Anna pulled away, suddenly afraid that Madame Durand would hang onto her. All that did was make the other woman look at her with a frown, the last thing she wanted. 'I'm still tired.'

How could she sleep, though? She sat on the bedchamber's balcony that overlooked the back lawn and the inlet beyond, certain that if she ventured down the steps, there would be only one torch lit now. Her mind took a leap. Was the torch Hector Durand's doing?

She touched John's pillow, hoping it was still warm, but no. She sat down, trying to summon serenity where she felt none. She sat there quietly, expecting no sudden flash of revelation or affirmation—none came. She was alone.

Not quite. She looked at the bureau to see Cathy Beattie's folded note. She stared at it, then put it in her dresser drawer, wondering why he had left it, then suddenly, wildly hopeful.

'Courage, Anna,' she said softly. 'It took a brave man to leave that with me.'

* * *

Three days passed; it seemed like an eternity. Inwardly calm, she rode with the children to St Matthews, and found herself distracted, thanks be to God, by Mr Brown.

He had his complaints. She dutifully listened to an earful about Port Mahon's inhabitants: child pickpockets, noisy women in the market, even the muezzin who proclaimed *Allah Is Great* five times a day from the mosque.

Should she? Why not? Hal Brown had no idea of the burdens *she* carried.

'I think the people here are charming,' she said. 'No child has picked my pocket, the noisy women are no louder than the women who shout through Plymouth's streets about Wellfleet oysters, and isn't Allah the Muslims' name for God? What's the harm in shouting His name five times a day?'

He stared at her, open-mouthed. 'Really, Madame Beattie!'

'It's Mrs Beattie, not *madame*,' she stated firmly.

Poor Hal Brown, an Englishman missing his country, or even just nearby Mallorca, that he had mentioned once.

'You'll get used to Menorca,' she told him, feeling like a sudden citizen of the quirky island. She looked around for inspiration.

Stodgy St Matthews sat so English and out of place on the waterfront.

She pointed to a dinghy tied close to the steps from the street where they stood. 'Perhaps you could take up fishing.'

He laughed and gave her a little bow, not a mocking

one, but somehow both awkward and charming. 'I believe you are right. The old Rector even thinks I should take Orders and replace him some day! D'ye think there is good English cod in these waters?'

She laughed along with him, in a better frame of mind, herself. Nice to know she wasn't as out of place as Hal Brown seemed to be. 'Good day, Mr Brown,' she said. 'Tell those rascals of mine to learn something today, eh?'

He gave her a playful bow. As Hector took her home, she watched that opposite shoreline, with its shops, homes and Menorcans going about their business as they probably had for centuries, war or not.

'I like it here,' she said softly to herself.

Nights were hard, she had to admit during that week. Funny how she had rubbed along so contentedly for twenty-nine years, only to change when the merest suspicion of love arose, not to mention two children. Here she was in a strange place, uneasy and in charge.

School continued as usual; everything did, as if mocking her suspicions. Her uneasiness continued after the children arrived home, deposited once more by Hector. *Does that man never smile?* she asked herself as she ushered Allan and Pru inside. She started to close the door.

'Stop, Mrs Beattie! I need you!'

She opened the door wide as another wagon trundled towards the house. Was that Captain Tyler seated beside the driver?

'Good God,' she whispered. 'Please, no.'

He leapt down before the wagon stopped and grabbed her arm. 'Mrs Beattie, we have a crisis on our hands and

I am about to dump it in your lap.' To her horror, he left bloody fingermarks on her sleeve.

'Is it Captain Beattie?' she managed before he tugged her to the side of the driveway.

'No, he is well. My *Hartford* tangled with *La Guerre* two days ago,' he told her, and she could tell he was condensing the story even as he spoke, whether to keep her from running away in fright or moving the matter along, she could not tell.

'And?' she prompted, her fear dissipating as she observed this exhausted man before her.

'Your husband found us and sent me here. I have three wounded men, one near death. I have no surgeon aboard.'

This was no time to quibble or argue, or even ask questions. 'Follow me.'

As Captain Tyler's crew carried in three men on stretchers, she ran to the sitting room, looked around and pronounced it serviceable.

'Set them down. We will move this furniture,' she directed, and picked up a side table.

'We can do that, ma'am,' a stretcher bearer said. He had a delightful, drawly sort of speech. Too bad there was no time to enquire about his home in faraway America.

To her relief, Madame Durand materialised, rolling up her sleeves and not wasting a moment. 'There are several cots in the room off the kitchen,' she said, and called for Hector.

Captain Tyler took Anna's arm again, but gently now, his head close to hers, as if suspecting the very walls of eavesdropping. '*La Guerre* jumped us. We managed to get away when *Swallow* sailed to our defence.'

'Was anyone on *Swallow*…'

'Injured, too? Nothing that *Swallow*'s surgeon couldn't manage.' He looked down. 'Except for this man. He's a private, a Royal Marine. It looks bad enough, and John—beg pardon, Captain Beattie—insisted I bring him here.'

She followed Captain Tyler to the first stretcher, where the Royal Marine lay, his uniform coat half on, half off, exposing a bloody bandage on his right arm. Anna knelt beside him and touched his shoulder lightly.

He opened his eyes. 'I told the captain it was nothing, but he insisted,' he said. She heard pain in his voice. 'Arguing with officers is against the rules. Breaking rules is what got me busted in rank, and I doubt I can get lower than a private.'

She couldn't help smiling at that. 'What's your name?'

'Private David Bartleby at your service, ma'am. I'll be all right.' He looked to the other stretcher, where Dan Tyler stood looking down at the occupant. '*He's* the one to worry about.'

'The Marine is right,' Captain Tyler said, speaking softly. '*This* man is here to die.' He passed his hand across his eyes. 'He's my second-in-command, my sister's husband and father of two daughters. I wish to God I could stay with him, but I must return to my ship.'

She knelt beside the wounded man, hesitated for the smallest second, then took his hand. He opened his eyes in that drowsy way that she had seen years before when her own father died.

'Joel Watt is his name,' Captain Tyler whispered.

'Joel,' she said. 'I'll take good care of you. You're on Menorca and in my house.'

Joel nodded like a dutiful child and closed his eyes. She made no objection when Captain Tyler's hand went to her shoulder. Obviously, more than one man needed tending.

'Beg pardon, Mrs Beattie.'

'No worry, Captain Tyler,' she said. 'I wish you could stay, too, but I know you must return to the fight.' She hoped she sounded calm and in charge, even as her heart raced as she thought of *Swallow* alone against *La Guerre*.

He pointed to the other stretcher. '*This* man from my ship has a leg injury. We both thought it best he come here, too. You're not in too bad a shape, are you, Billy?'

'No, sir, not at all,' was the cheerful reply, to Anna's relief. 'Can't move too fast, but you might argue that's my specialty, Captain.'

Captain Tyler smiled. 'You're a talented malingerer, but damned useful when sails flap and no one else climbs as fast as you do. Billy Whitlow is a foretopman, Mrs Beattie, damned cheeky and... Ah, here we are.' The Durands arrived with cots. 'Let me help.'

Anna hurried upstairs to her newly organised linen closet for sheets and pillows while Hector and Captain Tyler set up the cots. Madame Durand followed at a slower pace, ready to complain. 'More work and worry for us,' she said. 'I thought those ships had surgeons.'

'Some do, if large enough.' Anna remembered Grace Fillion of the Drake, and her calm message from what seemed like years ago, but which rang fresh in her mind and heart: *This is how we fight Napoleon.* 'I will tend the injured,' Anna said. 'You will cook more, and that is that.'

'I'm sounding like John,' she whispered to Captain Tyler after the housekeeper glared at her and turned on her heel with a great swish of skirts. 'When did that happen?'

'Ah, the fierce Royal Navy! Then we're all in good hands,' he joked, despite the circumstances. 'I'll help you.'

He was no expert at spreading sheets and tucking them just so, but she knew that wasn't Captain Tyler's lot in ordinary times. She stood quietly to one side when they transferred the wounded to cots from stretchers. She arranged pillows behind heads and got grateful smiles from the two less seriously wounded men. 'I'll be close by and you can tell me what you need,' she whispered to them as the captain knelt by his brother-in-law and kissed his forehead.

He stood there a moment, then turned towards her, his expression resolute. *I recognize that captain's look*, she thought, her heart going out to him.

She could almost feel his sorrow when he took her arm again in the doorway. She put her hand over his, and waited.

'He's a good man, my brother-in-law,' he began, not looking at her because she knew he couldn't bear eye contact at the moment—not this man. 'John told me to bring him here and said you would watch over him until death.'

'He was right. I will,' she replied, showing no fear because she felt none. This was *her* war to fight.

Captain Tyler squeezed her hand. 'He might call you Patience. That's my sister's name.'

'You said Joel and Patience have two girls.'

'Yes, Grace and Charity.' He did smile then, an apologetic smile. 'Aye, Mrs Beattie, we're of that firm Puritan stock with names you might consider quaint, but we can swear as good as your Royal Navy types.'

She smiled, too. He needed that. She waited.

'If you could tell him that Grace and Charity are well, and…and anything that comes to mind.'

'I will. Do not fear, Captain.'

'Bravo, Mrs Beattie. John says you're the kindest lady he ever met, and you have a cord of steel as a backbone. I would never argue with him.'

'Good thing.' No need for this sorely tried captain to even suspect that her backbone felt like blancmange right now.

He motioned his men out of the door. She stood with him, allowing him a moment of silence.

He surprised her then, leaning closer to whisper. 'This is for you alone. That Royal Marine? Nothing's wrong with him. John sent him for your protection. He said to trust no one. If you can tell me anything I need to know, now's the time.'

She whispered to him about the two torches that John had assumed meant a warship was in port. 'Pru confirmed those two torches when *Swallow* docked, and the one burning after he left. John was right in his surmise,' she said.

'He told me, and yes, he was right. We were jumped when *Swallow* was still in port. He put it together, but gives you and Pru all the credit.' He gave her a playful kiss on the cheek, that Yankee. 'Perhaps your Admiral Collingwood should summon you to his flagship for official duty.'

'Captain Tyler...' she began, then reconsidered. 'I trust you, too.'

He gave her a little bow, tears in his eyes.

Chapter Thirty-Five

'John Beattie, thank you from the depths of my heart,' Anna whispered as the wagon pulled away, taking Captain Tyler and the stretcher-bearing *Hartford* sailors back to the harbour, their ship, the sea, the war.

She stood in the doorway of the sitting room, watching her patients, who seemed to be sleeping. *I am no nurse*, she thought. *John, did you really tell Dan Tyler that I have a cord of steel for a backbone? I wish I did.*

What did wounded men need? Water, she told herself, and went to that Holy of Holies, Madame Durand's kitchen, where, to her astonishment, she heard the Durands in a heated argument. Maybe French just sounded more heated than English? Come to think of it, she had heard scarcely two words from Hector, and here he was, obviously holding his own. This shouting match carrying on behind a closed door reminded her how little she knew about the Durands, beyond Madame's questions, and the usually silent Hector.

She waited. When silence ruled again, she knocked on

the door and opened it with a smile. Might as well brazen it out.

'Madame Durand, could you please help me locate three carafes? I need water and a glass for each man. Heaven knows I get cranky when I am thirsty, so I can only imagine how they must feel.'

They both looked at her with frowns. As her insides churned, she gave them a calm face in return. Madame Durand yielded, with Hector pasting his usual morose expression back on his face.

'I will help you, Madame Beattie,' the housekeeper said, sounding less than eager. She added her own demand. 'I am no nurse. These men are *your* task.'

'I will manage them,' Anna said quietly. 'I would like you to make a cream soup, something to soothe patients used to much coarser fare. Consommé as well. The carafes, please.' She waited, knowing how easy to please she usually was, but hoping the caretakers heard in her tone that she also expected obedience.

'Very well,' Madame Durand said after a wait that Anna thought bordered on insolence.

'You are all kindness,' Anna replied coolly. 'I will take these glasses and you will bring carafes.' She left the kitchen, closing the door and waiting a moment to hear if the argument resumed. It did, but lower in volume.

I am in charge, she thought as she walked back to the sitting room. Every nerve in her body wanted her to throw open the front door and run and swim until she found the *Swallow*, but that was unwise and she knew it.

She watched three sleeping men. As she stood there,

the Marine opened his eyes and winked at her. She came closer to him, wanting to feel brave. He seemed to know, and whispered, 'Mrs Beattie, I will always be here between you and that door.'

She touched his shoulder, supremely grateful. He had given her the gift she needed: courage.

She looked at the foretopman, who snored, then sat beside Captain Tyler's brother-in-law. His breathing was shallow and his eyes half closed, as if he hadn't the strength to command his eyelids. *Poor man*, she thought, then murmured, 'Joel, I will stay by you.'

Madame Durand came in soon with water, which she set by each cot. She stood longest by Joel, shaking her head and saying, 'A hopeless case.' She must have spoken too loudly, because Joel flinched. Whether he heard her meanness, or just the loud sound, Anne could not tell, but she stroked his arm and he seemed to relax.

'Patience, I was hoping you would come.'

God in heaven, give me courage.

'Certainly, I did,' she said softly.

'You always do,' he replied sleepily.

'Just rest, my dear,' she said. 'Would you like some water?'

She put her arm behind his head and raised him slightly. He sipped, but most of the water ran out the sides of his mouth.

'So good,' he told her as she blotted his face. 'Patience, you're a wonder.'

He slept then, to her relief. Madame Durand was long

gone, and Anna knew the Marine was watchful. *I can do this*, she told herself.

Later, she heard the front door open and knew the children were home from the parish school. Hector must have warned them, because they came into the sitting room quietly, hesitantly, looking for her. She beckoned them closer.

'Papa and Captain Tyler want us to tend these men,' she said. 'Madame has luncheon for you. When you finish, come back to me.'

Allan nodded. Anna sighed to see his eyes so apprehensive, much like the first time she'd seen him.

Pru must have noticed. She put her hand on his shoulder. 'I'll take care of you,' she told him. 'Missy is busy, but she is here and she will never leave us.'

He nodded and hurried from the sitting room, that pleasant place where they had spent recent evenings reading and playing jackstraws and cat's cradle, while Anna mended and darned.

Pru took her time. 'What is his name?' she whispered, knowing far better than Madame Durand about keeping a quiet voice around the wounded.

'Joel Watt,' she whispered back. 'Pru, he thinks I am his wife, Patience. He has two daughters, Grace and Charity.'

Pru did something she had never done before; she kissed her cheek. 'When you are tired, Mama, I can sit here and be Grace.' She kissed her again. 'Or Charity, but now I am hungry. I'll be back.'

You called me Mama again. Anna closed her eyes in

gratitude, touched to her soul at the resilience of the child. She felt gratitude for even this terrible war, which had brought her a husband she knew she adored now, and a son and daughter she'd never thought to have.

'I can manage anything,' she whispered, her lips barely moving. 'I will never be alone.' She looked down at the gravely wounded man whose hand she held. 'You will not be alone either, Joel Watt. Your family is here from America.'

For two long days and nights, Anna kept her vigil beside the dying man. She wiped his face and read to him from *Psalms*, because one midnight during his agony he gasped, '...my shepherd I shall not want,' and she knew exactly what to say. There were moments when she wished him dead, not for her relief, but to liberate him from one more second of pain she could not subdue.

Joel rallied again and again, speaking to her in a nearly normal voice about good times he remembered, and reminding Patience, sitting beside him now, of their courting days. When Pru joined her after parish school, he called her Grace. Pru read to him so Anna could curl up on the floor beside the cot for a moment of sleep, and even weep because the real Patience wasn't there to hear her husband's declarations of love in a voice growing ever fainter.

Lying there but watchful, Billy Whitlow, *Hartford*'s injured foretopman, requested a length of rope for Allan to learn his knots. They all listened to stories from a wistful man who missed a rocky place called Maine, where winters were long and cold, and many boys went to sea because they heard of warm tropic lands with mermaids, if you knew where to look.

In his own way, the Royal Marine watched over them, reminding Anna to eat when Madame Durand, subdued now and nearly as silent as her husband, brought cream soups and puddings for them.

Pru even worked up the courage to ask Private Bartleby if he wanted her to change his dressing. 'Your bandage looks so bloody,' she said. 'If Mama teaches me, I could make it better.' He kindly assured her that it wasn't so bad.

When Allan and Pru went to their own beds, Private Bartleby assured Anna that his arm was perfectly fine, the bandage 'borrowed' from a sailor who didn't need it any more. 'Never think for a moment, dear lady, that I cannot protect you all.'

On the fourth day, even the Royal Marine couldn't protect Joel Watt, first mate on the *Hartford*, husband of Patience Watt, father to two fine daughters. Death came calling. It came gently, though, almost apologetically.

Joel had been silent all morning, after a long, long night of speaking to Patience, even urging her to remarry if she found another good man. 'Just remember, dear lass, that I will be waiting for you in a far better place than this one.' He pressed Anna's hand with surprising force. 'Never doubt that,' he said quite distinctly. 'You are my dearly beloved.'

He said no more. Weary beyond belief, Anna rested her head on Joel's chest.

To her everlasting gratitude, the Marine knelt beside

her and put Joel's hand on her head. 'There now,' he said. 'It will only be a moment. I've seen this before.'

Joel's slow breathing stopped, then started again. There was one last breath that when released like a long sigh took the *Hartford*'s first mate with it. Done. Peace.

Private Bartleby moved Joel's hand onto his chest and folded his other hand on it. He sat beside the cot and pulled a weeping Anna onto his lap. 'I've never seen such kindness as you have shown, you and Pru.'

'I didn't even know him,' she said into his chest.

'He never knew that. You were his Patience,' he assured her. 'I'm too worldly-wise to be amazed at women, but by God, I am.'

She sat up to see the foretopman watching them. Even in her mental and physical exhaustion, she saw nothing in his expression but determination.

He spoke to the Royal Marine. 'You and I are from different nations but we are not so different. Let's finish this fight with *La Guerre*.'

'That will depend on the next move Captain Beattie makes,' Private Bartleby said. 'It will be bold and right.'

And dangerous, Anna thought. *Please, God, I love him.* She thought of Cathy's note, left behind and probably missed, and her lovely portrait on the Swallow. *What about you, John Beattie? Do you love me? Can you?*

Chapter Thirty-Six

First Lieutenant Joel Watt was coffined and buried the next day. There was no funeral, only the quiet burial of a sailor far from his native land, watched over by Mrs John Beattie and her children, Pru and Allan.

Private Bartleby, Royal Marines, whispered to her that he wanted mightily to attend, to keep his word to Captain Beattie that he would watch over Anna with his very life. Ever practical, Anna reminded him that he needed to maintain the fiction that he was wounded.

'I am counting on you and the foretopman to be convincing invalids while we see a good man to his grave.'

'Are you always this stubborn?'

'I have only been this stubborn since a certain captain knocked on my door last January,' she told him.

'Very well then,' he grumbled, pulling up his blanket and facing the wall like a spoiled child. 'Mind you, if I didn't greatly respect your husband, I...'

'Private Bartleby, do shut up,' Anna said, but kindly. 'Trust *me*.' She thought she heard him laugh.

Hector glowered at her when she insisted they accompany him and the coffin to St Matthew's burial ground beside the church. She held firm. To her surprise, he relented, even though he made them sit low in the wagon bed next to the coffin, and not on the driver's seat.

'I don't mind,' Anna told Pru and Allan. She patted the side of the coffin. 'I feel as though we know Joel by now.' She couldn't help a smile. 'After all, Pru, you and I have been his imaginary relatives.'

'Monsieur Durand could have been less rude to you about it,' Pru grumbled.

'No matter. We'll hunker down here. I'd rather be out of sight than sitting up there and smelling Hector.'

When they pulled up to the Anglican burial ground beside St Matthew's, he climbed from the wagon seat, speaking loudly, as if he had no respect for the dead. '*Mon fils, enterrons cet homme.*'

Anna couldn't see who he was speaking to, sitting as they were on the other side of the coffin. The response of, '*Oui, père, comme vous voulez,*' equally meant nothing, except... *I know that voice*, she thought, racking her brain over 'feece' and 'pear', which sounded vaguely familiar.

She pulled both children closer, and whispered in Pru's ear. 'Do you know that voice?'

Pru nodded. 'Mama, I have wondered how Mr Brown knows French,' she replied, her voice soft as a breath. 'I have heard him speaking French to other men, when he is outside the classroom.' She frowned. 'Should I have told you?'

'Don't worry,' Anna whispered.

Pru is right, she thought. *Many people know some*

Spanish, French and English on a place like Menorca. It is nothing.

Except it was everything, because she did know *feece* and *pear*. She heard them often, mainly because Madame Durand was prone to drama. Only yesterday, she had gone quietly to the kitchen for more water, and startled Madame. The housekeeper had jumped and crossed herself, muttering something which had to be, 'Father, Son and Holy Ghost.' Madame Durand said it often, over both minor and major irritations. Father. *Père.* Son. *Fils. Saint Esprit.* Holy Spirit.

Hector Durant and Hal Brown are father and son? Surely, this cannot be, she thought, astonished and wanting to be wrong because it was absurd. Surely, she'd let her imagination get away from her.

The men spoke in lower tones. Anna peered around the coffin and put her hand to her mouth. Hector had finally removed his nasty cap and she saw two heads together, two red heads of that handsome auburn colour she'd admired on Mr Brown the schoolteacher.

Father and son whispered together before her eyes. Frightened of this knowledge and all it implied, she had no choice but to act as though she hadn't heard a thing. She sat back against the coffin, feeling a powerful sense of protection from the casket that harboured a good man gone too soon.

'Here I go,' she murmured. She coughed several times, waited a moment, then stood up in the wagon, making herself visible, where before she had been hidden from view. There they were, father and son. Hector must have replaced his cap when she'd coughed so deliberately, giving him time to do precisely that.

She willed herself to be calm, composed, and never someone demanding attention, the person she had been all her life until John had entered her life.

'Mr Brown,' she said. 'Do help me down, please. I have been tending poor Lieutenant Watt since the *Swallow* brought some wounded men to Admiral Collingwood's house. How fortunate we are to have an Anglican church here on Menorca for his burial.' She held out her hand to the teacher, willing it not to shake.

'How kind of you to come along, Mrs Beattie,' he said in that perfectly accented English she had heard for weeks and never questioned.

'We wanted to be here,' she replied as he swung down the children. 'The poor man is a long way from his home in the United States, but what can one do in this time of war?'

'Indeed.' He indicated the long inlet below them, then folded his hands. 'On the morning of the Resurrection, the American will have a welcome view from here.'

'I doubt there is a lovelier view,' she replied, and meant it. Then she noticed something that explained everything. Only the greatest force of will kept her from gasping.

Directly below them was that sailing dinghy, the one that had inspired her to suggest to Mr Brown that he might like to learn how to fish. She put the whole awful truth together in her mind. She looked towards Port Mahon proper from the burial ground, and found herself gazing directly at the slip where the *Swallow* moored for every call in port. The man who lit the torches must be Hal Brown, son of Hector Durand, the caretaker who knew what was going on in Admiral Collingwood's house. Father and son, *pere et fils*.

She looked down at the dinghy. It didn't take a genius to notice that anyone could see the Royal Navy ship dock, then, when it was dusk, row across the inlet in that dinghy and light two torches to warn some other ship further out, probably *La Guerre*. And with two flames to confirm the *Swallow* in port, the *Hartford* was fair game at sea.

So simple, so diabolical. What remained now was to mourn a good man, then casually return to Admiral Collingwood's house and talk to the Royal Marine.

Her heart racing, Anna watched the two gravediggers lean on their shovels as the old Rector of St Matthew's made a few comments about 'Ashes to ashes and dust to dust', then consigned this American, far from home and probably not an Anglican, to his final resting place. The gravediggers let down the coffin with ropes and packed down the dirt, standing back when the children spread their impromptu bouquet across the mound.

Anna watched them, forcing herself to appear the serene lady the Durands knew, and not a woman who had put together the truth. She left the daisies Allan handed her on the mound, wishing she could do more for Joel Watt.

'You're so far from home, you men who go to sea,' she said.

Hal Brown waved to them as they left the churchyard, after what Anna thought was a pointed look at the hunched-over Hector. Only moments ago, she would have thought she was imagining all this. She now knew she wasn't.

Madame Durand had luncheon ready on the sitting room's veranda this time. She took her time serving, as if not wanting to be out of earshot. Had Hector whispered something to her about father and son speaking in French and Mrs Beattie possibly overhearing? Anna prayed for a moment to speak to Private Bartleby, who was lying on his cot, watching her with a frown.

I swear I truly am a better actress than Sarah Siddons herself, she thought throughout the long afternoon. Rather than attempt a word with the Private, she took her basket of mending onto the veranda and darned stockings already darned. Pru and Allen weeded the flowerbed close by. Hector was not in sight. After an hour of this, Madame Durand shrugged and returned to her kitchen, but leaving the door open and peering out now and then.

Why didn't I notice that nosiness sooner? Anna asked herself as she took a moment to observe the other woman, then looked away, suddenly aware that Hal Brown bore a more-than-passing resemblance to their housekeeper, someone she trusted no more. It was a small thing, their cheekbones and the shape of their eyes, something she never would have noticed had father and son not stood together, heads with auburn hair nearly touching. *Now I know. How to tell the Royal Marine and not rouse suspicion, now that Madame is watching me?*

To Anna's relief, Private Bartleby found a totally innocuous way to end the impasse. 'Mrs Beattie, could you bring me more water?' he called to her. 'I know I should work up my nerve and have this nasty-looking bandage changed.'

Thank God. 'Yes, certainly,' she called back, dropping a thrice-darned stocking in the basket. 'One moment.'

In the kitchen, she drew water and chattered some inanity to Madame Durand about Marines who couldn't stand to touch a wound. She took her time leaving the kitchen, coming back with the small satchel John had left behind, which contained clean bandages and ointment. 'Would you care to help me, Madame?'

Remembering Madame Durand's revulsion at having anything to do with tending the men, Anna counted on that to be true, and not another Durand lie.

'*Mais non*, Madame Beattie,' she said. 'That is *your* task, remember.'

'I suppose it is,' Anna replied, pretending to make a face at the satchel.

She decided on a leisurely stroll back to the sitting room, pausing once to sniff the brightly coloured flowers in a vase in the front hall. *Be careful, Anna*, she told herself. *Take your time*.

She moved to Private Bartleby. As she unwrapped the bandage, she spoke softly of her knowledge that Hal Brown was no teacher, spoke beautiful French, and that it was probably he who lit the torches. 'I fear Hector has told his suspicions of me to Madame,' she concluded. 'I'm certain they are related to Hal.' She leaned closer. 'I'm covering your arm with a mere layer of gauze, then

I'm putting part of the bloody bandage on next, in case anyone checks to see if you have a wound.'

'Wise of you. Put several layers of clean bandage on top,' he said, 'although I doubt Madame will check.' He leaned closer, his voice as soft as hers. 'Does she suspect you know? Can you tell?'

'I don't think she does.' She managed a smile. 'She believes I am not so bright.'

'Then more fool her. Be wary.'

She finished the bandaging, leaving off plenty of the old bloody bandage to take into the kitchen and burn. 'There now, good as new,' she announced as Madame Durand entered the sitting room suddenly. 'Madame, would you throw this in the kitchen fireplace?' she asked, feeling great satisfaction when the housekeeper recoiled and backed away, making some excuse before she darted down the hall.

'That was successful,' Anna said to the Marine. 'Private Bartleby, what should we do?'

'First, call me David,' he said, which somehow calmed her mind.

He looked to the other cot, where the foretopman lay, propped up on his elbow, listening intently. 'Any ideas, Whitlow? We could use them.'

Oh, these cheeky Americans. Billy Whitlow, foretopman and apparent rascal, folded his arms across his chest. 'Private Bartleby, since you have no jurisdiction over me, I will confess that mine was a misspent youth. I stole and lied and raked around—beg pardon, Mrs Beattie—until my poor father sent me to sea, where I learned a trade.'

'I'm relieved,' the Marine replied. Anna heard the sarcasm. 'Say on, you miscreant.'

'I think tonight, when all is quiet, I will revert to my former trade and steal something.'

'What, pray tell?' Anna asked, almost—but not quite—entertained.

'A sweet little sloop I noticed in Port Mahon when Captain Tyler brought us here. Here's my plan: I will sail that sloop toward Mallorca, where, with any luck—and I might add that luck is *all* we currently have—I will encounter either the *Swallow* or the *Hartford* and tell them what is going on.'

He looked around, smiling beatifically. 'We're a rascally lot at times, we Americans.' He added, 'I wouldn't trust us, either.' His expression changed. 'Know this: I'm not badly injured at all. Captain Tyler wanted me here for the same purpose as you, Private Bartleby.'

'I'll be damned,' David said.

Billy turned serious eyes on them. 'I will never let you two down, nor any one on either of our ships. Word of honour.'

'And you have mine,' David said. 'I'd like to wring Hal Brown's neck, but that can wait. Can't afford to alert the Durands. Ending dirty doings on Mallorca is the bigger issue, where the French are assembling an army. We have to defeat *La Guerre*, but how?' He looked at Anna. 'Mrs Beattie? You have another thoughtful look on your face.'

Be careful, be careful, she wanted to say. *Oh, my, do we dare? Surely they've already thought of this.*

'What, Mrs Beattie?' David asked. 'Your husband told

me you have a fine mind. Nothing too audacious, though. We're mere mortals.'

'You might laugh...' she started.

'We could use a laugh,' Billy said. 'Say on.'

'Perhaps you audacious Americans could be the bait,' she said.

'Oh, harsh. And...?' he prompted.

'When you find your ship, tell Captain Tyler to dock in the *Swallow*'s slot. I suspect the two torches will flare, no matter which ship is there. Before he left, John told me he was going to sail close to the *Hartford*. Before Captain Tyler sails here, he can alert the *Swallow* to sail into our private inlet in the dark of night.'

'A lot of whens and ifs there, Mrs Beattie,' David cautioned.

'If you have a better idea, speak up,' she said sweetly, which made him wince.

'After a night here, Captain Tyler can sail out at dawn from Port Mahon. Normally, that would alert Mr Brown to cross the inlet to light one torch, which in turn would alert the watching *La Guerre* that the *Hartford* is coming out. The *Swallow* will still be nowhere in sight, but hiding here, in the inlet. Oh, dear, this sounds most unpleasant...'

David Bartleby was smiling now. 'Mrs Beattie, I believe you are a tactician worthy of Lord Nelson.'

'Nothing so grand,' she said modestly. 'You see what your role is to be, don't you?'

'I am to snap Brown's scrawny neck at St Matthew's before he can light one torch to indicate the one ship he knows of is leaving. *Hartford* will therefore sail out unexpectedly towards *La Guerre*, followed closely by the equally unexpected *Swallow*.' He laughed. 'Our battle begins, two to one this time.' David looked around, triumphant. 'We will have the advantage of surprise.'

'It's complicated,' she warned.

The three of them looked at each other. 'Is it aye or nay?' she asked.

'Aye, Mrs Beattie,' her heroes said in unison.

Chapter Thirty-Seven

Billy Whitlow, foretopman and reformed scoundrel, did indeed revert to his former ways. After a nearly sleepless night, Anna came downstairs in her robe and peeped in the sitting room. His cot was empty. David Bartleby gave her a thumbs-up. She tiptoed back upstairs, hoping the foretopman was as good a thief as he said he was, and hoping Hal Brown would take no interest in an ordinary sloop sailing from Port Mahon, something that happened all the time.

She dressed quickly, then hurried downstairs to the sitting room. 'David,' she whispered, 'has Madame Durand been in here yet?'

'Not yet,' the Marine replied. 'I suggest you make a big noise about Billy's disappearance so she is aware. I doubt the Durands will know what to do about this unexpected development.' He gave her a big smile.

She hurried to the kitchen, where the Durands were drinking their morning tea. 'Madame Durand, that American has left us!'

They ran into the sitting room, Anna right behind. 'I

came in here…' She turned to the Marine. 'Private Bartleby, did you hear anything?'

If she was the talented Sarah Siddons, then the Marine was Edmund Keane, Drury Lane's other darling. He groaned, sat up and rubbed his eyes. 'I had a bad night,' he said, pointing to his bandage, where blood oozed onto his wrist. 'It won't stop bleeding.'

Anna stared at the blood, and the odd whiteness of his face, the genuine look of a man in distress. She had no trouble bursting into tears, theatrical or not. The only thing that kept her functioning was his slow wink just for her.

'You are a rascal,' she said under her breath, when Madame Durand turned to her husband and spoke in rapid-fire French.

'But I am so damned good-looking,' he whispered back. 'Let's see how clever *you* are.'

So that was it? Wretched man. She glared at him, then, 'Madame Durand, please help. He is bleeding most profusely!'

That brought the response she prayed for. The housekeeper backed away. 'No, no! Hector and I must search the grounds for that American!' They ran from the room.

'Cowards,' David muttered.

Anna sat beside him on the cot. 'What did you do to your arm?'

'Nothing much. I stuck myself with this little penknife,' he told her, pulling it from under the sheet. 'Just a little poke. It has already stopped bleeding. Wipe it off after you smear it around a bit on the bandage. That should *keep* her away.'

'And what, pray tell, did you do to your face? You look like a dead man.'

'That good? Excellent. Allan had a stick of white chalk in his little drawing kit. He's copying that portrait of Admiral Collingwood over there, and I swiped it.'

'What should we do now?'

'We wait,' he said simply. 'If you're the praying type, you might encourage the Lord God Almighty to speed the foretopman on his way.'

It was a long, long day. Anna watched as Hector with surprising energy flogged his pony cart towards Port Mahon itself, more lively than she had ever seen him. She had no difficulty weeping and wringing her hands until even Madame Durand took pity on her and made her sniff smelling salts.

'Do let me know what Monsieur Durand learns in the port,' she begged as she batted away the assault of the smelling salts, nasty things. 'That awful Captain Tyler will blame me because I did not tend to his wretched sailor!'

Pru and Allan were regular rocks of Gibraltar. She calmly told them that the other invalid had decided to leave, and the Durands were hoping to find him. This was one time even Pru didn't need to know what was going on, and perhaps for Anna to remind herself that the stalwart girl was truly a child.

To keep him occupied, she asked Allan to continue his

chalk drawing of Admiral Collingwood. 'I think he will like that,' she told him.

This seemed like a good time to introduce Pru to embroidery, something Anna had no patience for, but had dutifully learned when she was Pru's age. 'We will begin with French knots,' she said. It quickly became a tangled mess, which gave them both the giggles. They blamed it on France, and laughed some more.

Two more days passed. Allan focused on adding Bounce the dog to his drawing, when he wasn't weeding the kitchen garden for Madame Durand, who took Anna aside after that first morning to whisper that Hector had learned the rascal had stolen someone's sloop.

'We won't see him again,' Anna agreed, sounding irritated, when inside she was collapsing with relief. Billy Whitlow had done what he'd said he would.

Two days. It felt like two years. At the end of the second long day she sat beside the Royal Marine, now pretending to run a fever, which kept Madame Durand further away from him. Another smear of chalk helped.

After tucking the children in bed, she returned to her vigil beside his cot. 'David, I have no patience with time,' she admitted. 'Don't laugh, but I keep wishing for some way to keep in touch with my husband.'

'You're a wishful thinker.'

'I told you it was ridiculous. Still…' she sighed '… I miss him. I worry.'

'Talk to me,' he said, and she did, telling him of the death of her brother after Trafalgar, how she had met her husband at his most desperate time, the scandal in Plymouth, and the kindness of Grace Fillion at the Drake.

She wasn't about to tell him how much she loved her husband. He knew enough. 'It's your turn,' she said after the clock struck midnight.

He told her he had been a sergeant in the Royal Marines, knocked down to private because he had married a girl from a Plymouth counting house. 'She's a grand lass, but I broke a rule. Marines may not marry without permission, and it is seldom granted.' He sighed. 'I should have been court-martialled and hanged, but your husband intervened. I am in his debt.'

She knew what to tell this man, sorrowing in front of her. 'You're repaying that debt now by keeping me from utter despair,' she said frankly, barely able to choke out the words. 'Where is your wife now?'

'I do know Maggie returned to her father's farm in Cornwall,' he told her. 'I may not write to her. It has been two years now. Dear God, so long.'

She took a mighty leap then, thinking of her husband, and gently put her hands over his eyes. 'There now. Go to sleep, David,' she said when she took away her hands, relieved to see that awful stare of war gone. 'Sleep now,' she said again, no command, but softly as she would to Allan or Pru.

'Only if you promise to do the same,' he said, then added, 'Thank you, kind lady.'

She left the room after a firm touch on his shoulder. Upstairs, she lay down and slept.

* * *

The third day began as the others had.

She sat quietly beside David, who, during the night, had rubbed more chalk onto his face and neck. It so unnerved Madame Durand that she refused to enter the sitting room. 'Mission accomplished,' he whispered to Anna.

She looked up from the sonnet she was reading aloud to hear banging on the front door.

'Friend or foe?' she asked him, frightened.

'Call the children over,' the Marine ordered. 'I'll defend you all to the death.'

She did as he said, gathering them close, then gasped when Captain Tyler stormed into the sitting room, dragging Billy behind him. The Durands peered over his shoulder.

She said nothing when Dan Tyler shook the chain binding the foretopman, at least until Billy Whitlow, thief of a sloop and perhaps the bravest man she knew, smiled at her. She glanced at Captain Tyler, who did the same and put a finger to his lips.

'Why did you bring this…this…rascal back to us, Captain Tyler?' she demanded, speaking for the benefit of the Durands, who stared from the doorway.

'I wanted you to know that this thief of someone's sloop—we have returned it to the port master—harboured the delusion that I would be happy to see him. Oh, no! I clapped this Yankee Doodle vermin in irons and I am taking him to the *Constitution*.'

'The *what*?' she asked, genuinely confused.

'The *Constitution*,' he repeated. 'It's a bonny man-o'-war, now in Tripolitan waters and sailing to America soon.' He gave the foretopman a good shake. 'He'll hang from the yardarm before we reach Gibraltar, if I have any say in the matter.'

His performance continued for the Durands as he addressed them. 'I want you to know, *madame* and *monsieur*, that my *Hartford* is now anchored in the slot reserved for the *Swallow*, and we sail in the morning. That is all. Come along, you wretched man! You have a date with a cat-o'-nine-tails, one hundred strokes at least!'

'We deeply appreciate knowing this,' Hector said.

'Thank you,' Dan Tyler replied. 'I will return to my ship, after I speak with this Marine.' He peered closer. 'He doesn't look so good, does he? Look at him!'

The Durands couldn't leave fast enough. Captain Tyler released Billy and knelt beside David's cot. 'Billy told me everything and all is well. I imagine that rascal teacher, who can see my ship from St Matthew's, will light two torches to inform *La Guerre*.' He motioned to Anna. 'Mrs Beattie, John knows. The *Swallow* will anchor tonight in your private inlet, as you suggested, all lights extinguished.'

She closed her eyes in relief.

'The *Hartford* sails tomorrow before dawn's light.' He turned to the Marine. 'I trust you will be at St Matthew's in time to prevent Hal Brown—or whatever his name is—from any signalling.'

'Nothing will make me happier than to wring a spy's neck,' David assured him with some glee. 'Both *Hartford* and *Swallow* will sail, with *La Guerre* none the wiser.' He rubbed his hands together. 'I'd love to watch that battle.'

'I wish you could. Private Bartleby, please assure me that you are actually healthier than you appear.'

'Sound of wind and limb, Captain Tyler. You needn't fear for Mrs Beattie and the children. I also have a good idea what I can do with the Durands right here.'

'Captain Beattie thought you might. Farewell to you all. If this venture goes as planned, we'll foul *La Guerre*'s anchor once and for all.'

Captain Tyler kissed Anna's cheek. 'Captain Beattie told me to do that for him, but really I did it for me!'

He left, dragging Billy Whitlow after him, cursing and swearing, in case the Durands were nearby. Anna sank into the chair by David's cot and pulled Pru and Allan close.

'Not a word of this,' she told them. 'We know nothing.'

'Not a thing,' Allan agreed.

Anna saw his anxiety; she felt it, too, but now was not the time to show anything but courage.

'I believe your father is close by.'

He hugged her. 'Mama, what if he doesn't return?'

'He will return, son,' she assured him, her heart full, the last barrier down. He had finally called her mother. She was his mama and knew, in the deepest part of her being, she always would be Mama to Allan Beattie. The strangeness of her life was sweetened and completed by that one word she'd never thought to hear from this child. Allan Beattie was her son, no matter what happened in the battle coming tomorrow. 'He will return, daughter,' she said to Pru, anchoring her, too, this wise child, this brave girl.

She looked at Private David Bartleby, no words needed. He had business with the schoolmaster.

Chapter Thirty-Eight

'After the children are asleep I need your help,' David whispered to Anna when she rose from the chair beside his cot, and sent the children to the veranda, promising them heaven knew what for dinner.

It was time to play the wide-eyed naïve lady again. She went into the kitchen, where the housekeeper stared at nothing, fidgeting with her household keys. Anna gathered every ounce of courage she possessed.

'Madame, I didn't expect to see Captain Tyler and that scoundrel foretopman again,' she said, striving for genuine amazement. 'Do you… May I help you provide some dinner for the little ones?' She shook her head. 'I do not think Private Bartleby is up for anything beyond consommé.'

Perfect. Madame Durand, no matter her level of plotting and secrecy, would always and forever be a cook. She banished Anna from her kitchen. Soon Anna heard the sound of pots and pans. The result was an excellent dinner that tasted like sawdust to Anna. The children enjoyed every bite.

She read to them in the sitting room, calm and serene, because she had no choice but to be the quiet lady the Durands thought wasn't bright enough to figure out anything. Let them think that.

She played cat's cradle with the children until thankfully Allan finally yawned, and even Pru started to droop. She took them upstairs and helped Allan into his nightshirt, one that only days ago she had cut down from one of his father's. *I will see you again, John, I will*, she thought fervently, even as the weight of the coming battle nearly ground her heart into powder.

She knew these clever little ones sensed something in the air and made a decision.

'Such a day this has been,' she said, holding their hands. 'I think you should share a room tonight. It's a nice thing to do when things are in a bit of commotion, don't you think?' She almost felt their relief. 'Goodnight, dears.'

She undressed slowly, not bothering to light even a candle in her room, thinking about her words and wishing she could share her own bed tonight. 'I honestly do not know what gets into women's brains when they decide to fall in love and marry a Navy man,' she announced to her mirror. 'It is a great malignancy.'

'Come now, Anna. You know you love me.'

Certain that wishful thinking was her downfall and she was sinking into imbecility, she took another look in the mirror and gasped.

There he was behind her, uniform flung onto a chair and looking pretty much as God had made him.

'John, would you mind if I pinch you?' she asked, coming closer to the bed. 'I really don't believe my eyes.'

'I'd rather kiss you here and there in random places. Will that do?'

He was right; the random places cheered her immensely. And who would have thought that the odour of brine was an aphrodisiac?

'I swear I am an easy mark,' she murmured as she settled herself next to him. 'Luckily, you're my husband and not some random stranger.'

He was silent, not wasting a moment as he gentled her onto her back. He kissed her lips, her breast, her stomach and that sweet spot that seemed to take on a life of its own. She sighed with relief when he moved inside her, and her legs knew exactly where to go. Sensible woman always, she knew nobody died of pleasure, not even a Navy wife without her man for too long. He kissed her when she started to moan. 'Shh, love,' he murmured, then buried his face into her shoulder to silence himself when his peak quickly followed hers.

If he had stayed like that forever she would have let him, but no. It was as though she saw Duty tapping his shoulder, maybe whispering in his ear as not long ago she'd wanted to whisper, *I love you*. But for once, Duty could wait. It was her turn now.

'John, I think I have loved you for quite a while, but…'

'I didn't make that easy for you, did I?' he asked grimly, and settled beside her. 'Anna, I owe you an apology.' He touched her face. 'I owe an apology to Cathy, too. What you said when you asked if I believed her when she told me to remarry…'

'It was wicked of me! I didn't mean to hurt your feelings,' she said. 'I shouldn't have…'

He stopped her words, a finger to her lips. 'You were entirely right. So was Cathy. I may have even used war and duty to avoid the simple fact that I am a good husband and I like being married.'

She kissed his fingers. 'John, don't you see?' she told him earnestly, and he smiled tenderly. 'Cathy only wanted you to be happy. You needed a little time to see it, too, and who has time to look during a war?'

'I *am* happy with you,' he said simply, and kissed her, wrapping himself around her. 'I will echo my late wife here: if something happens to *me*, don't stay a widow forever. What a waste of good love that would be.'

'I like being married, too,' she whispered in his ear. 'I love you, John Beattie.'

'And I love you, Anna,' he said. She heard his truth at last, as something finally settled in her heart, never to leave.

She felt him chuckle as he disentangled himself but didn't leave their bed. 'Now that you're not moaning in my ear, I hear Duty demanding my time.'

'Wretch! Ahem, I can be dutiful, too. May I assume that the *Swallow* is tucked away close by?'

'Aye, lass.' He laughed softly, keeping her close. 'In case you're interested in nautical matters now, my amiable wench, we're anchored in our inlet below the house.'

'How did you get into the house?'

'That veranda door leading into the sitting room never had a good latch,' he said. 'To be honest, I made sure it didn't when I left, and so informed Bartleby. He was waiting for me downstairs and helped me with something else that needed to be done.'

'Which was...'

'We must have been especially quiet.'

Anna sat up, nerves on edge. 'The Durands!'

He tugged her down. 'No worries. He met me with two hammers, long nails and three wicked-looking slats.'

She held her breath. 'Breathe,' he commanded. 'Monsieur was drunk so he was no problem. Marines are good at what they do! Bartleby stuffed a rag in Madame Durand's mouth and held her down with his knee on her back while I took off that rattling belt of keys and found the one to the pantry. I shoved the drooling Hector inside and Bartleby tossed in the woman. I locked them in, then we used those boards to secure the kitchen door. It's perfect. No windows. Food, so they can't complain we didn't feed them. Oh, and I took out a sack of bread for you three, and that wonderful stuff they make here and call *mahonnaise*.'

'Husband, you amaze me.'

He laughed and patted her shoulder. 'Anna, I never thought of myself as the swashbuckling type. I'm a captain in the Royal Navy, not a member of a pirate band. Believe it or don't, I am inclined towards modesty.' He shook his head. 'This adventure seems to have brought out my derring-do.'

'I'm not complaining,' she teased in turn. 'Write your

memoirs some day, if you have the nerve. Otherwise, when we're old and grey, no one will believe our sojourn on Menorca.'

He sat up. She knew what was coming and stood first, putting on her chemise, then taking his hand and kissing it.

'I know you cannot stay,' she said quietly, 'you and Private Bartleby.'

'He *is* staying here. I won't leave you defenceless. Thank you,' he said as she handed him his smallclothes. 'We of the *Swallow* owe him a great debt. He was there at the inlet when we sailed in, and told us to dock out of sight.' He shuddered. 'Good God, Marines. He cheerfully announced that he had twisted the schoolmaster's neck, so both torches would keep burning. Captain Tyler and the *Hartford* are pulling out about now. We're next.'

As he dressed, Anna tried to memorise everything about him, this confident lover, this highly skilled captain, who only months ago, as a distraught father, had knocked on her door and changed her life. There was nothing desperate about him now, and she rejoiced.

He held out his hand to her. 'Come, Anna. Toss on that dress and see me out.' He rubbed his hands together, partly, she suspected, to make her smile. 'I do like a good surprise. Imagine how surprised *La Guerre* will be.'

When he put on his uniform jacket, she tucked in Cathy's note. 'Keep it with you as long as you need it, dear heart,' she told him.

He patted the note. 'There is room for both of you, Anna.'

'I thought there might be,' she said softly. 'I do have a question, though.'

'You want to know how you are so lucky to have married such a prodigious lover? Eh? Is that it?'

'You are a rascal,' she said calmly. 'Where did Mrs Beattie go? You have called me that for so long.'

He bowed his head. When he looked up, she knew.

'Mrs Beattie was a convenient wife,' he said. 'She had her place. But Anna is my dear heart. And I am hers.'

Anna kissed him, just a simple kiss, until it filled their universe.

She went down the stairs with him, nodding to the Marine who stood at the foot. In fact, she held out her hand to him. 'None of this bowing,' she said simply. 'Shake hands with me, David.'

He shook her hand, glanced at her husband, then kissed her cheek. 'I'll keep them safe for you, Captain,' he said.

Her husband kissed her other cheek. 'You'll probably hear the battle, Anna,' he said. 'Be strong.'

'I will be. Go with God, dear heart.'

Chapter Thirty-Nine

Anna made herself comfortable on the steps, dozing as time passed, then waking when she heard the veranda door open. David stood there.

'It's done. We've just watched the *Hartford* sail.' He sat beside her. 'Your man is safely aboard the *Swallow*. I watched until they left the inlet.'

'I know you would rather be aboard the *Swallow*, but here you are.'

'I would rather,' he agreed, 'but I gave my word to a good man that I will protect you.' She saw his smile, even though the light was dim.

'Thank you with all my heart,' she said and gave his shoulder a nudge, which made him chuckle.

He stood up. 'Mrs Beattie, I am going to stay here and listen. I wish I could see *La Guerre* when it goes after the *Hartford*—prime bait—and finds the *Swallow* coming in right behind *her*.' He clapped his hands together once and loud. 'Your captain is probably smiling about that, because he knows there is not a ship afloat that isn't the most vulnerable when its stern is fired upon.'

'I'll sit with you,' she said. They sat in silence in the canvas chairs as the sun rose and the roar of cannon came with it, thunder from the sea by Mallorca and the village of Palma, because the sky was clear and it was another sunny day in the beautiful Balearics. He held her hand when she started to cry, worrying for her beloved husband, then gave it a squeeze when the roar grew fainter and finally stopped.

'Now we wait to see who won,' he said, mincing no words. 'The hardest part.'

When Pru and Allan woke up, Anna gave them an abbreviated outline of what had happened and made them sandwiches, which they ate on the veranda. Pru raised her eyebrows when she heard banging on the kitchen door, but Anna didn't comment beyond saying, 'The Durands are locked in.' Allan smiled and returned to his sketch of Admiral Collingwood. They were perfect Royal Navy children.

From the veranda, Anna waited. She prayed for a successful outcome, but braced herself for something else. She had two children to raise, no matter what, and so she stayed on the veranda, where she knew David watched her, too. The matter was out of her hands, so she bowed to Duty herself.

In late afternoon they heard the sound of carts coming towards Admiral Collingwood's wonderful house, bought for his family who never came to Menorca, and perhaps never would, but which had sheltered hers. She started for the front door, the Marine in front of her, Pru and Allen trailing after them. She stared hard at the door.

'You or me?' David said as the sound of carts grew louder.

She reached for the knob as she heard singing. It was the chorus of *Heart of Oak*, something her brother Will had sung every time he returned from sea. She always sang with Will and she sang now, the door still closed.

'... Steady boys, steady! We'll fight and we'll conquer again and again.'

She opened the door and there he stood. 'Dearest heart,' she said in her practical way and opened her arms wide.

As they clung together, sailors, officers and Marines poured into the house, all of them smelling of black powder and sweat. She looked around John's arm to see Admiral Collingwood himself, and ran to him, giving him a hug as he lifted her off her feet.

'Anna, earlier, I sent Admiral Collingwood my plan for battle,' her husband said, watching them. 'Who should arrive off Mallorca but our esteemed leader? And in a sloop-of-war, no less.'

'Aye, my dear,' the Admiral told Anna. He set her down with a bow. 'It took me back to my fighting days with the Royal Navy in Boston.' He rubbed his hands together. 'I like a fast sloop-of-war and never mind leaving my boring flagship.'

'Aye, the Frenchies were indeed building a fort near Palma. Shall we say they were less than happy to offer the sword of surrender to our admiral,' John said. Anna heard all his affection. *La Guerre*'s captain admitted that he had positioned his ship's sailing dinghy close to

Menorca, which kept him informed of who came in and out of Port Mahon.'

'Mrs Beattie, you should have seen us!' Admiral Collingwood said, then nodded to John. 'Captain, don't ever seek to be an admiral. All the fun is gone!'

From the comfort of her sooty man's arms, she sneezed at the powder and smiled to see Captain Tyler of the *Hartford*, followed shortly by Billy Whitlow, reformed sinner and foretopman and certainly not in chains. Soon the hall was full and the sitting room as well, with victorious men piling out onto the back lawn, most to simply lie in the grass, exhausted.

John welcomed them all in, then took her hand. 'Look who else we found, Anna.'

She turned to see Sofia Callona, who held out her arms for a tight embrace.

'We were more than lucky,' John said, and gestured in an older couple with that look she recognised now of people who had suffered greatly. 'These are Sofia's parents. They were being held in that fortress the French were building near Palma. Captain Tyler was so right about that.'

'I am heading back to my flagship as soon as I can gather my crew together,' Admiral Collingwood said. 'The Callonas will come with me to the *Queen*. A Fast Dispatch Vessel will take them to England and safety.'

I wish it could take you, too, Admiral, Anna thought, touched at the way he looked around, as if imagining his own family greeting him there in his Menorca house.

Anna kept her arm around Sofia, who shyly introduced

her to her parents. She whispered to Anna, 'I will never again compose a list of demands, no matter how irked I get.' She shuddered. 'The French did not treat us well.' But she was still Sofia. 'They are *not* good hosts.'

'I am certain you are right, Sofia,' Anna assured her, trying not to smile.

A few words from the admiral to his particular crew partially cleared out the room. He smiled at the good-natured groans from the more high-spirited among them, shaking his head when the Marines thought to move everyone along faster. 'Let them take their time,' he said. 'It was a glorious fight.' He slapped Captain Beattie on the back. 'There's a commendation coming your way, and I have a plan, if you and your pretty wife are amenable.'

'Sir?'

'I like the idea of the *Swallow* establishing a permanent base here at Port Mahon, perhaps with another ship as well—maybe the one I borrowed—to continue keeping an eye on things.' He nodded to Captain Tyler. 'I don't think your country and ours are quite ready to become allies, but you're welcome to drop in now and then.'

'Thank you, sir, but no,' Tyler said. 'All the same, I greatly enjoyed the privilege of working with Captain Beattie.'

'It was my privilege, too, Captain Tyler. We're both anchoring here tonight, Admiral. Captain Tyler sails for Tripoli tomorrow.'

'Oh?'

'Yes, Admiral. I have orders to rejoin the American fleet. The USS *Constitution* is sailing home, now that there is a treaty in place with the Tripolitan pirates. We are part of that escort.' His expression turned rueful. 'I will miss our particular war, Captain Beattie.'

'As will I,' John said. 'Thank you. That matter we spoke of?'

'I understand you,' Captain Tyler replied, then gave a nod to Anna. 'Take good care of him.'

'I will,' she said, resting her cheek against her husband's hand on her shoulder.

Captain Tyler didn't bow to Admiral Collingwood. Anna didn't expect him to. 'Admiral, I know our countries have had their differences. Things may change in the future.'

'Very well,' Collingwood said. 'We will leave it at that. You Americans are a bloodthirsty lot, born in battle. I saw that with my own eyes in Boston at Bunker Hill. Thank you for your service today.'

'It was an honour, Admiral.' As he left, Captain Tyler couldn't seem to resist. 'I'll give a good report of the Royal Navy to Tommy Jefferson!'

'Scoundrel!'

The *Hartford* and some of the *Swallow* crews climbed in the wagons to return to the port and their ships, safe now from flaming torches with signals. Admiral Collingwood lingered longer with his own crew, nodding his approval when his Royal Marines knocked down the barrier in the kitchen and dragged out the Durands.

'Clap 'em in irons when we're aboard the *Queen*,' Collingwood ordered. He whispered to John, 'I might just throw them overboard.'

'Not yet, sir, if you please,' her husband said. He took a battered letter from his uniform jacket. 'I will give this to you to forward to the Admiralty. Please read it, sir.'

As he read, Anna watched Collingwood's eyes widen, then narrow, making her suddenly grateful she never had to stare at him across an enemy deck in battle or at a court martial. He tapped the letter, cleared his throat and waved it in front of the Durands. 'Spies! To think that I hired you to take care of my house. I trusted you.'

She glanced at her husband to see him watching her, his eyes filled with that look of desperation she had hoped to never see again. *Betrayal of trust. I wish I could cover your eyes*, she thought, *and yours, Admiral Collingwood, and mine, and maybe everyone who is at war.*

Another glance at her husband proved that he knew precisely what she was thinking. He put his hand to his lips and to his heart. She did the same. It was enough for now in this public place, and it gave her the courage to ask, 'Admiral, who is the note from? Is it secret, or may I know?'

'My dear, it is signed with the initial N, from Napoleon himself.' He stared again at Madame Durand. 'It's brief, ordering you Durands to spy on us—I include your son and *La Guerre*—and cripple us here in Port Mahon, to give your master Bonaparte time to fortify Mallorca and control the Mediterranean. Damn you all.'

No one spoke. Somehow, it did not surprise Anna that Private Bartleby filled the awful silence by stepping forward and saluting. He had nothing to lose. 'Admiral, if I may speak to the Durands?'

'Why not? You here suffered more than most. Victory makes me inclined to let anyone say anything, especially to duplicitous scoundrels. Say on, Private.'

'*Monsieur* and *madame*, it gives me great pleasure to inform you that your son met a fitting end when I nabbed him as he was about to get into that sailing dinghy.'

Madame Durand shrieked in fury. Anna swallowed. Her anger subsided, but not entirely. She was not a lady to make a scene or call attention to herself. Still… She took a step towards the woman, this spy, who with her husband and son had caused so much death and commotion.

'I trusted you, Madame Durand,' was all she said.

'You fool!' came Madame's vicious reply. She stared at Anna, who did not flinch. '*Vive la France,*' Hermione Durand said, her voice menacing, then rising. '*Vive l'Empereur!*'

'He will not win, Madame Durand,' Anna said firmly. 'He will never possess these islands.'

'Get them out of our sight,' Captain Beattie commanded. 'Now.'

The Marines led the Durands away. Admiral Collingwood gestured to the door and John and Anna walked with him.

'Once I return to my flagship, you'll have official orders to remain in this town. Find housing in Port Mahon proper, where you can keep an eye on the *Swallow* when she docks.' He looked around. 'I am going to sell this place.'

Poor, poor man, she thought.

Collingwood lifted his hat to them. 'Carry on, Captain Beattie. It's a long war and there is more to come. I expect good things of you in this post.'

'I will never disappoint you, sir.'

'Neither of you will.' He touched Anna's cheek. 'Cherish this dear wife of yours, Captain. You are a very lucky man.' He bowed and left them.

John kissed her cheek. 'He has smoothed our way, my love. I doubt the world will ever revere him as it revered Admiral Horatio Nelson, God rest his soul. I will always honour Collingwood, too.'

John sent most of his crew back to the *Swallow* with the Admiral, assuring Mr Marsing that he would join them by morning at the dock in Port Mahon for a return to Mallorca, where the clean-up continued.

'They might be the enemy, but they deserve decent burials,' he told Anna. 'I'll find you and our children a good place in Port Mahon. I already have one in mind.' He nodded to David Bartleby. 'He'll stay with you, too. I want you protected.'

'You'll get no argument from me,' Anna said.

'Now I will have my steward cobble together a meal for us few remaining here.'

It was enough of a meal to satisfy them all. She listened as the remaining crew refought the battle, marvelling at the courage of the brave sailors of the Royal Navy performing a hard duty, with no end to war in sight.

With the meal over and dishes done—everyone pitched in, even the Captain—John sent his remaining crew to the sitting room. 'Rest for a minute, men,' he told them. 'I need a moment with two sailors, and then you can return to the *Swallow*. Baird and Catherwood, come with me,' he said. 'Come, too, Anna and Private Bartleby.'

She watched Baird and Catherwood, wondering if her husband was going to ask them to join their household on Port Mahon. When the sailors glanced at each other, she saw fear. David just looked puzzled.

John led them to the lawn, out of hearing, and wasted no time, surprising Anna by speaking to her. 'Peter Baird and William Catherwood are Americans. I know your brother spoke of impressing American seamen from Yankee ships we boarded, upon occasion. We forced them to join our crew when our need was great. We gave them no choice.'

'It seems unkind,' she murmured. 'That's what Will thought, too.'

'I know. We frequently argued about the matter. However, the needs of the Royal Navy must be satisfied, whether or not you or I like it.' He leaned closer. 'I hope you still love me.'

'John, don't be silly,' she chided, which made even the Americans laugh.

'It is this: Peter and William, when you return to the *Swallow* tonight, you will be a short swim away from *Hartford*, which you heard Captain Tyler say is returning to America.' He took a deep breath. 'If you swim to *Hartford*, I will miss your good work for *Swallow*, delivered even under duress. You may stay or leave.'

'Are you serious, sir?' Peter Baird said, as if he could not believe his ears.

'Completely.' He turned to Anna. 'You need to know

this, dear lady. If word leaks out that I engineered their escape—providing they choose to leave—I will be court-martialled and likely hanged.'

'Dear God,' she whispered, wondering at this husband of hers, astounded at such courage. No wonder Will had stayed with him until death. She spoke calmly, deliberately. 'I thought I could not love you more, but I do.'

'It's the right thing to do, Anna.' He looked at the Americans. 'You gave me your good work, even when you had no choice. Choose now.'

'I will swim,' Peter Baird said with no hesitation. 'I miss my country.'

'Godspeed you. Captain Tyler will be watching for you. He'll hide you, if needs be.'

John turned to William Catherwood. The sailor looked down, then at his captain. 'I believe I will stay, sir.' He smiled. 'There's a girl in Plymouth. I want to see her again.'

'Very well. Thank you both. Not a word to anyone, please.' He clapped his hands. 'Look lively now. Take the wagon back to the *Swallow* with the others. If anyone wonders what we talked of, say I gave you a royal scolding for some misdemeanour and it was brutal.'

'Aye, sir,' the Americans said in unison. They draped their arms around each other's shoulders and walked back to the house.

'Go along with them to the *Swallow*, Private Bartleby,' John said, 'then return here. But first, a word.'

'Sir?'

'Admiral Collingwood will endorse that your rank be

restored to Sergeant and forward his request to the Admiralty. Can you find that wife of yours in Cornwall?'

Anna couldn't help her tears now, not with all the devotion David Bartleby had shown her and the children, protecting them every moment her husband had been away, complaining about nothing, even though his own lot was bitter.

'Sir, I don't know what to say,' David said, clearly overcome.

'Knowing you, you'll think of something, Private Bartleby, and perhaps test my patience again.'

'Well, there's that...'

'I have another request.' He kissed Anna's head. 'The Admiral has given me leave to continue to provide protection for my dear ones. When you find your wife, she has my permission to come with you to Port Mahon and help Anna with our household.' He gave her a nudge. 'There might eventually be more children to tend.' He raised his eyebrows at the Marine. 'Perhaps yours, too? Go on with you now. Get my crew back to the *Swallow*. I'll join them in the morning.'

'Aye aye, sir!' David snapped to attention, turned and whistled his way into the house.

Anna put her arms around her husband. 'You make me weak-kneed.'

He picked her up and she wrapped her legs around him, not caring if anyone in the house was watching. It was dark, and she doubted that his young crew thought someone as 'old' as the captain had a body or passions.

'Does that help?' he asked. 'Anna, I could sleep for a

week, but I don't think I will tonight. The world thinks sailors are a randy lot and I believe I will keep proving it.'

They laughed. He set her down, and they started a slow walk to the house. Pru and Allan stood waiting by the veranda door. She stopped, wanting one more private word with her husband.

'John, do you ever feel lucky, I mean, really lucky? Even now, when the world is at its worst?'

'Lately, all the time,' he told her. 'No man could be more content.'

'You said before that we are the only two people in the universe. I understand that now and I rejoice, my dear Captain.'

'Anna—I have a favour to ask.'

'Ask away.'

'I know there is a portraitist in Port Mahon. When I return, would you have a portrait painted of yourself for me to take on the *Swallow*?'

Anna let herself be enveloped in her dear husband's embrace. 'I could stay like this with you forever,' she whispered. 'Yes. A portrait.'

'Know this, my love,' he said. 'You found a broken man on your doorstep in Plymouth, took him in and made him whole. I had no idea what would happen when I knocked on your door.'

'I didn't either,' she assured him, then couldn't help a laugh, because she was still Anna and prone to humour. 'I would like a portrait of you, too, you know, just to remind me how handsome you are, if, well, someone else knocks on my door and you've been at sea too long.'

They laughed together. 'I can see we will need a secret knock,' Captain Beattie teased in turn.

'Do be serious,' she joked.

'All right. As for those only two people in the universe?'

'Anna and John?'

'So we are, my dearest love. So we are.'

Epilogue

October 9, 1806

Dear Grace,
My friend, since my last letter, such good news! I'm sick every morning. If John is in port, he winces, then grins like a Rock Ape. 'It will pass, dear heart,' he says. 'Let me get you some ship's biscuit. You'll keep that down.' Then, drat his hide, he adds, 'Weevils and all.'

We have informed Pru and Allan. Imagine my delight when Pru told me, 'Mama, I will be a big sister again!' I cried. Who wouldn't? John tells me I cry at everything now. He exaggerates.

Late May is the time of my confinement. I expect we will still be here on Menorca, as Admiral Collingwood intended, the Swallow patrolling, with occasional assistance here and there in the Mediterranean. John groused to Admiral Collingwood about showing the flag but just patrolling, until the admiral pointed out to him that is precisely what keeps the French bottled up in Toulon.

John's little fleet does not keep a predictable schedule, lest any French observers notice a pattern. They also patrol the many inlets found in these islands. 'There will be no more flaming torches,' John states. 'We learned that lesson.'

Admiral Collingwood and Bounce visit here occasionally, which delights our children. I think the admiral feels the most content when he and John—if he is in port—chat about small matters in the sitting room. I mend and darn, which still relaxes him. Poor man. I do not know why the Admiralty forbids him even a quick visit to England. It saddens me.

He sold the house and wants to purchase another closer to Port Mahon itself, where we have taken up residence. For myself, I enjoy our own place, right in the centre of Port Mahon with an excellent view of the docks.

We are all protected by Sergeant David Bartleby. He is much happier since his recent return from Cornwall, wife in hand. Maggie Bartleby is a welcome help to me—a wonderful cook and a friend already. I know there will be more babies in this house!

You asked about the Americans. Captain Tyler and the Hartford sailed two months ago. He made port to see us and our new house before following the convoy with the Constitution. I asked John what he thinks of the Americans. He shrugged. 'I trust *them, for the most part, but we might find ourselves at odds again. Mind you, Yanks are better friends than enemies.'*

There you have it, Grace. We are content here on Menorca. The 'war' I fight now against Napoleon consists of keeping morale high. Captain Beattie tells me that a happy captain means a happy ship. He's far removed from the desperate man who knocked on my door. I hope to never see that particular captain again. This one suits me right down to the ground.

Much love from all of us, dear Grace.
Anna Beattie

* * * * *

Author Note

Admiral Lord Cuthbert Collingwood, Royal Navy (1748–1810) was ten years older than the more-famous Admiral Lord Horatio Nelson, but an equally talented commander. While Horatio Nelson's genius led to stirring victories, Cuthbert Collingwood's talent lay in navigation and gunnery, and his insistence on the proper order of things.

Following Lord Nelson's death at Trafalgar (21st October 1805) Collingwood assumed command of the Mediterranean Fleet. The Admiralty deemed him too vital in the Mediterranean to permit him leave to visit his wife and daughters in England. In the hope that they would visit him, Collingwood did indeed purchase a home near Port Mahon on Menorca, one of the islands comprising the Balearics, today popular vacation spots, and in the possession of Spain.

Collingwood's family never visited. Years of constant warfare and sea duty exhausted him. His faithful dog Bounce aged along with him, dying in late 1809 by falling overboard. By 1810, Collingwood's poor health reached the point where the Admiralty allowed him to resign. He sailed for England on 6th March 1810, and died a day later at sea off Port Mahon.

Admiral Lord Collingwood was laid to rest in St Paul's Cathedral, close to Admiral Lord Nelson, whose coffin lies in a most prominent position, high above other caskets in that famous crypt. Collingwood's plain coffin calls no attention to itself. He was a man of duty, not show.

My Menorcan research turned up a minor tidbit, but one that most readers are familiar with: mayonnaise. Everything points to the delightful fact that this concoction did indeed originate in Mahón, Menorca. *Bon appétit!*

If you enjoyed this story, be sure to read these loosely linked titles, also by Carla Kelly:

The Wedding Ring Quest
Marriage of Mercy
The Admiral's Penniless Bride
Marrying the Captain
The Surgeon's Lady
Marrying the Royal Marine
A Naval Surgeon to Fight For

And check out some of Carla Kelly's other historical romances

'A Father for Christmas'
in A Victorian Family Christmas

'The Captain's Christmas Journey'
in Convenient Christmas Brides

MILLS & BOON®

Coming next month

ACCIDENTALLY WED TO THE PRINCE
Lucy Morris

What should I say? Magnus had made his decision in the library earlier, but now he was at a loss for words. The next sentence would seal his fate and that of his beloved Thrudheim forever.

He supposed he should just get it over with. 'Miss Mortimer, in light of our recent…accident. I think it only best that I ask for your hand in marriage.'

'What?' Miss Mortimer screamed the word so loudly that his ears rang and he winced.

She glanced up at the stagecoach, and he noticed that several people had gathered at the windows and doorway. Staring down at them expectantly like a nest of hungry chicks. Miss Mortimer scowled back at them and they hurried back into the shadows.

'Have you lost your wits?' She hissed, and then added, 'Your Serene Highness.' Belatedly and with a perplexed expression, as if she wasn't sure how she could remain polite and question his sanity at the same time.

'As we are going to be married, you may call me by my Christian name, Magnus, at least in informal settings such as this.'

She blinked with a slack expression as if she couldn't quite comprehend his words. After a moment of blankness, a strange iron-will seemed to take over her. She raised her chin and her spine stiffened, that odd conviction hardening within her eyes like granite. It was spectacular to watch, a goddess emerging from a fiery pit. 'I did not agree to your proposal!'

Continue reading

ACCIDENTALLY WED TO THE PRINCE
Lucy Morris

Available next month
millsandboon.co.uk

Copyright © 2026 Lucy Morris

COMING SOON!

We really hope you enjoyed reading this book. If you're looking for more romance be sure to head to the shops when new books are available on

Thursday 21st May

To see which titles are coming soon, please visit
millsandboon.co.uk/nextmonth

MILLS & BOON

TWO BRAND NEW BOOKS FROM
Love Always

Be prepared to be swept away to incredible worldwide destinations along with our strong, relatable heroines and intensely desirable heroes.

OUT NOW

Four Love Always stories published every month, find them all at:

millsandboon.co.uk

FOUR BRAND NEW BOOKS FROM
MILLS & BOON MODERN

Indulge in desire, drama, and breathtaking romance – where passion knows no bounds!

OUT NOW

Eight Modern stories published every month, find them all at:

millsandboon.co.uk

LET'S TALK
Romance

For exclusive extracts, competitions and special offers, find us online:

- **f** MillsandBoon
- **X** @MillsandBoon
- **○** @MillsandBoonUK
- **♪** @MillsandBoonUK

Get in touch on 01413 063 232

For all the latest titles coming soon, visit
millsandboon.co.uk/nextmonth